To Jack –
From Lou
Christ.
Thanks!

D0590912

The
Proteus
Pact

The Proteus Pact

A Novel by
Geoffrey St. George

Little, Brown and Company
Boston – Toronto

COPYRIGHT © 1975 BY GEOFFREY ST. GEORGE

ALL RIGHTS RESERVED. NO PART OF THIS BOOK MAY BE REPRODUCED
IN ANY FORM OR BY ANY ELECTRONIC OR MECHANICAL MEANS IN-
CLUDING INFORMATION STORAGE AND RETRIEVAL SYSTEMS WITHOUT
PERMISSION IN WRITING FROM THE PUBLISHER, EXCEPT BY A REVIEWER
WHO MAY QUOTE BRIEF PASSAGES IN A REVIEW.

FIRST EDITION

T 04/75

LIBRARY OF CONGRESS CATALOGING IN PUBLICATION DATA

St. George, Geoffrey.
    The Proteus pact.

    I. Title.
PZ4.S138Pr [PS3569.A452]   813'.5'4   74-26561
ISBN 0-316-76670-4

Published simultaneously in Canada
by Little, Brown & Company (Canada) Limited

PRINTED IN THE UNITED STATES OF AMERICA

For Anita

The
Proteus
Pact

«1»

Late in the afternoon, on a very hot day at the end of
August, 1939, a man — tall, handsome, and smartly
dressed — appeared at the registration desk of a small inn
located near the town of G——, close to the Polish-German
border. The innkeeper, a man named Rudolf Heiber, realized that he must have been extraordinarily preoccupied
with his financial record books, for he had not heard the
guest approach the inn. In cold, clipped tones the man
asked him if there were any rooms available for the night.
Herr Heiber assured him that there were several rooms
available and that he could, after looking them over,
choose whichever one pleased him most. The guest
decided quickly. On the second floor, at the rear of the
inn, there was a room which afforded the occupant a
particularly pleasant view of the surrounding countryside.

"This one," the man said.

Herr Heiber escorted him downstairs once again so that
he could have him sign the registration book. The man did
so, putting down the name Reinhard Kleist. Kleist then
turned and started to walk away, but he stopped suddenly,

faced Herr Heiber, and asked if he could pay his bill immediately since he intended to depart at an unusually early hour in the morning. Heiber agreed to this readily enough and took the money. Did Herr Kleist have any baggage with him?

"No," was the response.

"Very good, sir," said the innkeeper, and those were the last words exchanged by the two men. It was not until two days later that Herr Heiber noticed that Kleist had failed to write down a home address next to his name in the registration book.

Heiber always slept in a room on the ground floor of the inn. On this particular night, he did not sleep at all well. He was troubled by chaotic, frightening dreams. Fiery images passed before his mind's eye. Perhaps the rumors about another European war disturbed him more than he knew. At 3:30 A.M., he woke up. Unable to fall back to sleep, he lay flat on his back staring at the ceiling. Half an hour later, Herr Heiber began to hear sounds outside the door of his room. At first he was alarmed, but then he remembered that the guest named Kleist had said something about an early departure. It was, indeed, an early hour for someone to be checking out of his room. Heiber got up and walked to the window which faced out on the road directly in front of the inn. Kleist emerged and walked toward an automobile parked on the opposite side of the road. The first traces of dawn were visible in the distance. In the faint light, the innkeeper could discern enough to tell that his guest had undergone an unexpected transformation. Kleist was dressed in the uniform of an SS officer.

While Herr Heiber fell back into disturbed, image-laden sleep, Kleist drove nearly twenty miles. He stopped at the side of a rough, dirt road. He had arrived at a point only several hundred yards from the Polish-German border.

4

Getting out of his car, Kleist walked toward the top of a gentle slope off to the left of the road. A large pair of field glasses hung from around his neck. Dew lay thickly on the ground. The moisture collected on his boots as Kleist proceeded to the top of the rise. In the eastern sky, the light of dawn continued to increase in intensity. Kleist waited, surveying the peaceful landscape all around him.

Then, the nearly perfect silence of this perfect rustic dawn was disturbed by a sound, barely audible at first, which came from the west. At the outset it was a distant rumble, the type of sound that suggests the beginnings of an awesome natural catastrophe. This rumble grew into a droning roar.

Kleist scanned the heavens.

They came from the west — scores of aircraft stacked up as far as the eye could see against the ever-brightening sky. The elliptical wings of Heinkels. The angular ugliness of Stukas. The pencil shape of Dorniers. Steel birds, on their way to Poland, on their way to war.

It was 5:00 A.M., September 1, 1939, and the Second World War was about to begin.

Kleist rode with the invading armies. He was everywhere, moving from one armored division to another, observing, with clinical coolness, the rapid progress of the destruction. Riding, during the opening phase of the invasion, with List's Fourteenth Army, Kleist sat on top of an armored personnel carrier and watched the systematic elimination of pockets of resistance. The whine, the grating metallic shriek, the whistle of concentrated artillery fire. The unrelenting waves of Stukas. The hordes of tanks. Kleist witnessed all of it. He watched and listened, sometimes pointing to a particular scene of battle and commenting on it to some panzer officer or brigade commander who happened to be standing nearby. Always with field glasses, Kleist, along with other officers, scanned the skies for the close-support fighters, scanned the fields for enemy armor, scanned the roads to the rear for the supply vehicles. Riding for a while with Kluge's Fourth Army, Kleist was sitting in an officer's vehicle when two machine-gun bullets tore through the windshield and killed the driver. Blood splattered Kleist's uniform. On every field, in every town, on every road, men fell. Victory has its price. Kleist observed in silence when the wounded, the bandaged, those without limbs, walked or were carried past him. Traveling with Reichenau's Tenth Army, Kleist drove down a road littered with shattered, burned-out tanks. Burial details removed the bodies of men who had been partially incinerated inside their vehicles. A terrible stench filled the air.

Four miles southwest of Radom, there occurred an incident not at all unusual during the course of the campaign in Poland. A motorized unit operating with Reichenau's Tenth Army was held up just outside a small village. The unit was caught on a road which approached the village from the west. Two of its tanks had hit mines. Each had lost a tread. Four hundred yards from the road, a tree line, marking the edge of a forest, concealed a strong Polish unit. This unit, in battalion strength, resisted the German advance with grim determination. From the road on which the mechanized unit was stalled, the land sloped gradually up to the tree line. The Poles fired down on the Germans, keeping up a constant barrage of mortar and machine-gun fire. German heads were pinned down behind protective armor plate.

Four hundred yards off to the other side of the road, standing on another rise, four SS officers watched the battle below and in front of them. These men were traveling with the Tenth Army. Two of them, Holscher and von Heim, were prepared to organize the job of occupation immediately upon the cessation of enemy resistance. They were getting a feel for the local topography. A third officer, named Schlink, was involved in intelligence work with the Abwehr, Luftwaffe branch. These three men stood grouped together near an SS command car, observing the battle through field glasses. The fourth man was Kleist — SS Gruppenführer Reinhard Kleist. He stood apart from the others, some sixty yards from the command car. He too was observing the stalled column on the road. Directly to his right, not more than ten yards away, one of Joseph Goebbels' newsmen, operating a motion-picture camera mounted on a tripod, methodically filmed the raging battle.

Kleist lowered his field glasses and, after having reflected for a moment on the scene before him, wheeled completely about so that only his back faced the embattled armored column. Once again he raised the glasses to his eyes.

Where were the dive-bombers? Where were the close-support fighters?

Nearly half a mile away a Polish mortarman fired off a round. It exploded one hundred yards from Kleist. Other shells followed. Someone was trying to hit the SS command car. Shrapnel whistled through space. Chunks of earth hurtled through the air. The three officers threw themselves on the ground. Kleist remained standing. His face did not show the signs of concern, the symptoms of fear. Turning so that he could face the battle once again, Kleist examined the distant tree line in an effort to locate the exact source of the mortar fire.

All this had happened before. Kleist's colleagues had not failed to notice, and to admire, his absolute imperturbability in the face of the dirt, the roar, the chaos of battle. Holscher had once remarked to Schlink that Kleist, never far from a battle, seemed to observe warfare as if he were the director of a minutely planned, well-staged spectacle. With mortar rounds crashing in on the slope, Kleist did not seem to be "bearing it," he did not give the appearance of a man consciously and tenaciously maintaining a militant posture in the midst of the discomforts of combat. The hellish sights and sounds of battle did not disturb this man. But then, wasn't the SS supposed to represent a new breed of human being?

The Polish mortarman gave up. The tanks were more important targets. Between the distant bursts of machine-gun fire and the crash of artillery rounds, Kleist could hear the faint whirring sound of the motion-picture camera.

Then, from the distance, came the noise of the approaching Stukas. The fighters were on their way too. At 11:07 A.M., the Poles, thinking that they had the German column at their mercy, launched an infantry attack across the downward-sloping field. It was at this moment that the aircraft arrived. The Polish infantry, backed by small armored vehicles, were halfway across the field when the Bf-109's swept in for a strafing attack.

Kleist followed the air attack through his glasses, his head moving slowly from side to side.

How can one adequately describe the nearly symphonic splendor of intermingling cannon and machine-gun fire?

The rapid, staccato chatter of the lighter weapons.

The duller, persistent thudding of the cannons.

Kleist heard all of this against a background of shrieking, whining aircraft engines. The fighters raced in, one after another, barely fifty feet off the ground, wings rocking from side to side. They went into climbing turns after completing each firing pass, gaining altitude in preparation for another attack.

And there, before Kleist, were the striking, visible results of this initial howling assault from the air. As each fighter raced in for a pass, guns firing, shells and bullets tore into the ground, kicking up patterned lines of dirt, mud, clay and grass. An invisible artist etched geometrical lines of destruction on a natural canvas. A flowering meadow was enriched with the fiery orchards of machine guns. The ground was relentlessly lacerated by an invisible shower of steel.

Caught in the open, enemy infantry fell in waves.

At ten thousand feet the Stukas waited in stepped-up echelon formation. The new architecture . . . geometrical formation flights. The dive-bombers wheeled over into their dives. Their brakes slowed them down until, seen from below, they appeared to drift, to float toward the earth. Kleist could see five cylindrical objects fall away from each aircraft. Here too he could observe the aesthetics of a perfectly natural geometry of destruction. As each aircraft pulled out of its dive, combined descent and ascent describing a gigantic "U" in the summer sky, the steel cylinders fell away, hurtling toward the ground in nearly straight lines of descent.

The field blossomed out as explosions miraculously darted across its surface. The mad force of bomb blasts ripped apart enemy vehicles. Jagged pieces of grotesquely twisted armor plate cartwheeled wildly through the air.

The motion-picture camera dispassionately recorded the spectacle.

Kleist surveyed the results. The Polish infantry and armor were in disarray. The survivors retreated hastily.

Otto Schlink appeared at Kleist's side. He was clearly pleased by the Luftwaffe's work. But it was Kleist who spoke first.

"There seems to have been a failure in coordination here."

Schlink wondered if Kleist was referring to the delay in getting the air support. But surely one could overlook that now. Mark III tanks were already preparing to pursue the remainder of the shattered enemy unit. German gunfire split the air and dominated the field of battle.

"Next time," continued Kleist, "make certain to

9

coordinate the Stukas and fighters for maximum effect. Send in the dive-bombers first. Let the fighters follow up with their strafing attack. Catch the enemy as he retreats from the bombing runs. Don't you agree with this view?"

"In this situation, Gruppenführer Kleist, it was not possible to coordinate so precisely."

"May I suggest that you tell regional Luftwaffe headquarters that its aircraft await more explicit instructions from ground unit commanders?"

Schlink barely refrained from making a hostile remark. In fact, Kleist had nothing to do with Luftwaffe operations. He was not part of the Luftwaffe chain of command. But, on the other hand, Schlink thought that Kleist's point was not entirely incorrect. He turned away to survey the scene of battle. The column had started to move again, and, in a matter of minutes, the village would be in German hands. Why, at this point, should anyone become engaged in a technical argument? He decided to explicitly acknowledge the validity of his colleague's criticism, but when he turned to face him, Kleist had gone. He was moving off to the right in order to attain higher ground. No matter, Schlink said to himself.

Kleist had another problem on his mind. He stood alone. The dust and smoke of battle were gradually settling in the shallow valley spread out before him. His fellow officers, now gathered at their vehicle, wondered whether or not he was considering the danger implicit in standing on open, high ground. Enemy snipers were, no doubt, still concealed in the forest. Shots were still ringing out. But the Gruppenführer was utterly indifferent in regard to this danger. Off by himself, he was engrossed in the matter that continually preoccupied him. Shattered, burning vehicles lay on the field before him. The grotesque, graceless postures of the dead testified to the violent manner in which they had died.

How would it be possible, thought Kleist, to increase the scope, the range, the efficiency of the means by which one creates destruction?

It was just after 4:30 P.M. on a mid-December day, 1939, and throughout the city of Frankfurt am Main lights were going on as darkness began to creep across the cold German sky. People, many of them on their way home after Christmas shopping, dressed warmly, for the winter was, in this first year of the war, unremittingly unpleasant.

A man clad in a heavy, gray winter coat stepped out onto the sidewalk in front of number 839 F____strasse. He paused momentarily, glanced up at the generally overcast sky, placed his cumbersome briefcase down on the sidewalk, and proceeded to close the top of his coat around his already chilled neck. The fur lining felt good against his skin.

This man's name was Otto Kessler.

The weather over and around Frankfurt had been persistently drab and gray for at least two weeks, and although Kessler was certainly aware of this fact, it did not fail to happen that at the end of each workday, as he emerged onto the street, this drabness, this grayness, struck him anew as something slightly oppressive. Otto Kessler was not in the least prone to reflecting on atmospheric conditions. He did not spend his long, concentrated days looking out the windows of his office. When anyone told him that there could be really strong correlations between meteorological conditions and people's emotional states, Kessler found this difficult to imagine. At this moment, however, having completed the securing of his neck against the cold, Kessler picked up his briefcase and started down F____strasse at a leisurely pace.

He was tired. By four-thirty in the afternoon he was glad to be leaving his place of work. Number 839

F——strasse was an imposing, four-floor concrete structure containing a large number of offices and laboratories. On this particular afternoon, the color of the building matched perfectly the color of the overcast sky. On an iron-framed pane of glass mounted directly above the main entrance, ornate black letters spelled out the words "University Research Center." Above these words, fixed onto the wall of the building, an iron eagle, an indefatigable bird, wings folded stiffly back in military fashion, stared out into the distance as if he were proudly surveying an infinite, private domain. An iron swastika, Germany's twisted cross, symbol of the Third Reich, was mounted just below this militant bird. Above this bird, lights continued to burn in office and laboratory windows.

Dr. Otto Kessler, professor of metallurgy on the faculty of the University of Frankfurt, was a tall, impressive-looking man. He was just over six feet and decidedly stocky. Indeed, one might almost have called him barrel-chested. The observer sensed an incongruity in this, for if there is a physical stereotype implicit in the conception of a university man, Otto Kessler did not resemble that stereotype. Kessler was a scientist, but he had the physique of a laborer. Brown eyes, set beneath thick eyebrows, radiated sharp intelligence. Brown hair, beginning to grow thin around the temples, testified to premature aging. The nose was slightly too broad for the rest of the face and, unfortunately, destroyed that potential balance which would have permitted one to judge Kessler a handsome man. He was fifty-one years old, but the lines around the eyes and mouth made him look more like sixty. Perhaps he spent too many hours thinking out difficult problems. His work consumed him. He was a man incapable of any form of extended, genuine relaxation.

Invariably, he walked home each afternoon after work. Kessler followed a route which took him through a residential district of the city. Old, three-story, dark brown apartment buildings lined both sides of the street. In front of these buildings, unattractive by any standards, large numbers of children were usually playing. Some sat on the steps which led up to the entrance of each building unit, while others, blissfully unaware of the cold, ran wildly through the streets. Christmas decorations were already visible in the windows of many apartments. Human existence proceeded on these streets much as if there were no war going on at all. But the Party was visible too. Occasionally, Kessler would see a boy wearing the uniform of the Hitler Youth organization. But it was the last part of the walk that he liked best of all. It took him around the perimeter of a small park. There was something about the trees, even the bare winter trees, which gave him a momentary sense of composure, a sense of escaping, for just a brief period of time, from the pressures of work.

It is unlikely that any of the people who passed Kessler on the street each day knew who he was. Specialists in alloys do not ordinarily achieve any form of widespread public recognition. But this all too common anonymity did not disturb Kessler any more than it disturbed any of Frankfurt's many inhabitants. Anonymity has its virtues. There were many people who recognized, intuitively or otherwise, the advantages of a well-cultivated alienation. Could anyone bring himself to say, with a sense of certainty, that one human relationship was absolutely safe, whereas another might be fraught with danger? Cultivate a friendship with a waiter in a favorite restaurant? Seek out further contact with such and such a pleasant fellow whom one had met at a party last week? How could one be certain? In fact, it really did not matter at all whether or not the waiter was taken into one's confidence, the pleasant individual introduced into one's small circle of friends. What really mattered was that these questions

13

were in the air. The uses of terror are unpredictable. Into what bizarre "whole" could the innocent part one was playing be integrated by the fertile imagination of the secret police? A question like this was virtually inseparable from the order of things, and Otto Kessler, very much a part of the order of things in Germany, certainly knew enough to ask himself this kind of question. Trust no one. At the same time, keep all human relations strictly and "sincerely" confined to the sphere of the trivial. In this way, everyone can sacrifice, on the altar of these principles, the whole of his humanity.

But there was another sense in which all of these considerations remained curiously objective from Kessler's point of view. His alienation, and his authentic indifference toward that alienation, had other sources as well. He knew only what he thought he had to know. When politics crossed the sphere of his personal life, he cared about politics. In the early 1930s, Kessler had been just as much a victim of Germany's economic disorder as anyone else. He had voted for the Nazis, not because they had touched off some deeply rooted passion, but because the severity of the nation's overall situation had convinced him that only radical-sounding, strong policies could create order and political balance. Kessler had grown bored with predictable rhetoric and conventional political programs. He did not like the complex and seemingly unresolvable arguments which grew out of sophisticated discussion of major issues. In addition to this, when the banners of the N.S.D.A.P. proclaimed "Germany Awake," Kessler, with the soul of a scientist, responded affirmatively to an exhortation ostensibly directed against the dead weight of the past. A true bourgeois, Kessler could be impressed as much by the appearance of order as by real political and social order itself.

He walked around the perimeter of the park. This day,

as always, he looked forward to going home. There, his wife and his housekeeper awaited him. Kessler had been married for twenty-five years. He had met his wife Karin in Leipzig just as he had been finishing his advanced studies. From his point of view, to say nothing more, Karin was the perfect wife. She shared absolutely none of his professional interests. This situation allowed him to feel, more certainly than anything else, that there was an autonomous dimension of his world that he could retreat to each day which bore no obvious resemblance to the world of his work. In this respect too, Kessler was an utterly conventional man. Karin was an attractive, bright, and totally unassuming person, the kind of wife who was quite content with sitting at home, reading light fiction, and going on shopping trips with her friends. In regard to looking after the house, Karin could rely on the housekeeper, Ingrid. The latter was a devoted, diligent, efficient woman who, in the last analysis, made it all the more imperative that Karin find ways in which to entertain herself. Karin would not have been pleased if she had known that Otto, on his walks home, really looked forward to seeing Ingrid. She was the one who actually provided Kessler with immediate attention when he walked through the front door. She took his briefcase, removed his coat, got him a predinner glass of wine or beer. It was Ingrid who prepared the satisfying meals. These things always generated sensations of well-being in Kessler's tired mind and body. They were the cornerstones on which his sense of reality depended.

He bought a newspaper on a street corner and glanced at the front page. Kessler rarely did more than this. All the papers were still acclaiming the spectacular triumph over Poland. No one expressed any concern over the fact that a state of war existed between Germany and the English and French. The western front was quiet.

15

Kessler approached his home. In front of it, two dogs were scrapping with each other over a bone. A third stood by and watched the struggle with an air of contempt. Kessler didn't care much for animals. He passed them by and, having ascended the front steps and crossed the porch, entered his home.

Kessler knew, from the moment he closed the door behind him, that something was different. He stood in the entrance foyer and waited, but did not hear the sound of Ingrid scurrying out of the kitchen in order to greet him and help him with his things. He placed his briefcase on the table that stood against the right-hand wall of the foyer, removed his coat, and then placed it carefully next to the case. He glanced up the staircase directly in front of him. No sound emanated from the second floor, even though Karin was usually up there each day at the time of his arrival. To the left of the stairway there was a hallway which, continuing off the entrance foyer, led directly to the kitchen.

"Ingrid?"

There was no response. Kessler decided to have a look in the kitchen. He passed the entrance to the darkened living room on his right, and the equally dark study which was just off to the left. Once in the kitchen he perceived immediately that Ingrid had, in fact, been in the process of preparing dinner. Several pots, cut vegetables and potatoes already in them, stood on the counter next to the stove. Several knives, already dirty from use, lay across a wood carving board. It was conceivable that Ingrid had gone down to the cellar in order to procure a bottle of wine. He checked the cellar door on the far side of the kitchen. It was locked. Puzzling. Perhaps Ingrid had left the house because she had forgotten to buy something called for by a recipe. Kessler thought to himself that Ingrid could be a forgetful woman, but he did not stop to realize what a petulant and gratuitous judgment this was, for the occasions on which she actually forgot something, thereby disrupting the predictable sequence of events that constituted Kessler's ritualistic evenings, were really quite few in number. These disruptions, however, acquired special, annoying significance for this man. He remembered, quite suddenly, the morning during the preceding summer when Ingrid, for no apparent reason, had forgotten to bring him his breakfast. "My mind must be going," she had said at the time. But the memory of this event had no sooner fled from his mind when Kessler, already halfway down the hall on his way back to the living room, was startled by the clear sound of footsteps coming from the study. Within seconds he could see someone standing at the point where the light from the entrance foyer and the darkness of the study met to form an imperfectly defined area of twilight.

"Dr. Otto Kessler?"

Kessler was now positioned in the middle of the hall facing the unannounced guest. Behind the man there was only the blackness of the study. Four or five feet separated the two men.

"Yes, I am Dr. Kessler."

"Good evening, Herr Kessler. I am sorry to have to intrude on you in such an irregular manner. Pardon me — if you can. Just the same, I thought it would be better to hold this meeting in the privacy of your home."

A pause, slightly too long to be natural, followed this stiff opening speech.

And then, unexpectedly, the guest bowed from the waist. It was not a deep bow. At the lowest point of the gesture, while maintaining the upper half of the body in its rigid and forwardly inclined position, the man, raising his head slightly, looked Kessler directly in the eye and proceeded to identify himself.

"Gruppenführer Reinhard Kleist—from SS headquarters in Frankfurt."

He bolted back into his former upright position.

"Perhaps you can spare me some of your time, Herr Kessler."

Kessler was still recovering from the initial shock he felt at finding this man in his home. Already, as he stood momentarily rooted to the spot, fear began to replace his feeling of surprise. Kessler managed to mutter something about his guest being welcome. Turning awkwardly with the upper part of his body, he made an attempt to invite Kleist into the still-darkened living room by making a half-confused, half-purposeful gesture with his left arm. Kessler entered the room first and crossed over to the far right-hand corner. He turned on a large, ugly floor lamp. Even before he could turn around, Kessler could hear his guest settling into the heavy leather chair that stood just to the right of the entrance to the room. Kessler was preoccupied with his own anxiety. Accordingly, as was his way, he began to pay attention, excessive attention, to trivial details. That lamp in the corner, for example, the one he had just switched on—did it provide enough illumination? Would this man, this SS Gruppenführer Kleist, think that he was trying to conceal something? An absurd question. Kessler found himself obsessed with it. The dark wood, ornate coffee table with ash tray and silver serving platter on top—the oak desk off to the right, still covered with papers—the bookcase behind Kleist's enormous chair—the thick, floor-length green curtains covering the windows—the ceiling-high cabinet filled with good china—all these objects simultaneously emanated, and were bathed in, a brooding heaviness which suffused the room. An incalculably great, immovable mass seemed to fill all space. It was because of the light. There was not enough light.

Kessler assumed that Kleist's visit was directly related to Ingrid's absence. Or was his wife the reason for Kleist's presence? Where was she? Kessler had still heard no sound come from the upper floor. And yet, the idea of Karin, or of Ingrid, engaged in any form of activity that would merit the attention of the SS was, on the face of it, untenable.

Kessler sat down on the sofa opposite Kleist.

"As you can see, Herr Kessler, I have requested that we be left to ourselves for the duration of this meeting. Your wife and housekeeper are down at my headquarters where they will be entirely safe. No cause for alarm. They will be back in two hours. I have personally arranged for transportation."

SS officers were not without a certain cold charm. This quality, in combination with the actual substance of Kleist's statement, provided Kessler with a source of emotional relief. The anxiety he had been experiencing dissipated almost completely. Being a normal human being, once his fear had subsided, Kessler was capable of allowing full sway to the presumption that Kleist, but another human being, was probably a decent, reasonable man. The doctor resolved that he would try to serve this officer in a cooperative spirit.

There could be no question about how essentially intriguing this SS officer was. Even Otto Kessler, who was not particularly insightful about people, would have willingly conceded this point after five minutes' close contact with the stiff, formal Kleist. There were many SS officers in Frankfurt. Kessler saw them nearly every day. At a single glance, Kleist was in no way remarkable, but at a single glance it was difficult to respond to anything other than the striking, dramatic, deliberately macabre SS uniform. There is necessarily no such thing as a uniform that can aid in refining the sense of the unique, the individual, for it is part of the function of a uniform to blunt that form of sensibility. Kleist looked like the others. The shining, reflecting, highly polished black leather boots which came up to the knees — the smartly tailored black pants and matching jacket top — the swastika armband with its powerful red, black and white color scheme — the pistol strapped into a bulky, black leather holster. Was there not genius of a perverse kind in the design of this outfit? The aesthetics of power. Do not violate this sacred sphere. Do not trespass on hallowed ground.

But this man — this SS Gruppenführer Kleist. Kessler did not doubt that Kleist had gained easy acceptance into the élite cadre. He obviously met all of the physical requirements — the light-colored hair, the light eyes, the supposedly Nordic physique — all of it was there. But Kleist became interesting at precisely the point where discrepancies arose between the concrete realities of the man and the ideal, recruiting-poster image of the SS man. The hair was light, but not blond. It contained streaks of a darker color. The eyes were light, but not pure blue. They were tinged with green. The nose was aquiline and yet it was a trifle too broad at the base. The mouth was thin and moist, but by no means either hard or cruel. Kleist wore a pair of gold, wire-framed glasses. There was something more, however, something beyond departures from an ideal physical type. This additional quality suggested the presence of a personality that one could never adequately grasp or define through platitudes about the SS, the Party, nationality, cultural type, and so on. These notions would never reflect the essence of the man's special aura. Kleist's eyes radiated a piercing intelligence — the terrifying dialectical intelligence of a grand inquisitor. Kessler could imagine a police interrogation with Kleist as interrogator. Confronted by those eyes, one would have to despair of attempting to lie successfully. And yet, even though the eyes seemed to afford one a glimpse into an unfailingly acute mind perennially engaged in sharp calculations, razorlike processes of judgment, the rest of the face was inscrutable. Nothing stood revealed there. The mouth, just at the corners, might have suggested a hyperrefined callousness, but never did it snarl or sneer or assume some other unambiguously cruel form. No — nothing was written in lucid terms on this astonishing face. Wasn't Kleist, then, an epitome of characterlessness, of impersonality? It was not that simple. Indeed, it was precisely this very quality of the inscrutably impersonal that paradoxically gave one an insight into the bizarre aura Kleist radiated all about him. The individual, the strictly unique, the absolutely personal, arrived at, as it were, on the "other side" of personality as we know it. That was Kleist. Take this or that particular quality — intelligence, detachment, coldness — refine that quality until it is pure and abstracted out of any actual human manifestation, and then imagine that quality breathed back into human flesh. That was Kleist — the living spirit of inquisition.

But the doctor had nearly forgotten himself. He offered Kleist a drink. The latter accepted. Kessler got him some brandy and returned to the sofa.

"What can I do for you, Gruppenführer?"

"I take it for granted, Dr. Kessler, that, as a German citizen, you were interested in the successes of our armed forces during September's operation in Poland."

"Certainly . . . certainly."

"Our overall state of preparedness made those successes possible. We were capable, as the entire world learned, of coordinating the use of aircraft and armor in a simple, but completely effective, manner. Polish defenses crumbled away in the face of this effort."

Kleist paused. Then, as if in summation, he added, "Truly modern warfare began in Poland this past September."

Kessler could not see the point of this review of recent

history. Everything, thus far, had been merely introductory. Kessler shifted slightly on the sofa.

"However, Dr. Kessler, this phenomenal campaign, so impressive from nearly every point of view, will have negative, or shall I say reactionary, effects if considered from a different perspective."

Kleist paused again, as if to let his words produce their intended effect. He raised the small brandy glass to his lips and sipped silently. Kessler said nothing. Kleist, elbows positioned on the armrests of his chair, held the glass with both hands directly in front of his face. He gazed into it as if it were a crystal ball.

"A striking victory breeds complacency, Herr Kessler . . . an unwarranted contempt for an opponent's true capabilities. In military matters, as in scientific ones, a man can never rest. There is always more to be done."

That was perfect audience adaptation.

"Agree . . . I agree absolutely," said Kessler, and he nodded his head vigorously . . . a trifle too vigorously.

"Already, you know, there are people who believe that German military technology completely outstrips the level of technology found anywhere else. One cannot deny that there is some . . . there is a bit of truth in this position. If you consider the pace of weapons development in the Western democracies, I think you would have to say that they have not put in the time, the effort, required for developing, let us say, first-class armored vehicles."

Kleist stopped. Again he sipped from his glass. Kessler, becoming increasingly restless as his guest's preamble grew in length, started to rise from the sofa, partly in order to get Kleist some more brandy, partly in order to relieve his growing psychic discomfort.

"No . . . no . . . I am fine," said the Gruppenführer. "Stay where you are." Kessler froze, still seated, on the edge of the sofa.

"German air power, Herr Kessler . . . German air power, to take one more example, has obviously benefited from years of careful planning. If the performance characteristics of our equipment are compared to the performance characteristics of comparable items in the arsenal of any European nation, it becomes clear that we have attained a remarkable superiority. The fruits of the Polish campaign are convincing enough evidence on this point. Now, Herr Kessler . . ."

Kleist stopped again, this time in midsentence. Then, rather than bringing his glass to his lips, he reached over with his right hand and placed it on a small table that stood next to his chair. Both the pause and the gesture marked the moment as an important one.

"Now, Herr Kessler . . . why is all of this true?"

Kleist did not expect an answer. He was the authority on military affairs.

"Hard work? Concentrated effort? Meticulous planning? The will of the Führer? No one doubts that these things are crucial. They have all played a part, but there is more to the question than that. I spoke just now of unwarranted contempt for the enemy. The Führer himself has proceeded diplomatically on the assumption that England and France did not want to fight. Already, in that assumption, we see a variety of contempt. Oh, it is true . . . it is true . . ."

Kleist began to wave his right hand as though he were physically warding off an objection about to be raised, an objection he had heard many times before.

". . . it is true that this diplomatic posture, in spite, mind you, in spite of the fears of the General Staff, has won Germany several astonishing bloodless victories."

And Kessler was puzzled, indeed, he was amazed by this remark.

"The occupation of the Rhineland."

This man Kleist was openly speaking about the secret fears of the General Staff.

"The annexation of Austria."

If the SS intended to give him trouble in any way, if they had their suspicions concerning him, then Kleist would never be speaking to him about these issues.

"The Sudeten crisis . . . the Munich agreement."

Kessler sat motionless.

". . . So we can all happily admit to these victories, but this policy, founded on contempt, was really only workable, if workable at all, during peacetime. The English and the French are not so prepared as we are because they did not choose to face the very possibility of war. But now a state of war exists. Striking victories are a product of relative strength . . . that is all. We can no longer assume that our opponents will remain uncommitted to technology, to weapons research. We can no longer permit our hitherto contemptuous attitudes to determine our actions. The gap between German and enemy military strength will begin to close."

"And yet, Gruppenführer, our research should allow us to maintain a sizable, perhaps a commanding, lead. Surely you do not anticipate our losing the advantage that has been accumulated during past years."

"No, Herr Kessler. I am sorry. I do not share your easy optimism."

And who was this man, Kessler wondered. What was there about him that entitled him to speak with such conviction about scientific matters?

"The point is that our first military success has had the effect of convincing the Führer and the more fanatical element of the Officer Corps that German arms are literally invincible."

As he said this, Kleist once again rested his elbows on the arms of the chair and brought his fingertips together. He had finished speaking . . . or so it seemed. His arms moved slowly back and forth. The fingertips bounced off each other three times. Suddenly, with the left hand clenched into a fist, and the right hand sweeping outward in a wide gesture, Kleist inclined forward and stared at Kessler with special intensity.

"Of course, there are bound to be a few more such victories. We can easily imagine the soporific effect these will have on the more important, less competent authorities. What I am trying to tell you is that soon the necessary internal impetus will be lacking — the impetus with which to expand our research programs. When that day comes it will be, quite invisibly at first, the beginning of the end for Germany."

There was a brief silence. The Gruppenführer possessed the sensibility of a dramatist. He timed his pauses carefully.

"That is why I have come here to see you."

Otto Kessler had been expecting this moment. He had been expecting it for some time. Kessler was highly respected by all those who comprised the German scientific community. Therefore, it could hardly surprise him if someone among the members of that community, someone with strong pro-Nazi attitudes, recommended that he organize a special research project or direct an agency engaged in such research.

"Are you interested in having me direct an agency —"

"No." Kleist cut him off sharply. "We want you to direct a project. You will be in complete command of the research team. We, of course, will set you the problem."

"This is to be weapons research?"

"You may call it that," said Kleist.

Kessler got up and walked toward the large oak desk. This move was instinctive, prompted by symbolic considerations. There, behind the desk, Kessler hoped, he could regain the sense of authority, of being in control of the course of events, which he had felt slipping away from him during the predominantly one-sided conversation.

Kessler stood directly behind the desk.

"But I've never done such work before."

With that, he sat down in the brown swivel desk chair.

"Furthermore," he added, "I have very little interest in that kind of work."

Kessler's notion of cooperating with the SS did not yet extend to voluntarily abandoning his career.

Kleist stared at him. He said nothing. Tension began to charge the atmosphere in the room.

"To be candid," continued Kessler, "I don't see how I can be of any help to you with weapons research. There are literally scores of men who are better qualified to direct projects involving aerodynamics, ballistics . . . matters of that sort. If you want, I can . . ."

Kessler coughed twice at this point. He cleared his throat.

"Excuse me, Gruppenführer," he said. "If you want I will gladly provide you with the names of some of these men."

"That will not be necessary, Herr Kessler. We have something else in mind."

Kleist stood up. The move, entirely unexpected, shocked Kessler. The conversation was clearly far from over and Kleist, perhaps as a way of inaugurating the next phase of the discussion, seemed determined to maintain total control over the proceedings by counterbalancing Kessler's move to the desk.

"Please follow me," said the Gruppenführer.

Kleist left the living room, crossed the hall, and entered the study. From his seat behind the oak desk, Kessler could hear the snap of a light switch, the rustling of papers, and the sound of Kleist seating himself once again. When Kessler entered the study, Kleist was reaching into a black leather case which lay open on the enormous plain wood worktable which stood on the right-hand side of the room. The Gruppenführer placed several folders, each containing an impressive number of papers, on the worktable. He opened each folder and looked hurriedly through the documents. Kessler watched. Outside, a driver persistently honked an automobile horn.

Kleist chose papers from each folder and, with meticulous care, placed them on the wood table facing Kessler. Hesitating for a moment, uncertain as to whether or not these documents were meant for his eyes, Kessler waited until Kleist, with a gesture of the right hand, indicated that he was to approach and examine the documents. Then, after picking up the papers, Kessler crossed the room, seated himself, and began to read.

The first paper contained a full description of Kessler's educational background. The schools he had attended were listed. Beside each school were the names of the teachers he had worked with. Next to the name of each teacher there was a series of letters and numbers. Dr. Bernhardt Grubner — XJ1045. Dr. Ulrich Hess — XJ4233. Some twenty-odd names. Kessler conjectured that these numbers and letters were references to additional documents bearing on each of the listed individuals. Perhaps there was a full dossier on each person. Perhaps each person had written an evaluation of Kessler himself. One could not be certain about any of this. The possibilities were legion.

Kessler turned to a second document. It contained a list of his publications in scientific journals. Books were also listed. One item caught his eye. There was a star next to it. *High Temperatures and Metal Fatigue Phenomena,* Leipzig, 1931. Next to this entry was the name of the English translator, Basil Parks. This work was, unquestionably, the most important Kessler had done.

Had Kleist actually read these articles, these books? That was unlikely.

In a third document Kessler read a list of all of the men he had worked with on numerous research projects. No — that was not entirely the case, as he noticed at a second glance. The list started with the year 1925 and simply ignored the work that he had done before that. This struck Kessler as an exception to the remarkable thoroughness demonstrated in the other documents. He did not doubt that these omissions were deliberate on the part of the SS. They had their reasons.

He did not look further. Allowing the papers to settle on his lap, Kessler's gaze wandered to the bookshelf on the wall to his left. He did not focus on anything, but rather stared into infinity while his mind, beginning to race uncontrollably, attempted to assess the realization that Kleist, and the organization he represented, had been observing him methodically for some time. Kessler could not entirely dispel the terrifying feeling that his past fifteen years, perhaps even more, had been lived under an illusion, for it now seemed, at least for a moment, as if the hidden but true function of all those years had been nothing other than to provide the information recorded in these SS documents. These people knew everything about him. Otto Kessler was unaccustomed to the experience of being unable to control his emotions. Now, for the first time, a cold terror began to seize him. With the onset of this distressing feeling, a strange idea occurred to Otto Kessler, professor of metallurgy. He thought that terror, the feeling of terror, rather than being a phenomenon internal to a man, was actually something in the objective order of the world itself, and that at certain moments a man could come across or discover this phenomenon.

Kleist was patiently awaiting a response. The roles had been reversed. Now Kessler would have to speak.

"So, I can see that you know a great deal about me, Gruppenführer. Very impressive . . . very thorough. My compliments."

He coughed again. It was a nervous cough, a purely psychosomatic episode rooted in the magical belief that he could arrest time long enough to think of some ideal response.

"I can imagine what's in the rest of those papers."

Kessler was trying to sound informal, detached, indifferent — a common reaction on the part of intelligent people caught in these circumstances. Now he stood up, walked over to the worktable, and placed the documents next to the open folders. Striving still to maintain a tone of indifference, Kessler continued.

"Tell me. Why does your list of my former research colleagues extend back only as far as 1925? Are there other documents covering the earlier years?"

"We are concerned, Herr Kessler, only with your post-1925 activities. In July of 1925 you began your work on steel alloys and fatigue phenomena in metals. That is what interests us."

This explained why they had starred the 1931 publication. Kessler felt relieved. Evidently, no matter what happened, they weren't going to ask him to leave his favorite work, the work that was the object of his deepest devotion and which elicited his greatest intellectual passion. Was it possible, then, that Kleist would adapt to Kessler's needs? Kessler wondered if the Gruppenführer understood him even more fully than the sheer facts on the SS documents indicated. Here was an officer who had studied the documents closely, but what precisely did he know about the human reality behind the facts?

"You are concerned, Herr Kessler, about the sacrifices I

might ask you to make. That much is obvious to me. It is said that National Socialism means sacrifice. That, at any rate, is its chief selling point. However, a man who has devoted a lifetime to the refining of a particular form of intelligence is rarely willing to surrender the exercise of his peculiar capacities. I know this. I have seen this principle demonstrated many times. But I ask you to hear me out. I know you for the gifted man you are. For example, Herr Kessler . . . your 1928 essay."

"You have read it?"

"Yes, Herr Kessler,"

"The one on steel alloys?"

"You treat the problem of the destruction of the molecular structure of steel alloys when they are exposed, for prolonged periods of time, to extreme temperatures."

Kessler returned to his chair, turned around, and sat down slowly. Should he ask Kleist about the mathematical calculations contained in the essay, or would that move constitute too obvious an attempt to test his knowledge? Could he risk offending this officer?

"In June of 1936, Herr Kessler, you delivered a lecture in Berlin on the same subject."

"You had someone following me?"

"No, Herr Kessler."

Kessler knew what he was about to hear.

"I attended your lecture."

"To be entirely candid, Gruppenführer —"

Again Kleist did not let him finish.

"You are surprised by the extent of my interest in you?"

"Yes."

"It was an admirable performance, Herr Kessler — the lecture, that is. I sat in the rear of the hall. I came in civilian clothes so as to attract little attention. Perhaps that's why you don't remember me?"

30

"That was some time ago. My memory . . ."

"Yes . . . yes . . . it was. In 1938 too . . . in February of 1938."

Kessler's eyes had wandered to the bookshelf again, but Kleist's recitation of the new date compelled him to look at the Gruppenführer with a heightened sense of anticipation.

". . . You gave another talk on special properties of steel-tungsten alloys. You know, Dr. Kessler, what is most impressive about your talks, aside from your sheer expertise, is your transparently clear dedication to truth . . . to scientific truth, I should say. Anyone who observes you closely must come to recognize this. It is astonishing. No. It is more than that. It is moving."

Many others had made the same observation. Kessler was a dedicated man. Whenever it happened that an uncontrolled, uncalculating spontaneity broke through the conventional forms of Otto Kessler's scientific-intellectual way of life, the force of his normally well-contained passion radiated outward with a fierce intensity. It was this phenomenon that Kleist had referred to as "moving." This happened frequently when Kessler lectured. If he was asked a question from the floor of a lecture hall, a difficult question which would tax the finest intellect, an audience could see Kessler harness and devote his passionate energies to precise calculation. Effort, concentration, true dedication would be written in the lines of the brow and in the playful, lively gleam in the eyes.

Now Kessler found himself moved to respond. The conversation had turned to the subject of science and the scientific way of life. Otto Kessler detected the chance to regain his composure, to redirect the discussion into familiar territory, to let Gruppenführer Kleist know that secret police intelligence work could never adequately assess his true value.

"There is no point, Gruppenführer, in spending one's life as a scientific bureaucrat, as a mindless technician who applies tired methods to problems set him by the reigning establishment. Man and Nature are participants in a game . . . a cosmic game, so to speak. When I succeed in my work it is because Nature has permitted it. Each and every achievement, every triumph of imaginative method, is a gift granted by Nature in response to the one thing that matters, the one thing that Nature respects . . ."

Kessler paused, in order to frame his point. He too could dramatize his world view.

". . . the mental act of penetrating to the heart of a mystery . . . the imaginative leap which takes one to the very order that lies at the heart of things."

"The order that is . . . that *is* the heart of things, Herr Kessler."

"Correct . . . absolutely true. That is the heart of things."

Kessler stood up.

"You see?"

"Yes, Herr Kessler."

"Metal . . . gauges . . . presses . . . all of these material objects count only in that they lead us to this mystery . . . you understand when I say mystery?"

And now the doctor strode over to the bookshelf as if he could, right at that very moment, open one of the finely bound volumes and locate the key, the answer, to the mystery of Nature of which he spoke. His step displayed new confidence.

"I understand you perfectly, Herr Kessler. You are a religious man . . . of a kind."

"Yes, Gruppenführer," said Kessler, turning so that he could look directly at his guest. "I suppose you could say that."

"Dr. Kessler . . . we are interested in developing and

32

producing a virtually impenetrable metal alloy. The substance we have in mind is to be something —"

"An impenetrable substance?"

"Yes."

"That isn't possible."

"We spoke just now of a mystery . . . of an order in Nature. You must think of our goal as an Ideal, Herr Kessler."

There were sounds again, sounds coming from outside. This time it was the screeching of automobile brakes.

"As you already know, to build a vessel, or a tank, or a fortification capable of withstanding great punishment requires the use of large quantities of whatever substances are now available to us. A tank capable of withstanding a direct strike from a seventy-five-millimeter gun must weigh at least fifty tons. If we are talking about a battle cruiser, then it becomes necessary to equip it with eleven- or twelve-inch armor plate if combat with a comparable vessel is to be feasible. We are speaking, then, Herr Kessler, of fantastic weights and enormous quantities of material. The problems created by these simple facts manifest themselves at all levels of military operations. If a tank is damaged in battle, if it's lying in a field, we are faced with the problem of getting heavy maintenance equipment to the tank, or, in the case of a badly damaged vehicle, getting the tank back to a repair depot. That involves all types of heavy equipment. You see? The complications are endless. Beyond this, there are types of weapons for which we have not been able to design really protective armor. The weight problem is insurmountable. A fighter pilot must rely on his own skill if he is to avoid the effects of cannon fire. We cannot weigh down a fighter aircraft with armor plating thick enough to stop such shells. It would be a self-defeating measure. However, I don't think we need multiply examples any further."

33

Kessler nodded his agreement.

"And so, Herr Kessler, we are looking for a substance, a true miracle substance, if you will, which can meet two requirements. It must be capable of withstanding great punishment, as I have said, and it must be lighter, by far, than anything we now have. Twenty times the strength of steel, and one-tenth the weight of steel. A goal simple enough to state . . . very difficult to attain. The strength of this hypothetical material will have to lie in its peculiar molecular structure. If we can achieve this, then it is patently obvious that we will not be forced to use vast quantities of the material in order to build new weapons. Think of the advantages of building warships with four-inch armor plate capable of sustaining hits from a twelve-inch gun. An impressive prospect — is it not?"

But Kleist fell silent, unexpectedly silent. Kessler was prepared for several more minutes of this monologue, for the Gruppenführer had been developing a driving momentum throughout his impassioned description of the possibilities inherent in the miracle substance. The very abruptness with which the silence came left the atmosphere in the study charged with the excitement that had animated Kleist's voice. A strange energy pervaded the room. Kessler was strongly affected by the description of the ideal substance. What a perfect — what an economical conception — as perfect, as economical as Nature herself. A light, but incredibly strong substance. It was not that he had never thought of this before. He had. What was so compelling for Kessler was not simply the idea of this substance in the abstract. No — what impressed Kessler, although he was not fully conscious of the fact, was the force of the situation in which he found himself. This man, this unannounced guest, actually sat before him, bringing, with his words, a semblance of reality to a hitherto fantastic idea. The dream idea of this ideal sub-

34

stance seemed to hover in the room, threatening, at any moment, to be driven into material reality by the sheer force of Kleist's description. The vision of this substance beckoned to Otto Kessler.

Kessler stood at the window of the study. Frankfurt was already in darkness. Street lights cast their soft glow across the pavement. Not intending it at all for Kleist's ears, Kessler muttered to himself.

"I see . . . I see."

He stood in silence. A minute passed — a long silence between two people. Then, he walked back to his chair and sat once again.

"And what, Gruppenführer Kleist, will be the conditions under which I would work?"

"First, let us consider the research staff. Do you have colleagues at the university with whom you would like to work?"

"Yes. There are several such men. I also know three or four others . . . former research associates."

"If they are based in other cities," interrupted Kleist, "we will arrange to have them moved to your new facilities. If that doesn't please them, then some other way of coordinating your efforts can be found. In any event, Herr Kessler, within the parameters of normal security measures, you will have complete freedom in choosing your staff."

"And the assistants for each of these men?"

"Each, in turn, will be able to choose his own subordinates. In that way, each participant will feel that he is not constrained to abandon his personal style of work. Do not fear, Herr Kessler. I understand the need to provide the scientific mind with the proper atmosphere."

Kessler relaxed in his chair, stretching his legs out fully. He placed his hands behind his head.

"What of the arrangements for testing our conceptions?

We would, at some point, want to produce test samples and subject them to combat condition stresses. Are you going to ask Krupp to convert part of his present resources?"

"No. In terms of maximum security we cannot do that. It would be wiser to build a new, but small, factory just for the purpose of producing these test samples. If we meet with success, expanding to full production will be easily achieved."

"Where will this be done?"

"The site has yet to be determined. We will settle the matter shortly."

"Gruppenführer Kleist, this work will necessitate a full-time effort. I can only assume, after all you have told me, that you consider this an urgent matter, a top-priority project. At the very least, several years will be needed before we can reasonably expect positive results. I will have to leave my post —"

"Of course, of course. But we are prepared to pay you the equivalent of your present salary plus two thousand marks a year. Will that suffice?"

Indeed it did. Kessler was satisfied. Actually, the generosity of the offer surprised him.

"And we are prepared to do something more. In the event of your successfully completing the project, the Reich will pay you half a million marks. That sum will be free of any form of taxation."

Kleist watched Kessler closely for a response to this last statement. It was a truly fantastic proposition, the kind of offer that Otto Kessler had never heard before. But Kessler's face betrayed nothing of his inner reaction. Perhaps he was attempting to conceal his emotions. Perhaps the offer was too fantastic to seem real.

"And what of the actual research facilities? The laboratories? The offices? You said something before about new facilities? Will they be specially built for this project?"

"Precisely. New facilities, a project headquarters, will be constructed."

Kleist paused. Kessler was searching for further questions, exploring the situation in an attempt to discover reasons for doubt.

"You understand, Herr Kessler, that the Reich will meet all the financial demands which arise during the course of your work. I pledge to you total support. If you require equipment, transportation, materials, anything at all — it will be provided. Money can be found for anything."

The ease, the obvious readiness with which Kleist had been answering all Kessler's inquiries made it clear to the doctor that his guest had thought out everything well in advance of their encounter. The organization that stood behind Reinhard Kleist had anticipated every question, every doubt, every desire, and that organization was fully committed to the achievement of the one goal that the Gruppenführer had so persuasively described. How many others were involved in the machinery of this operation? Who stood behind Gruppenführer Kleist?

"I trust that you will not be offended by what may seem to be excessive curiosity, but there are still several matters that disturb me. First, who are the other people participating in this project?"

"Ah — a good question, Herr Kessler. At this moment there are only four other people who know anything about this scheme. I am afraid that I cannot give you their names. That is a security precaution. Of course, you have not joined us yet — have you? I could hardly reveal to you the identity of these individuals at this point. Once, however, the full machinery of this project begins to move, many others will become involved. But names do not matter, Herr Kessler. They are unimportant. Instead, let me articulate for you a major principle. Very few people will be in a position to understand our final aim. Everything, including the construction of facilities, laboratories, factories, and the rest will be executed in a manner that maximizes security. Surely you can sympathize with me on this issue."

"Then perhaps I failed to put my question properly. Who is the ultimate authority behind this project?"

"The ultimate authority, Herr Kessler? The highest authority. That is all I can say."

Kleist smiled. Thus far, this was the only distinct facial expression the man had made. But the answer itself could only leave Kessler confused. Hadn't Kleist said that even the Führer was suffering from an excess of confidence over Germany's military capabilities? If that was true, then what sense could be imputed to Kleist's reference to a "highest authority"? Was this one of the Gruppenführer's security precautions? This cryptic remark would have to stand unchallenged. Kleist would say no more.

Thus, one troubling issue remained — the question of Kessler's freedom. Was he really free to make whatever decision appealed to him most? Was a Gruppenführer of the SS actually going to give him a choice between significantly different options? What if he refused? Had he not just examined documents from a dossier that the SS was keeping on him? Even if they did not arrest him for refusing, the kind of information they had (and he had seen but a small portion of it) would enable the authorities to make his life very difficult. Kessler thought of his wife. He had been so involved, so caught up in the dialogue with Kleist, that the thought of his own private world had virtually disappeared for a while. His wife, his housekeeper, were still at SS headquarters. Was that the form of intimidation Kleist was going to use?

"Gruppenführer Kleist. What happens if I refuse to join this project as research director?" He stood up energetically as he asked this question. With a sense of purpose, he walked back to the study window. Kessler had done this before during the conversation. He felt strangely confined, as if the path between chair and window were the only one he could legitimately use. Looking out the window, he spoke on.

"Yes — what happens if I refuse? What are the reasonable options for me? You have extensive intelligence materials which can be used against me should I prove to be uncooperative. That much is undeniable. Shouldn't I rather ask — how can I possibly refuse?"

"On the contrary, Herr Kessler, it is entirely possible for you to refuse. In fact, I insist that you do so if that is your genuine inclination."

Kleist's voice was uncharacteristically soft, unusually accommodating.

"There is no coercion implicit in this situation. Let me put your mind at rest. I will gladly leave this dossier here with you even if you refuse the position. Destroy it if you like. There are no copies of these documents."

Kessler turned and looked intently at his guest. It was as if the man could read his mind.

"But you do not believe me. You think that there are other copies and that my offer is fraudulent."

Kessler was caught completely off guard by this. He was still undecided about what to do, but Kleist's disconcerting habit of preemptively voicing Kessler's doubts before Kessler could speak them forced him to conceal his uncertainty. Kleist was shrewdly manipulating the situation, forcing Kessler into a position in which it would be acutely embarrassing to suggest, even implicitly, that Kleist was being less than truthful. Kessler turned away from his guest and walked, hands in pockets, along the bookshelf-lined wall. Upon reaching the corner of the room, he was about to speak, but Kleist anticipated him once again.

"You are still concerned, Herr Kessler."

There was a phone behind Kleist on a small shelf built

into the wall. The Gruppenführer reached for the receiver, picked it up, and dialed a number.

"Give me 318," he said.

There was a short silence.

"Hello . . . this is Gruppenführer Kleist. Could you connect me with Hauptsturmführer Muller? Yes . . . correct."

Another pause.

"This is Gruppenführer Kleist. Muller . . . are you busy? Ah . . . good. Listen to me. May I suggest that you bring Karin Kessler back to her home? Yes . . . and the housekeeper too. They are unconcerned, I trust? Good. Yes . . . I am sure your immediate superior will approve. I will speak to you later."

Kleist hung up.

But would the dreaded intimidation, some terrible reprisal, should he refuse, occur at some future time? Kessler wondered how he could secure a guarantee against that. Could it be that the entire arrangement — the unexpected meeting at home, the disappearance of his wife and housekeeper and the staged return — could it be that all of it had been calculated as a way of inducing him to take the position by generating a false sense of freedom? But surely that thought was mad. Kessler silently accused himself of paranoid thinking. The SS could, in fact, force his hand; and yet here they were, going out of their way to allow him the room for a free choice. It was really not necessary for them to do that.

"Let me say one more thing, Herr Kessler. There would be absolutely no point in our forcing your participation in this project. If you decide to join us, the decision must be taken willingly. That is crucial from my point of view. If your work on this project is to be of the highest quality, if it is to be creative and productive, then you must work with us of your own free will. I cannot help but think that you agree with me fully on this point."

This was perfect. As a scientist, as a man dedicated to finding truth, Kessler believed in his heart that all important work, all truly great work, came from men who dedicated their lives freely, completely, single-mindedly to the pursuit of one overriding goal. Kleist understood this. He would not corrupt the spontaneous force of Kessler's intellectual passion.

"Then I will work with you, Gruppenführer."

"Good . . . good . . . very good, Herr Kessler. I am pleased. You will not regret this decision."

Kessler felt as if he were in a bizarre, unreal state of suspension. In making a major decision, nothing can be certain, and it must have been this inevitable residual uncertainty that created, for Kessler, this peculiar state of inner suspension. When he announced his decision to work on the project, it had seemed to him that someone else had spoken the words. Time seemed to stop. Was there some force, some invisible agent, freezing time, holding back history, so that he could reverse his decision? And yet, when he examined his decision from every rational point of view, Kessler could find no clear argument against it, he could locate no concrete cause for this unaccountable feeling of schizophrenic detachment from the real.

"You recognize, of course, that what we have said today must reach no one's ears. That holds true even for your wife. From this moment on, we shall continue to have considerable contact with each other. I will be the chief intelligence officer for the project. Now, however, let me provide you with a kind of guarantee."

"Guarantee?"

"Yes, a guarantee, or, if you prefer, a contract concerning your . . . shall we say . . . prize?"

Kleist reached into his briefcase and took out a two-page document. He placed it on the long worktable. Kessler examined it. The paper was a contract between the government of the Third Reich and Otto Kessler signifying, among other things, that in the case of successful completion of I-P 9, the code designation for the project, Kessler would receive half a million marks. His salary was stipulated. The conditions under which Kessler would work were also listed — the research staff appointment procedure, construction of new facilities (site undesignated), construction of a factory for producing test samples (site also undesignated) — it was all there.

Kessler read the document twice. It seemed clear enough. The sheer presence of such a document reassured him concerning his decision. He had not expected to be presented with a formal contractual agreement.

A car stopped outside the house. His wife?

Glancing out the study window, as if turning over in his mind some last and dimly apprehended consideration, Kessler saw only the darkness of the sky, the glow of the street lamps, and several cars moving in the distance.

That was all.

He signed.

«2»

Trevor Grey took the tube each morning on the way to his office. He left his flat at 6:30 A.M., walked six blocks to the nearest station in Knightsbridge, bought a *Times* on the corner before descending the steps, and then vanished for a while into the subterranean complexities of the London underground system. He rarely read the paper on the train. The act of reading, combined with the motion of the train, invariably made him sick. Instead, Grey enjoyed holding before his mind's eye an imaginary map of the underground transport system. In this way he could mentally follow the progress he made across the city. This kind of imaginative exercise gave Grey a special pleasure.

After riding for fifteen minutes Grey would emerge onto the streets only four or five blocks from Westminster Abbey. He worked near what is perhaps the most famous, the most historic section of the city. Big Ben, the Houses of Parliament, 10 Downing Street — they were all close by. In March of 1940, in spite of the fact that the war was on, the life of the city continued much as if nothing out of the

43

ordinary were happening. The people who walked to work through Trafalgar Square, past the National Gallery, the people who lived near St. Paul's Cathedral and who drank beer in the pubs — most of them did not display the level of anxiety and fear which one would expect to find in a people just embarked on the bloodiest conflict in human history. It was the period known as the "Phony War." Poland was gone, but all of Western Europe was still intact. In some of London's streets sandbags had been piled up in preparation for air raids, fires, or other war emergencies. Still, there were many people unconvinced that it would ever be necessary to use them. The Battle of Britain would not begin for another four months.

Grey breakfasted regularly at a small corner restaurant not far from his place of work. After that he walked another five blocks and entered a nondescript building located on G____ Street. Grey had a small office in this building on the third floor, a small, unattractive office in which, each day, from roughly 8:00 A.M. to 5:00 P.M. he attended to the delicate and complex tasks set him by his superiors. Grey was employed at M.I. 6. He handled espionage work in foreign countries.

Some people would have called Grey a stereotypical Englishman in that, more often than not, he wore a trench coat and carried an umbrella. But appearances did not concern him much. The coat was always heavily wrinkled. He lost at least one umbrella a year. Like many others who rode to work each day, Grey carried a brown leather bag. In this bag he kept various unclassified documents related to the cases he was working on. He liked to have this bag with him at all times so that if an idea struck him which necessitated checking on some fact, he would have a chance of finding it among the papers he carried. Grey was short, only five foot eight. He was also slender, slender to the point of forcing his doctor to encourage him to eat more. Not all of Grey's colleagues liked him. Some thought him too reserved, even for an Englishman. They interpreted this quality as a form of unfriendliness. Others found him positively strange. The latter judgment was most often based on Grey's peculiar way of "vanishing" into his own world. When this happened, his blue-green eyes glazed over. Grey was only thirty, and that too served to him apart from most of his older colleagues. He had come to the Secret Service straight from Oxford. No doubt intelligence work provided him with the means for participating in the war effort without radically altering his life-style. One might have called Grey a student, a critic of literature who applied interpretive techniques to espionage work in much the same way that he applied them to novels or poems. Perhaps some of Grey's colleagues suspected that he had no active appreciation for the fact that, in Europe at least, real people were dying real deaths, and that intelligence agents were not fictional entities in syllogistic plots. Curiously, Grey's university teachers might have leveled a parallel charge against him in regard to his scholarly work. "Grey — you must confine yourself to what's on the page," one of them had told him. He had a nearly uncontrollable penchant for explaining literature in terms of bizarre theoretical speculations, speculations which frequently left the hard evidence far behind. Just the same, no one, neither his teachers nor his Secret Service colleagues, could have accused him of intellectual incompetence. Grey was an exceptionally bright man.

He also loved to play chess. For him, his work was akin to a real, living chess game. Grey knew very well that the analogy between chess and espionage, or chess and murder mysteries, was a cliché, but that knowledge did not make the analogy any less a compelling, living reality for him.

On March 3, 1940, Grey arrived on the third floor of the

office building at 8:02 A.M. He greeted the secretary, Mrs. Phillips, who handled all the paper work for the agents stationed on the floor. She offered to make him a cup of tea. He gratefully accepted and asked her to bring it to his office.

He stopped by the office of the one colleague with whom he maintained a friendship, Harry Forsyth. The latter had arrived unusually early. Grey peered in, remaining at the threshold of the office.

"Good morning, Harry."

"Ah, Grey. It's you. Have a big day ahead of you?"

"I should think so. What brings you here at this hour?"

"Atkinson rang me up last night. He says he wants to see the files on some local people. I've really got no idea what he has in mind."

"Who ever does? Lunch today?"

"Sorry. I've got to get this done. Tomorrow?"

"All right."

"One o'clock?"

"Good."

Grey crossed the hall, spent thirty seconds fumbling around looking for his keys, finally located them, and let himself into his office. He went through the usual ritual — hung up his coat, unlocked some file cabinets, cleared papers away from the center of his desk, and sat down in order to think out what he had to do. The secretary arrived with the mug of tea. This diverted Grey for several minutes as he looked for sugar. He found it in a bottom desk drawer. Grey sipped the tea while staring blankly out of the single dirty window directly behind his desk. I've got to remind someone to get that bloody thing cleaned off, he said to himself.

He decided on his first task.

He got up, closed and locked the door to his office, went to one of the steel file cabinets, and removed several dark brown folders. These items were each marked "Secret." Placing them on his desk, Grey unclasped the outer covering of each folder. A second inner cover was revealed. On each of these inner coverings two words were printed — Early Riser. These two innocent words were the code designation for a special operation to which Grey had been assigned by his superior, Anthony Atkinson. Grey's branch of the Secret Service handled many kinds of espionage work, but the operation that went by the code name Early Riser represented a uniquely promising endeavor.

In June of 1933, a mere five months after the Nazi seizure of power, a man named Gunther Florstedt had contacted a minor bureaucratic functionary who worked at the British embassy in Berlin. Florstedt was a forty-one-year-old railroad official stationed at the marshaling yard near the German capital. Walking casually among people at a cocktail party, Florstedt had struck up an innocent conversation with the embassy employee. He suggested, in an offhand manner, that a meeting between himself and a higher-ranking British official might be profitable for His Majesty's government. He had something interesting to say. Word of this exchange was passed along. The embassy staff considered the idea for several weeks. Then, figuring that there was nothing to lose, the meeting was set up as requested. Florstedt announced to an attaché on the embassy staff that he was a dedicated anti-Nazi. He claimed, furthermore, that a major European war was absolutely inevitable. The attaché objected to this judgment. Florstedt repeated his conviction. The British, he said, did not really understand Hitler and his Party. In any event, wouldn't it be convenient if a German, involved in railroad communications, perfectly placed in terms of observing troop movements, equipment transports, could be relied upon to get information about these matters to the British? Florstedt then gave a code name to the attaché — "Black Diamond." He said that, in the future, he would both contact them with, and respond to, that name.

The Secret Service was informed about this strange transaction. Men in intelligence work, accustomed to the discriminating uses of blackmail, threat and intimidation, do not react positively to the idea of self-sacrifice. The notion that a citizen of some other potentially hostile nation will voluntarily provide information to a foreign intelligence service will always strike the professional as a move that is part of some larger scheme. But, in this special case, the British underestimated the depth of Herr Florstedt's profound hatred for the Nazis. They did not know that in 1931 two of Florstedt's best friends had been killed by SA storm troopers in a Munich street-fighting incident. His own life didn't mean very much to him. British Intelligence decided to play along for a while in spite of their initial doubts. They contacted Florstedt through several cooperative traveling bank executives. He gave them information about the shipment of newly manufactured armored vehicles. All of it was accurate. For years these contacts continued. The clinching piece of information concerned the movement of troops to the German-Polish border just prior to the invasion in September, 1939. That had convinced the M.I. 6 staff that this "turnaround" German citizen was playing an honest game.

The Florstedt experience was the model for fifteen similar cases. Between June of 1933 and November of 1936, fifteen additional German nationals, all fanatically anti-Nazi, all well placed in terms of access to interesting and valuable information, and all imbued with a darkly prophetic, if not positively apocalyptic, turn of mind, had volunteered to give information to British Intelligence. By 1939, five of these people had been frightened off by the increasingly intense activity of the Gestapo, two had been caught and executed, four continued to send information, and five had been "turned off" by Secret Service headquarters. This meant only that the British felt that it would be wiser to wait until these people could be used in an important, decisive manner. Why risk losing them before that? Trevor Grey was one of two British controllers responsible for running these agents — the Early Riser agents.

Grey was examining the extensive materials he had accumulated on these agents. He was pondering a problem that had been bothering him for several months. Could it be, Grey asked himself, that the war would spread no further? One point of view held that Hitler really admired the English, that he did not want to fight a major war with them. The idea was appealing, although by March, 1940, with a state of war already a complete reality, the notion of real peace seemed hopelessly remote. Ideally, everyone might still have hoped for a negotiated settlement between the antagonists. They had done this in regard to the Czechoslovakian question in 1938. Grey, however, was not an expert in political affairs. He was not in the best position for assessing the chances one way or the other. For him, the force of any calculation could be felt solely in reference to the one issue — what should he do with the Early Riser agents? Should he risk them at this time? If he could get himself to believe that the Germans were preparing a next military move, then it could prove wise to proceed with the activation of the "sleeper" agents. There were people who argued that if Hitler had been opposed forcefully and dramatically in 1935, or 1936, or 1938, then the war itself would never have become a reality. What if England and France, through a precise anticipation of Hitler's next move, could demonstrate a fierce willingness to oppose Germany. Could "sleeper" agents provide the information which would make that kind of preemptive opposition possible? But what if the Germans were really intent on expanding the war? Perhaps calling diplomatic bluffs was no longer possible. In that case, thought Grey, it would be far better to save the agents for a time when a decisive conflict was at hand.

Grey thumbed through his files.

Karl Graml — in charge of production at an aircraft factory in Regensburg.

Jurgen Maier — a colonel in German army communications.

Dr. Wolfgang Buchheim — a leading chemist working for I. G. Farben in Essen.

These people, and others, were awaiting a simple code word which would "activate" them. Grey could not decide. No matter what he did risks would be entailed.

At 11:15 A.M. part of his decision was made for him.

The phone rang. It was Douglas Trenchard on the line. He wanted to see Grey immediately.

Trenchard worked for Section V, the counterespionage division, of M.I. 6. Early in 1935 he had taken a markedly strong interest in the Early Riser operation. Speaking to his own superior, a man named Michael Green, Trenchard had convinced him that the agents who were working with the espionage branch as Early Riser operatives possessed untapped potential for counterespionage work as well. Green readily accepted this line of argument if only in that shared responsibility for Early Riser agents would permit his branch of the Service to participate in a broader range of activities. Green liked power. He, in turn, had called Tony Atkinson and had persuaded him, after an enervating two-hour argument, that in spite of the jurisdictional complications implicit in the suggestion, Trenchard had a good point. Would Atkinson mind if Trenchard served in an advisory capacity on the Early Riser project? Why not make it a joint show? Atkinson agreed to this. Grey didn't care one way or the other, at least not at first. He didn't mind consulting with other people.

Grey went to number 34 W____ Street, the location of Trenchard's office. He brought his brown bag with him.

Trenchard worked in a large, poorly lit room on the first floor of the headquarter's building for the Secret Service, counterespionage branch. There were two odd and strangely disconcerting things about this office. First, three of the walls were lined with bookshelves. There was nothing necessarily peculiar in that, only the books themselves had nothing to do with Trenchard's work. English, German and Russian novels filled the shelves on one wall. There were no translations. Everything in the original languages. Along the second wall there were volumes on physics, chemistry and theology. The combination was arresting. When anyone suggested to Trenchard that he shelve these books in a more reasonable order, he always responded by saying that he couldn't afford the time. The shelves along the third wall were empty. "There . . . someday," said Trenchard, "I will put the books that I will write." People laughed when he said this.

The second odd thing about the office was the dark mahogany desk which sat directly in front of the only bare wall. This desk was kept absolutely clear with the exception of whatever document Trenchard happened to be studying, two telephones which were positioned neatly along one edge of the desk, and a bottle of mineral water and a glass which sat along the opposite edge. Thus, the peculiarity of the desk lay in the resolutely Spartan sense of order which emanated from it. Behind the desk, and breaking the bare monotony of the wall, were two windows. Two floor lamps, placed in front of and to the sides of the desk, provided the only illumination in the room, for the heavy curtains, drawn completely over the win-

51

dows, effectively kept out the daylight. A heavy, maroon leather chair sat almost dead center in the middle of the office.

Douglas Trenchard was a decidedly quiet man. When he did choose to speak, he was most economical with his words. His subordinates all agreed that he was not at all difficult to work for. Indeed, Trenchard apparently had a gift for getting others, technically his inferiors, to forget all matters of rank. People worked for him because they wanted to, and if they did not want to, he was more than eager to let them go. Consequently, those who did stay were extremely productive. Trenchard was tall, thin, and dressed always in an immaculate fashion. Every day he wore a blue suit, raincoat and bowler hat. His eyes were brown and narrow, the hair jet black. What was most striking about Trenchard's appearance, however, were the cheeks and the entire lower facial structure. The narrowness of the face, the white pallor of the skin, and a slight sunkenness of the cheeks seemed to betoken ill health. It was as though the sides of the face were about to collapse into a cavernous hollowness. One asked — is the man sick? Is there some disease, some force, eating away at his physical substance?

"Good to see you, Grey," said Trenchard. "I hope you've been keeping busy."

"Hmmm . . . don't you worry about that."

"Sit, will you?" and Trenchard gestured toward the maroon chair. Grey was always impressed by the distance between the chair and the desk, and by how lonely and isolated the chair looked sitting in the center of the room. It was unnatural.

"I have something rather provocative to show you." Trenchard pointed to the single document which lay on his desk.

" I have here a report from one of our people in Essen.

It was transmitted last night and decoded early this morning. I realize you'll be getting your own copy soon enough, but thought there'd be no point in delaying our chat until tomorrow. Really . . . it's very curious. It concerns one of our Early Riser agents, the man named Buchheim . . . Wolfgang Buchheim."

"Yes . . . he's a sleeper. He has been for several years."

"That's correct."

"Do they have him?"

"Have him?"

"Yes . . . you know. The Gestapo. Have they picked him up?"

"No . . . no. I should say not. You are glum this morning, Grey. It seems that he has initiated contact with us without waiting to be put on assignment."

"Unusual."

"Oh yes."

"What do you make of it?"

"I thought you'd find that interesting. Buchheim reports that he received a visit from someone in the SS. They want him to move . . . just like that. From Essen to Frankfurt. It's an indefinite sort of thing. They don't say what it's for."

Grey thought about this for a moment.

"You really don't think that they've found him out?"

"No. Absolutely no. I see no reason to suspect that. He's too careful . . . and he's been inactive for too long."

"Is he staying with his firm?"

"No, Grey. A fascinating point. I. G. Farben is releasing him so that he can join a special, independent research team. That's all they'll tell him . . . and one more thing. The name of the man he's to work with. Kessler. Otto Kessler. Heard of him?"

"No."

"The two of them worked together in the late twenties

. . . sometime around 1927 . . . before Buchheim took his position with the firm."

"It's still possible, Trenchard, that they're on to him."

"How untrusting of you, Grey . . . really. I think we can afford to wait a while before writing him off. He's been quiet for several years . . . so let's give our man a chance. My intuition tells me that they would have picked him up a long time ago if they knew he's with us."

Grey gestured with his head in a way that indicated only halfhearted acceptance of Trenchard's point.

"In any event, Grey, even with all you have to do, wouldn't it be a good idea for you to watch this one closely?"

"Yes . . . all right, Trenchard, but we really haven't got much of anything yet . . . have we?"

Trenchard chose to ignore this purely rhetorical barb. Grey stood up and walked toward the door. He was, in fact, a trifle annoyed by having been called by Trenchard. They did, as Trenchard had mentioned, get the same information across their desks. In asking him to come over to his office, Trenchard was simply exercising a kind of political power. He was taking the initiative in a manner that seemed to imply that the case in question was his, rather than something that they had to share equal responsibility for.

"I'll look into Kessler," said Grey. "Maybe we can find something interesting."

"Good, Grey . . . very good."

Less than an hour later, Trevor Grey was in the British Museum. It was there that he intended to begin his research into the Kessler-Buchheim affair. The fact that he had displayed little enthusiasm during Trenchard's recitation of the fresh developments meant very little. This reticence bore no relationship to Douglas Trenchard's trustworthiness, for Trenchard was a man for whom Grey had the greatest professional respect. No — Grey was undemonstrative because he had truly internalized the impulses intrinsic to his profession. Let the voice reveal nothing. Keep the muscles of the face relaxed and unresponsive to the soul's inner, spontaneous voice. Grey had found Trenchard's report genuinely interesting. He placed the Kessler-Buchheim matter on the top of his list of priorities.

In Grey's view, expertise at intelligence work entailed adherence to two general principles. First, the professional must learn how to note, to observe, those subtle phenomena which everyone else, hopefully even an astute adversary, will tend to ignore. Sherlock Holmes represented the literary precedent for this principle. Second, the professional, in his passion for minutiae, must not sacrifice his sensitivity to the grosser, more obvious aspects of reality. He must learn not to develop the trained incapacity, the overeducated blindness of a second-rate sleuth. This methodological consciousness was a healthy counter to Grey's more instinctive occupational neurosis — a penchant for believing that much of the world conspired to conceal its purposes from him.

It was in accordance with the second principle that Grey went to the British Museum. As a Secret Service employee he was entitled to use the museum's extensive holdings whenever he chose to do so. There, among the books, the catalogues, the journals and monographs, Grey could, even as a Secret Service agent, indulge his scholar's passion for the search for truth. He told a member of the museum staff that he wanted to see works by a twentieth-century German named Otto Kessler. There were two men with that name listed in the catalogue — one was a theologian, the other was a metallurgist.

So Grey examined the 336-page volume entitled *High*

Temperatures and Metal Fatigue Phenomena, Leipzig, 1931 — English translation by Basil Parks, Cambridge University Press, 1933. He flipped through the pages rapidly and decided that there could be little point in reading it closely. The thing was quite unintelligible. Still, the fact that the English translation had appeared only two years after the first German edition made an impression on Grey. Kessler had spent precious little time looking for an interested foreign publisher. Both translator and publisher had obviously been prepared to rush the English version into print. Kessler's importance was further confirmed by a second fact. Grey was handed a volume containing the full texts of papers which had been presented at a symposium held in Freiburg, Germany, in December, 1934. Most of these papers, written by American, British, French and German scientists, had dealt directly with the implications of Otto Kessler's work on metal fatigue.

And what about Basil Parks, the English translator of Kessler's greatest work? He was on the faculty at Cambridge.

"Basil Parks?"

"Ah . . . yes . . . that's me."

"Grey . . . Trevor Grey."

"Grey?"

"Yes . . . I phoned you earlier."

"That's right . . . that's right . . . come in please. You certainly don't waste your time — do you?"

Grey was standing just outside Parks' office, brown bag in hand. Parks reached out, took his visitor by the arm, and nearly dragged him into the office.

"There . . . there . . . come in. There's no need for you to stand out there."

Parks was a disconcertingly impetuous man, a man whom Grey found impressively comic in appearance. He was short, no taller than five feet two; and wore closely cropped black hair and dark-rimmed glasses. The glasses were broken. One stem was missing completely. The man's nose was grotesquely large. He moved in short, energetic bursts, much as if strong electric currents periodically passed through his body. Parks puffed away furiously at a cigarette which he held between pudgy nicotine-stained fingers.

"Would it be possible for me to ask you a few questions?"

"Indeed it would."

"I'm with M.I. 6. I believe I told you —"

"Yes . . . we've been through that."

Grey started to reach into his inner jacket pocket in order to produce an identification card he could show Parks.

"No need for that, really . . . no need at all . . . hmm. Here . . . sit." Parks rapidly moved a pile of books off a chair located next to his well-cluttered desk. Next, he grabbed Grey's bag out of his hand and placed it on the floor in a far corner of the office. He motioned to the empty seat.

"Thank you, Mr. Parks."

Parks sat down in his own desk chair, leaned over the desk, and tapped the ash off his cigarette into a large and oddly misshapen ash tray which was perched precariously on top of yet another pile of books sitting along the far edge of the desk.

"At your service, Mr. Grey."

"Would it be possible for me to get at my —"

"Ah, of course. It was foolish of me to grab it away from you like that" — and Parks had to get up again, retrieve Grey's bag, and hand it to him. Grey reached into the bag and brought out a book. He placed it on the desk in front of Parks.

"You've read my translation? Really? You are a metallurgist as well as a secret agent. A fascinating combination I must say."

"No, Mr. Parks. I am not a metallurgist, but this volume interests me just the same."

"What would you like to know?"

"I want to learn about the author of this volume."

"Kessler . . . old Kessler."

"Yes . . . perhaps you can tell me about him. You worked closely with this man?"

"Indeed yes . . . I had to . . . we didn't waste any time on that thing, you know." Parks pointed to the book. "Kessler sent me the pages of the manuscript while he was writing it. Thirty, forty pages at a time. Translated right along with him."

"Have you met him, or was this all arranged and done through the mail?"

"Oh yes . . . I met him. I worked with him. In 1927 . . . no . . . 1928 . . . that was the first meeting. I was in Germany at the time doing some research on steel production. We met in Essen and became fast friends. Actually, we formed the idea of our little joint effort while drinking beer in one of those noisy beer cellars . . . or beer halls . . . you know the type of place."

"Yes."

"A bit too raucous for me."

"Yes."

"Hmmm . . . well . . ."

"By joint effort you mean this book?"

"Right . . . the book. He told me about his work, about his plans to write, and we agreed that I'd do the translation. Dry stuff, you know . . . not like doing Goethe's *Faust* . . . but it's an important work . . . a major work . . . quite thrilling in its own way."

"And you had no trouble getting the university press interested in the project?"

58

"Good Lord no. They positively jumped at the idea."

"An important man . . . this Kessler?"

"Yes, as I said . . . you heard me . . . a major work."

Parks puffed at his cigarette, making a sucking, then a smacking, sound as he first inhaled, then removed the cigarette from his mouth. He looked at Grey, his eyes growing suddenly wide with curiosity. It was as though he realized, for the first time, that he had an agent from M.I. 6 in his office.

"What is this about? Is Kessler an agent of some sort?"

"No . . . no . . . I can tell you that Kessler is not an agent. Not so far as we know."

"Exactly as I thought. Exactly. That would really be too much. That would be perfect . . . really," and Parks expelled an explosive, snorting laugh. "The idea of Kessler working for some secret service . . . the Gestapo, or whatever it is they have over there . . . that would be terrifically absurd."

"I take it that your feeling for the ridiculous is stimulated by that idea."

"Oh yes . . . exceedingly."

And again he tapped the ash off his cigarette.

"Because Kessler is apolitical? He's indifferent? Is that it?"

"Not exactly, Mr. Grey. He's no more, no less political than anyone else, I suppose. Kessler is simply dedicated to his work — that's all. He hasn't the time, the energy for anything else. I trust that you understand me. Kessler is really quite a charming fellow in his own way . . . a peculiar stumbling way . . . but he is like the rest of us . . . jealous of his time. He keeps to himself. His wife is like that too. But you know, time slips away, Grey . . . just like that. One really must dispense with nonessentials. We're all like that, more or less . . . jealous of our time . . . there's nothing to be done about it."

"Yes, I see," said Grey, and he could not, for the moment, think of a suitable continuation for the conversation. Parks was one of those people who intones his words as if they are utterly the last to be said on the topic under discussion. Grey really didn't like the man. He was too frenetic.

"Mr. Parks, I am interested in Kessler's work . . . in his potential . . . his capabilities. What he can do . . . you see?"

"What he can do? Well, I suppose there's no question about that. He can probably do whatever he wants to do. I don't think one would overstate the case if one called Kessler a genius. Anyone can see that. All you need do is read the book . . . but that's right. You can't, really . . . can you?"

"No."

"No matter, but it is absolutely true. He is quite something."

"Would it surprise you then to learn that Kessler may have been chosen to lead a team of research people?"

"So! They've done that . . . have they?"

"It appears to be the case."

"It's about time."

"Let's speak of this as a hypothetical matter, Mr. Parks."

"But they have done it, haven't they? Kessler is in charge of a project — isn't he?"

"Mr. Parks."

"Yes . . . yes . . . no, not at all. It wouldn't surprise me. Would it surprise you?"

"But what would they have him do? You've worked with him. What would the Germans set him onto?"

"Oh . . . now that's another question. I can't say. It could be anything — research on alloys for gun barrels — fatigue studies on metals used in aircraft production — water pressure on submarine hulls. It could be any of those things. I would have to know more."

"Does the name Wolfgang Buchheim mean anything to you?"

"It is vaguely familiar."

"He's a chemical engineer."

"No . . . not really. I can't say that I've heard of his work. But that means nothing. He could be a first-rate man. One can't know everything and everyone."

Parks smiled.

Grey left Cambridge shortly after this last exchange, totally convinced that he had exhausted Parks as a source of useful information. But he hadn't been in his London office more than five minutes when the phone rang. It was Parks.

"I've been trying to reach you, Grey."

"I just got in."

"Ah yes . . . well it's a good thing you left me your number."

"Yes . . . we always try to do that."

"Did you see my ash tray, Grey?"

"That odd thing on top of the books?"

"Right, Grey . . . that's the thing . . . now that could be a possibility."

"What could be a possibility, Parks?"

"Five, maybe six, years ago, Kessler told me he was trying to think out a formula for a special metal . . . a new kind of alloy . . . something extraordinarily strong . . . just a pet project of his . . . a hobby you might say. The point was for it to be both strong and light. In any event, he played around with it for a while . . . tried an experiment or two . . . just for the pleasure of it."

"Yes, Parks."

"That ash tray was the product of one of those experiments. He gave it to me three, four years back. The experiment was a failure. The substance is hard, but weak . . . not unlike a diamond, if you follow me, Grey."

"Yes . . . cleavage planes."

"Right, Grey. It splits along cleavage planes."

"I see . . . yes."

"But still, that is a suggestion worth thinking about. Maybe they've put him onto that one again . . . producing a new variety of metal . . . you see?"

«3»

Reinhard Kleist told Otto Kessler that there would be some delay before their project could achieve the status of a fully operational institution.

"You see, Herr Kessler, there is nothing so difficult as the problem of organization. This will take time."

The Gruppenführer had said this while standing in the entrance foyer, just before departing from Kessler's home on the evening of that first meeting. During the undefined interim period, Kessler was to conduct his life as if nothing had happened.

"Go to your office each day . . . come home each night . . . invent whatever explanation you like about the significance of my visit."

"I can say that you were making inquiries about a colleague at the university."

"Correct, Herr Kessler. As you know, people are prepared to imagine the worst about the SS and its activities. It is a hated, a feared organization. It prides itself on this. Now, however, I suggest that you start working on the conceptual foundations of our project."

To work and to wait. That would be Kessler's responsibility. Kleist promised that he would be in touch with him very soon.

But the delay persisted for longer than Kessler anticipated. How could he know that Gruppenführer Kleist was an extraordinarily busy individual? In April of 1940, just four months after the interview with Kessler, he accompanied German troops as they invaded and occupied Norway. In May of the same year, the Gruppenführer rode along with Hoth's Fifteenth Panzer Corps as it struck across a helpless France. The indefatigable Kleist reenacted, time and again, the scene which had occurred southwest of Radom. Perched on a hillside, peering through powerful field glasses, he would observe the thrust of the panzers, the pulverizing Stuka attacks, the collapse of the enemy. Kleist — the overseer, director of surrealistic spectacles staged, as it were, for the viewing pleasure of some invisible audience. He told his colleagues that these battlefield excursions represented a form of recreation.

"I tire easily of desk work," he said.

Kleist sent Kessler brief letters in which he commented on military progress and encouraged the doctor to go forward with his work.

And then, at the end of June, 1940, Reinhard Kleist returned to Frankfurt.

Now, the Gruppenführer possessed a rare gift for coping with that "problem of organization" he had referred to in his talk with Kessler. Indeed, organization was no problem at all to him, if by "problem" one meant only an annoying obstacle, a set of bothersome details. In each organizational problem Kleist perceived the key to further power, to further forms of total control. To him, the organizing of human beings represented the purpose of existence.

64

Asked for an objective appraisal of himself, Kleist might simply have called himself an artist. He considered himself an individual with refined aesthetic sensibilities. Form thrilled him. He was a lover of music. Enormous, late romantic orchestral compositions aroused his greatest passion. But what, precisely, was the object of this aesthetic taste? Was it the sound itself, the tightly organized series of tones that moved him, or was it not rather the mechanically organized human aspect of this sound production that stirred him most deeply? A wooden stick raps on a music stand, it is poised tensely in space, and one hundred hearts, minds and bodies prepare simultaneously to obey the slightest command, to respond to the subtlest gesture. That is the form of human organization in art, the totalitarian impulse in beauty.

Kleist, the overseer-director, the conductor of SS organization, applied his aesthetic passions to the purely human sphere in a peculiar way. In human affairs, there must always be something that is whole, complete, and organically perfect. There must be form. But only a few can be permitted to possess a thorough knowledge of the "whole." That was the key to power. Indeed, Kleist believed that only he should know the "whole," possess the Truth, the Truth that lies in organization. Before his mind's eye he could project his personal vision of the Ideal — an enormous chart spread out on an equally enormous wall. On this chart would be drawn a complex series of lines linking together the names of myriad offices, agencies, and headquarters — all arranged in a hierarchy of superordination and subordination, each in a well-defined relation to the others. What would be the real point of this strange vision? It would be that only he, Kleist, the sole possessor of the gigantic chart, would understand the internal mechanics of this labyrinthine universe. And the participants in this ideal world? Each would know something, but no one could know everything. Each could envision, as it were, a limited portion of the chart, but only Kleist would be able to grasp the whole. This was the Gruppenführer's personal application of the Christian principle which holds that the left hand should not know what the right is doing.

"Remember this well," Kleist had once told an SS leadership class. "Observe every organization from a position of omniscience. Work everything so that no one else can ever glimpse the totality of which they are a part."

A genuinely totalitarian principle, and Reinhard Kleist was its master.

Otto Kessler was summoned to SS headquarters at the end of July, 1940. Kleist wished to speak to him, for it appeared that the project, code designation I-P 9, was about to be formally activated.

Gruppenführer Kleist sat behind a large desk in an office on the first floor of SS headquarters. On the wall behind him a swastika banner hung from ceiling to floor. A framed, autographed photograph of Hitler sat on the desk.

"Herr Kessler, in spite of my absence, my staff has seen to your request for research personnel."

"Yes . . . I'm delighted to hear that. Wolfgang Buchheim has personally contacted me. He is a puzzled man."

"But you've told him nothing?"

"No, no . . . nothing at all for the present . . . as we agreed. But he is anxious to learn something about the assignment."

Kleist's staff officers had already contacted many of the men who were to participate in the project. Throughout Germany, scientists were learning that they would have to move to new locations.

Dr. Gerhard Reitlinger would go to Rostock.

Dr. Ernst Bennecke would move to Hamburg.

Dr. Helmut Schallmayer would leave for Ludwigshafen.

Each of these men, and others, knew nothing of the ultimate purpose of the move. "That you will learn later," each was told. "Fear nothing. The rewards will be commensurate with the sacrifices." Kessler had named some of these men. Kleist, working with a list of his own "chosen," singled out others for purposes of his own.

"A project of these proportions, Herr Kessler, entails a great deal of work . . . some of it trivial . . . the rest fundamental. I have arranged all these project-related tasks so as to achieve a maximum diffusing of responsibility. Various branches of the SS will handle different components of I-P 9."

And Kleist informed Kessler about some of these organizational details.

For example, a branch of the Reichssicherheitshauptamt, the Reich Security Main Office under the special command of Standartenführer Kurt Schreyer, would issue the orders, the documents, pertaining to the relocation of all concerned parties.

"A very efficient officer, Herr Kessler, although lacking somewhat in imagination. He will think that I am recruiting people for research into the race question."

Yet another branch of the SS bureaucracy, part of the SS Führungshauptamt, or Operational Main Office, under the aegis of Hauptsturmführer Ulrich Huber, would see to the job of contracting and securing all building materials required for project facilities.

"You will see, Herr Kessler, that, in this way, all of our construction needs can appear as related to Waffen SS training. This will be convenient for us as a method of forestalling interbranch rivalry."

And yet one more item (Kleist so obviously enjoyed describing his organizational maneuvers) — a section of the SS Wirtschafts-Verwaltungshauptamt, or Economic

Administrative Main Office — a command under Oberführer Erwin Prinz — would arrange for transportation, food, and all the basic necessities for those engaged in project activities.

"An innocuous operation, Herr Kessler. It can hardly generate suspicion, and, in any case, my old friend Prinz lacks all genuine initiative. A dull colleague can be very helpful. I cannot imagine that the same principle has any application in your kind of work."

"No . . . I'm afraid not. None at all."

But Gruppenführer Kleist had yet to reveal to Kessler the particular stroke of genius that he had meticulously prepared. He always prepared at least one such stroke for that dimension of his work which lay closest to his soul — the dimension of deception, of Intelligence. All Germany — if possible, all occupied Europe — would constitute the game board on which Reinhard Kleist would play out the elaborate moves he had designed as a foil for enemy intelligence. If they were at all competent, the British would learn something about I-P 9. Kleist would be ready for them when they did.

So Otto Kessler was informed that much of the organizational structure of I-P 9 would be, in effect, entirely extraneous to the project's real purpose.

"Competent as they might be, not all of the men assigned to this project will work toward the result which is our true aim."

"What do you mean?"

"It is quite simple, Herr Kessler. A certain portion of our effort will have one function, and one function only — deceiving enemy intelligence. The British will be watching us. Their secret service is a reputable organization. Do not doubt my word on that. Therefore, we are going to establish one real research center. That one will come under your supervision, and it will be located here, in Frankfurt."

"But we would be better off, wouldn't we, if the center were set up in a more isolated, a less urban, setting?"

"No, Kessler . . . not at all. A poor conception in my view. A research center located, for example, in the country, would be subject to clever, daring attacks by the enemy. British Intelligence finds us out, a commando team is sent in, a low-level air attack is staged, and our work is set back at small cost to our opponent. That will never do. You see, Herr Kessler, your notion is excessively melodramatic. No. We will build our main research center here, directly in the middle of the city, right in the center of a business district. That is the type of idea which intrigues me. Who would suspect it? We can use an old building. Remodel it according to our needs. An aura of innocence, of the conventional, will surround our operation. If you consider my proposal, you will recognize that an advantage is to be gained by choosing a location which is, on the face of it, absurd. Your research will be conducted next to a department store."

Kleist smiled. He was unashamed to display pleasure at his own ideas.

"Coffee, Herr Kessler?"

"What? Excuse me?"

"Would you like coffee? I can send for it."

"No . . . no. Please continue."

"Good. Next there will be a set of additional locations involved in our project. Essen, Lübeck, Rostock, Cologne, Stuttgart, Saarbrücken. There will be others. In these cities we will operate decoy projects. Our purpose will be to run them in a style that will attract the attention of enemy intelligence while simultaneously making it apparent that each case is a top-security matter. A delicate undertaking. Making the unimportant seem significant. You understand? We let the English believe we are conducting rocket research, or investigation into the use of poison gas.

69

This strategy guarantees us, at the least, that our real project does not become dramatically highlighted. If we are fortunate it will appear as if the real thing is a decoy, while the decoys are the real thing."

"But why . . . why do all this? It is surely wiser to devote our energies to tighter security around Frankfurt."

"It is better to have two lines of defense than one. My scheme does not preclude your point. Let us have the best of both worlds. We cannot conduct the I-P 9 project without attracting attention. My aim is to diffuse that attention."

But Otto Kessler had some questions about the implications of Kleist's baroque security arrangements. Was it, for example, really the case that the talents of a large portion of the professional men asked to participate in the project would be wasted? Would most of these men be called upon to do nothing, or rather, to do nothing more than idly occupy positions in decoy stations?

"No, Herr Kessler. I do not favor such conspicuous counterproductivity. Some of the men will be encouraged to pursue work they were previously engaged in. Others can be encouraged to begin fresh research. Each, however, must be made to believe that his effort is but part of some larger undertaking. That, in itself, will increase the likelihood of the enemy stumbling across a tantalizing, although misleading, clue."

"And yet, Gruppenführer, it seems to me that the fundamental thing —"

"Yes . . . the major aspect will be that each man will be playing an active role in the greater effort — my decoy scenario for I-P 9. So, you see, we will not actually be lying to these men when we ask them to join us."

"No, that is true. You will not actually be lying to them."

"But then, Herr Kessler, all of this is an intrinsic part of my work. Is it not?"

"Yes . . . yes it is."

"Your code of professional ethics is violated by my scheme?"

"In some way . . . yes . . . I suppose it is."

"As a scientist, you are interested in truth. As an intelligence officer, Herr Kessler, I am interested in half-truths."

Briefly, Kleist drummed with his fingers on top of his desk.

"Reichsführer Himmler," he continued, "a true plagiarist in my view, reminds us that no task exists for its own sake. You must approach everything in that spirit, Herr Kessler."

"And my own staff, Gruppenführer. Will they be in a position to know the truth?"

"You have provided me with the names of four men with whom you wish to work closely."

"Correct."

"Three of them will be permitted to do so."

"And the fourth?"

"Let us speak about him."

"Who is the fourth?"

"Dr. Wolfgang Buchheim. I would suggest, if you have no objection, that we give him a subsidiary task to begin with."

"But why?"

"We are uncertain regarding his status as a security risk."

"Has he done something to arouse your suspicion?"

"Now understand, Herr Kessler, that this is really not my responsibility. It was one of my staff officers, a methodical young man, who raised this issue with me. He says that Buchheim may lack the appropriate zeal. Herr Buchheim joined the Party later than the other men on your list. His attendance at Party functions is sporadic. To be honest with you, I do not believe that these things are significant in this case. Still, I refuse to contradict a dedicated staff officer who stands by a strong conviction. I cannot do it. It is bad for morale. So bear with me, Herr Kessler. I have worked out a compromise. Wait only for a while. Buchheim will be on your staff, but in a lesser capacity. Make use of his capabilities without telling him everything. Is this agreeable?"

"Yes, but these are conditions —"

"Conditions which you had not anticipated? Not precisely, Herr Kessler. Recall, for a moment, that on the evening of our first conversation, I said that all project appointments would be subject to approval from a security standpoint."

"I don't quite remember . . ."

"It is true. I do not misrepresent myself, Herr Kessler. This is an unfortunate development; however, I know I can rely on your understanding, your tact, your patience."

Kessler could not object further. Surely, he thought, Buchheim would prove himself to be a trustworthy, reliable and, above all, indispensable man. In any event, it was growing late. Kessler did have work to do and had no desire to waste an entire day discussing bureaucratic details. One additional matter. The factory. Where would it be located? Had a decision been made?

"We will build it in the east, in Poland."

"A purely arbitrary decision, I suppose."

"No, Herr Kessler. If British bombers want to reach it, then they will have to cross the entire Reich in order to do it."

"Ah yes . . . correct. Foolish of me not to think of it."

"And then there are labor costs."

"Labor costs?"

"Yes, Kessler. Factories cost money."

"Indeed they do. Well, I suppose that the Poles are in no position to negotiate wage settlements — are they?"

"No."

". . . The disadvantages of losing, rather than winning."

And now Kessler prepared to leave SS headquarters. He rose from his chair.

"Work beckons to me, Gruppenführer."

Kleist, always thoughtful, ordered a car for him. They agreed to meet again soon so that Kleist could keep him informed about the progress in constructing the needed facilities. Standing at the entrance of the building, Kessler thought of one last question. It was just curiosity.

"What does the code designation mean? Is it a standard form, one of a series of SS security designations?"

"I-P 9. It is something I thought of myself," said Kleist. "The letter 'I' stands for 'infernal,' the letter 'P' for 'Proteus.' Fitting, I think, Herr Kessler. Infernal can be understood as a description of the effects our project will ultimately have on our enemies. Proteus refers to the protean quality of our end product, the ability of the metal to be molded and shaped into myriad forms."

Was this a touch of poetry added, unnecessarily, to an otherwise dry scientific endeavor? Not for Otto Kessler. He liked this strange symbolic-poetic designation, for scientific truth was both beautiful and poetic to him. The Gruppenführer was a bureaucrat, but not a dull one. He was not insensitive to higher values.

The following day, Reinhard Kleist was on the phone with Brigadeführer Kurt Heiden of the Totenkopfverbände in Berlin. He had a favor to ask of him. Kleist informed the Brigadeführer that he was arranging for a special labor force to work on a project in the eastern occupied area.

"This will be a dispensable force?" asked Heiden.

"That is correct," said Kleist.

The Gruppenführer said that he needed a guard detachment for assignment to this group. The only thing which distinguished this request from thousands of similar requests was not its substantive content, but the style in which it was made. Reinhard Kleist emphasized, unequivocally, that under no condition did he want the Brigadeführer to disrupt his schedule of prior commitments. He should cooperate only if it was convenient. The manner in which certain officers assumed that all other operations should cease because they had, invariably, "higher priority" affairs to attend to, was outrageous. Heiden understood perfectly. He chuckled knowingly. He knew about these other officers. No names need be mentioned. He truly appreciated Kleist's effort to be considerate.

"Leave this to me," he said. "I will attend to it."

Within three days it was all arranged. Whenever the Gruppenführer wanted the guard detachment placed on active duty, he need only give Heiden a call.

Otto Kessler scrupulously heeded Kleist's suggestion. He lived as if nothing at all had happened. His friends and colleagues detected no change in his behavior. But Kessler could not repress fully a growing impatience with the failure of the project to achieve operational status. He worked on his own, but that did not satisfy him. He found himself looking forward intensely to the prospective team effort. Good minds working together — he enjoyed that. But Otto Kessler discovered that he harbored another, more surprising, feeling — a kind of secret, barely to be acknowledged pleasure at being a key participant in a nearly conspiratorial, therefore "history-making" enterprise.

And then there was Karin Kessler. Imperceptibly at first, a subtle tension began to develop between them. Gruppenführer Kleist had told Kessler that no one, not even his wife, was to learn about the project. He acquiesced in this condition without any uneasiness. Kessler was not indifferent to his wife's feelings, but he believed also that Karin did not even pretend to an interest in his work. Unfortunately, this was a miscalculation. Yes — she was not interested in his work, but she cared about the condition of secrecy that obtained between them. She began to develop obsessive fears.

"Ever since the visit from the SS, Otto, you have been different," she said.

This was inaccurate. Kessler had not really changed, but Karin hoped anyway to force the truth out of him by suggesting, however vaguely, that he was being poisoned or corrupted by the new situation. Still, from another perspective, she did indeed have some reason to think he was different. Kessler grew increasingly preoccupied with the conceptual problems intrinsic to the project. In itself, this state of preoccupation was nothing new for Otto Kessler. Karin, however, who had hitherto been quite capable of ignoring her husband's absorption in his work, now found that the condition of secrecy riveted her attention on this preoccupation in a new way. She imaginatively participated in his private states of mind. What was he really thinking? Was there something happening related to the safety of either of them? Was he being watched by the police because someone suspected him of unpatriotic activities? Was he protecting her against a potentially terrible contingency by saying nothing?

"I'm sorry. I've been sworn to secrecy," he would say.

It did not help that, at first, he had tried the cover story about the SS and a hypothetical colleague at the university. Karin had not believed it. Then he had broken down and confessed to as much of the truth as he could reasonably admit. This too was unsuccessful.

"If it were really only your work, you could tell me about it," she said.

75

He apologized for himself, for the situation, but it was useless.

"I don't understand your work anyway," she added, "so what harm could it do to tell me about it?"

"Yes . . . yes, I know. But there are others who will understand it."

She was not satisfied.

"Listen to me, Karin," he said with overworked patience, "you must get completely out of your mind the idea that we are in danger. We are not in danger. No one we know is in danger."

But Karin Kessler could not wish this idea out of her consciousness. She decided to suppress, as best she could, the external signs of her anxiety. Realizing that Otto would continue to be unrepentantly silent, she scrupulously avoided any further mention of her feelings. But the secret continued to exert its presence.

Kessler went to the office each day at the University Research Center. He worked and waited for Kleist to call him with news about the project facilities. Weeks went by. The summer of 1940 passed and the fall came. The newspapers carried stories about fantastic air battles over the English Channel. The Luftwaffe, according to these reports, was clearing the skies of British fighters.

One brilliant October afternoon, while shopping with Karin in downtown Frankfurt, Kessler noticed that a large building next to a department store had been closed down. Formerly, it had housed a series of shops on the street level, and, on the floors above, the offices of a law firm. Kessler could see a man scraping the lettering off the windows of the upper stories. Workmen were continually entering and leaving the building. The amount of activity, in addition to the kinds of materials being carried by the men, indicated that the inside of the structure was undergoing renovation. Kessler's intuition told him that this place was going to be the new research facility. He was right.

Time passed. Kleist did keep in touch with Kessler as he had said he would. He even invited the scientist to lunches at an officers' club located in the SS headquarters building. Kessler felt out of place at this club even though everyone treated him with great civility. He heard discussions about weapons, armored warfare tactics, the problems of the occupation in conquered territories. He was bored by all this.

Then, in late November, the word came from Gruppenführer Kleist. The facilities were ready. The first full meeting of the research staff could be held.

Kessler resigned his post at the university.

The initial meeting occurred late in the afternoon on a damp, cold November day. Otto Kessler radiated excitement now that the research facilities had been completed. The other three men who comprised the central staff expressed relief to each other, and to Kessler, for this first meeting meant the end of months of suspense concerning the nature of the project. They gathered in a small conference chamber on a subbasement level of the renovated building. Reinhard Kleist sat in a corner of the room, waiting to say whatever he had come to say.

Kessler began. Dr. Bernhard Gastner, Dr. Helmut Neumann and Dr. Wolfram Siemens listened attentively while he explained to them the goal of project I-P 9. The presentation took twenty-five minutes. Kessler stopped. The others, out of a sense of the occasion, applauded briefly. Kleist was silent. Kessler, assuming that the Gruppenführer would have some statement to make, introduced him to the staff.

Reinhard Kleist stood stiffly behind the lectern and spoke for half an hour, explaining, with exemplary care, the top-security status of I-P 9. "No one is to know anything," he said. That stipulation allowed of no exceptions. Kessler, hearing this once again, wondered how it would affect the other men. All telephones used by the staff, said Kleist, both home telephones and phones at the research center, would be tapped. Upon entering or leaving the building, every individual would be potentially subject to search procedures. Certain documents could not leave the building and would be locked away at the end of each day. Did everyone understand these regulations and the rigor with which they would be applied? No one, of course, was to feel personally affronted by any of these measures. They were standard procedures for any top-security project and were not, in any case, aimed at the present audience. That was all that Kleist had to say other than that he was the officer in charge of security and that any problems related to project secrecy should be brought directly to him. The Gruppenführer paused. Questions? There were none. He turned the meeting over to Kessler.

Now, what would the staff be doing first? Kessler had the advantage of having known about the project goal for many months before the others learned of it. He had already devoted many hours of hard thought to the problem of creating a lightweight, extraordinarily hard substance. Consequently, he thought it would be wise if, at first, he spent several weeks lecturing to the staff on conceptual progress he thought he had made. Thus far, he had focused on the effects of chemical composition on fatigue strength. Kessler wished to explicate the question of phosphorous content in low-alloy steels. Gastner, a specialist on the effects of heat treatment and microstructure on fatigue and tensile strengths, would be certain to find Kessler's remarks stimulating. Everyone agreed that the opening lecture series was a superb idea. Such exploratory sessions would maximize creative interchange among the men. They would try it and see. One can never predict the course that complex solution-finding will follow. It could take ten weeks. It could take ten years.

The meeting was adjourned. All were tired, both from the release implicit in terminating the prolonged period of suspense, and from the length of the opening session. The real work would begin the following day.

"So . . . good day, gentlemen," said Kessler. "I assure you that it will be a great pleasure for me to work with such a distinguished group of men."

But Kessler, instead of going directly home after this first meeting, conferred briefly with Wolfgang Buchheim. The two were delighted to see each other. After exchanging recent personal histories, Kessler told Buchheim what he wanted.

"Look, Wolfgang, I am tired," he said.

"Yes . . . I can see."

"We can meet again tomorrow, so let me get business out of the way first. I would like you to write a report on all of your findings on stress conditions and corrosion fatigue. Your work in that area is exemplary."

This request, thought Kessler, would keep Buchheim occupied for several weeks while, simultaneously, it would allow the SS time in which to discover that Buchheim simply did not represent a security problem. It would also spare Kessler the embarrassment of telling Buchheim he was not fully trusted by the authorities. Buchheim was satisfied with Kessler's request, and the two men parted after agreeing to lunch together during the week.

And so, Otto Kessler lectured to his inner circle of colleagues. Each morning, at 9:30, he would start, and by noon the blackboards in the large basement conference chamber would be filled with the fruits of Kessler's complex ruminations. Within ten days, they had decided that any form of steel-tungsten alloy could not possibly yield the characteristics they were looking for. Each day, following the lunch break, which was usually taken outside the building, the group would methodically discuss Kessler's work, pointing out, wherever possible, the flaws in his thinking. One afternoon, Kessler pulled out of his briefcase an oddly misshapen ash tray which normally stood on a bureau in his bedroom. An Englishman named Basil Parks also possessed one of these grotesque items. Those were the only two objects in the world, according to Kessler, which were made out of an experimental alloy he had concocted some years ago. This alloy was a sensationally tough substance, but its tragic flaw was that, just like a diamond, it tended to split along cleavage planes.

"No, gentlemen," said Kessler. "We cannot build tanks out of this material."

He had come to recognize the nature of his error, his failure of vision. It was quite useless. The entire approach had been misconceived.

Then, early in the morning on December 4, 1940, an event, innocuous and entirely innocent in itself, marked a radical break in Otto Kessler's existence.

He was sitting in his office thinking about the relation between rotating bending fatigue strength and tensile strength of aluminum alloys, when the phone rang. It was Kleist.

"Herr Kessler, does your staff have enough to do to keep it occupied for three or four days?"

"Yes, easily," replied Kessler. "They're still busy absorbing the results of my work. Our initial review seminars are going more slowly than I had anticipated."

"Very good. You see, there is something I should like to have you examine while we are still in an early stage of development."

It was the factory. Kleist wanted Kessler to look over the construction site and comment on the building plans. If he had any suggestions concerning the incorporation of testing equipment into the structure, the construction engineers would have to learn about them quickly. Kessler was flattered by the Gruppenführer's request although he did not think he would be capable of making many suggestions. He figured that a minor request might be a nice gesture. He could ask for a small office-laboratory arrangement in the rear of the structure, but no more.

"Good, Herr Kessler," said the Gruppenführer, "then we will leave in the morning." With that, Kleist had hung up.

This abrupt termination of the conversation surprised Kessler. No specific arrangements had been made concerning transportation. Nothing at all had been said about a departure time. Where was he to meet Gruppenführer Kleist? He tried calling him back, but Kleist had left his office.

That evening Kessler said very little while he ate his meal. He chose the moment when Ingrid served dessert to inform his wife that he would be gone for three or four days.

"Where?" she asked him, not even bothering to look up from her plate.

"I don't exactly know myself. In the east, in Poland somewhere." He did not expect that this would satisfy her.

"I see," she replied dryly.

"But it will only be for —"

"I know . . . you said three or four days."

He was silenced.

Karin slowly arose from her chair and left the dining room. She was not frightened by the prospect of Otto's leaving for a couple of days. Gradually, during the preceding half year, she had succeeded in convincing herself that Otto spoke the truth when he said no one was in danger. If the Gestapo or the SS thought he represented a threat, then they would have arrested him some time before. In her view, that was the way they worked. Otto's secret, then, did not involve danger, but the impenetrable reality of that secret remained intact. Surely, it was nothing other than the scientific project Otto said it was, and yet, the extent of his apparently limitless preoccupation with it, the fact that one evening he had told her that their phone would have to be tapped, the fact that so much of his life space was filled completely by this matter about which he refused ever to say anything — all this combined to generate an alienation that was growing between them. He would be gone for three days? He could have gone for ten. It would make no difference. He could say nothing about the trip. She could do nothing about it. Karin might have spoken to Otto about this distance that daily increased between them, but that too was impossible. His secrecy engendered in turn, and against her will, a like response in her. The sense of openness that is a precondition for intimate communication had vanished. His silence effectively thwarted her desire to speak. She could not intrude on him. So, Karin left the dining room table.

Otto sat there and drank two more beers. Then he retired for the evening, telling Ingrid that she needn't bother to help him in the morning. He would be rising at a very early hour.

The next day, Otto Kessler awoke even earlier than usual. It was dark outside. Black clouds were swirling about in the skies over Frankfurt. He could hear a constant, rapid drumming sound. A driving mixture of sleet and rain was pounding relentlessly against the roof and walls of the house. The sound came in irregular, undulating waves, increasing and decreasing in intensity, seeming, at one instant, to recede into the distance, then leaping forward in a fresh, wind-driven burst of energy. Kessler got out of bed. He did not know precisely what was supposed to happen. Therefore, he decided to quickly pack a traveling bag so that the arrival of the SS or a call from Kleist would not catch him unprepared. He made his preparations in the bedroom while hurriedly eating a breakfast roll obtained from the kitchen. Kessler discovered that he felt no anxiety about the mysteriously vague travel arrangements. For Otto Kessler, a man of habit, a creature of routine, this was unusual. He knew, however, that his relationship with Kleist was untroubled. He could rely on the Gruppenführer. Therefore, the journey would work out correctly. It was astonishingly dark in the house because of the storm outside. The rain and sleet continued to pound against the walls. The sound was merciless. Karin, either asleep or feigning sleep, lay on her side with her head buried deeply in two large pillows. Kessler considered waking her, but quickly decided against it. He thought to himself, unaccountably, that she should be left alone, that she had nothing to do with his journey. When he finished his preparations, he closed the clasps on his bag, and then, as if this had been a prearranged signal, he heard knocking coming from downstairs.

Gruppenführer Kleist stood on the front porch, rain water dripping off the bottom of his black cape, tiny drops trickling slowly down the lenses of his wire-framed glasses.

"Herr Kessler."

"Yes . . . I am ready." He walked out onto the porch.

"Is your bag heavy, Herr Kessler?"

"No . . . I can manage."

A Mercedes drove them to the railroad station through largely deserted streets. The storm kept people inside. Those few people who were visible walked with difficulty, their heads down, their bodies inclined forward and straining against the wind.

Kleist led the way onto the station platform while the

driver, a corpulent Oberscharführer, carried Kessler's bag. Four other SS officers, each a Sturmbannführer, awaited them on the platform. Kleist introduced Kessler to these men. One of them, a tall man who was holding an ivory cigarette holder in one hand, examined Kessler with a faint look of contempt in his eyes. The others, equally unimpressed, nodded a quick greeting and then resumed talking among themselves. A German shepherd, property of one of the officers, prowled impatiently around the group.

"I am going to be riding in a compartment by myself, Herr Kessler."

"Yes . . . fine. I've brought reading matter."

"We shall meet later in the dining car." Kleist boarded the train.

Kessler hoped that he could ride alone, but he was ushered into a compartment occupied by two other SS officers. He thought of initiating a conversation, but what could they talk about? What could they possibly have in common?

At 9:50 A.M. the train pulled out of the Frankfurt terminal.

Kessler made an abortive attempt to read a scientific journal. The words and numbers danced before his eyes. It was impossible to focus on the page. The incessant clicking of wheels on tracks distracted him completely. He let his eyes wander to the window. The velocity of the train and the strength of the wind lent terrific force to the rain and sleet slamming against the glass. He could barely glimpse the landscape as it rushed by.

He decided to sleep. Unconsciousness would be better than boredom. Now he concentrated willingly on the clacking of steel against steel, hoping that the sheer compulsive rhythm of the clamor would put him to sleep. That wonderful twilight state, half sleep, half consciousness, was just stealing over him when the two officers began to speak. The officer directly across from Kessler was participating in operations against Polish partisans. He made no effort to conceal his boundless, indiscriminate contempt for all eastern peoples. Poles stood near the bottom of his carefully articulated racial ladder. Kessler listened to a litany of racist comments — a rehearsal of National Socialist principles. Part of this officer's contempt seemed to find its roots in frustration, for it sounded as if the partisan activities were difficult to stop. Kessler, still oscillating between sleep and consciousness, caught phrases of the conversation.

". . . radical measures . . . eventual domination . . . rich spoils."

The other officer was with the occupation in France. He agreed with the first man and spoke with equal contempt for French resistance. It was outrageous, he said, because only apolitical troublemakers were responsible for the chaos. The discussion continued for a long time, the officers chatting about personal matters in between their reflections on professional problems. Finally, the motion of the train, the rhythm of the clatter, and the repetitiousness of the talk brought unconsciousness to Kessler.

A sharp jolting of the train woke him up. Outside, the rain and sleet had stopped. It was midafternoon and Kessler could see that they had pulled onto a siding in order to allow the passage of a military transport. Ammunition cars and vehicle-laden flatcars rolled past in a monotonous procession. Almost against his will, Kessler began to count cars. He reached twenty, then forced himself to stop. An annoying compulsion, he said to himself. He looked at his watch and figured that he had slept for over four hours. Then he noticed for the first time that the two officers were gone. Thank God for that — a tedious pair.

He decided to step out into the corridor and stretch his cramped legs. His body was wracked by the fatigue that comes of the constant vibration of train travel. Four compartments down the corridor stood Gruppenführer Kleist, leaning against a window, speaking to two officers.

"Herr Kessler," he said. "Will you join us?"

"In the dining car?"

"Yes. We are going to be delayed. Let us entertain ourselves."

"But the . . . uh . . . this military train should pass us in a moment. What is the delay for?"

"Partisans — Czech partisans I am told have blown the tracks somewhere up ahead. Our direct route has been cut. We will have to confirm a new one. So . . . please come."

Kleist, Kessler, and a party of officers walked forward to the dining car. It was not a public car as Kessler had imagined it would be, but rather a private SS officers' car decorated in shockingly extravagant, gaudy taste. Scarlet red curtains, hanging down to the floor, covered the full width of every window. A soft, thick red carpet, imperfectly matched with these curtains, covered the entire area of the floor. In between the windows, mounted on the walls, large gold ornate gas lamps covered by blue-tinted glass cast their glow. The walls themselves were covered by a light red, nearly pink, angular-patterned wallpaper. Dark wood tables lined both sides of the car. At each of these tables there stood four hand-carved, gothic-style chairs. Each armrest terminated in a weird, composite, reptile-headed monster. A circular bar, draped with a swastika flag, stood at the far end of the car. Officers were already gathered around this bar.

"The decor, Herr Kessler, is largely the work of Sturm-bannführer Ritter."

Kleist pointed to one of the men leaning on the bar.

"Ritter!"

"Yes, Reinhard."

"What special treat do you have for us today?"

Sturmbannführer Ritter, a mild-mannered officer from an upper-class background, smiled and said,

"Champagne, Reinhard. It is excellent . . . excellent."

Ritter had brought it with him from France.

"You realize," he added, "now that I am to be stationed in the east, I will have to provide my own entertainment. Weep for me, Reinhard. Lublin is not Paris. But five cases of de Saint Marceaux . . . five . . ."

Ritter rolled his eyes back into his head.

A riotous scene followed. Waiters, coming from a kitchen car, brought plates of potato and sausage to the tables. Champagne, wine and beer flowed copiously. Kessler, relieved now that he had found a way to pass the time quickly, drank with the officers. There were jokes about the Poles and the French. There were other jokes, the in-jokes, about some of the leadership. Kessler, feeling the pressures of the social environment, laughed at almost everything. Kleist introduced him to other officers as they entered the car, but he was indifferent to these introductions. He had no memory for names.

Sturmbannführer Eckstein, sitting across the car from Kessler and unable to contain himself any longer, burst into song.

". . . certain rat, dans une cuisine . . . Etabli comme . . . comme un vrai frater . . ."

He was too drunk to articulate either words or melody clearly. As he sang, he pounded his beer stein on the table.

". . . dans le fourneau le pauvre sire . . . crut pour . . . pourtant se cacher très . . . oh . . . très bien."

Kleist turned around.

"Where did you develop such tastes?"

"Ah! Disait-elle comme il grille . . . do I . . . do I have it right, Reinhard? You know it?"

"Une puce gentille chez un prince logeait."

"Ah! That's good . . . that's good . . . you do know it . . . you do . . ." and Eckstein pounded his leg with the stein. Beer stained the carpet.

Kleist did not drink. When asked why, he responded. "I don't need wine, gentlemen, in order to enjoy a good one about the Poles."

This comment evoked convulsive laughter from everyone, including Kessler. He was high enough to join in spontaneously with the others.

"You must understand, Herr Kessler," said the Gruppenführer, leaning across the table, "many of these men have simple tastes. Here you can observe nothing more than a little innocent brutality."

The trip to Krakow took twenty-one hours. There were many delays. Arriving at 6:45 A.M., Kleist told Kessler on the station platform that although a rest stop in Krakow would be enjoyable, they had better leave without delay for their ultimate destination. SS headquarters in Krakow provided them with a car.

"It is only an hour from here, Herr Kessler . . . tired?"

"Absolutely."

"You will be able to rest soon."

They drove into the countryside west of Krakow. Little more than an hour later, they came to a set of wooden barracks set back in a forest out of sight of the main road. The barracks area was partially surrounded by damp, muddy ground, half frozen by the cold of the Silesian winter. Other wooded regions were visible in every direction. A mist hung low over the ground. The Gruppenführer directed Kessler to one of the buildings and told him that he would be quartered there for the duration of their stay.

"If you would care to rest now, feel free to do so."

Kessler accepted this invitation. It was, after all, only

8:30 A.M., and the two agreed to meet again at noon for a first look at the construction site.

For the last time, Otto Kessler slept soundly.

At noon, Gruppenführer Kleist handed Kessler a pair of heavy hiking boots.

"You'll find that you need them out here," he said.

Kleist was right. The area was filled with partially frozen puddles and thick mud. They walked off into a dense forest directly behind the barracks and, emerging on the other side of the trees, hiked laboriously up a sharp incline. Kleist explained that they were taking a shortcut and that other people ordinarily used a road that circled around the woods. As the two approached the top of the incline, voices could be heard coming from the other side. The tone and patterns of intonation of these voices indicated that someone was shouting.

Kleist stopped on the summit. He was giving Kessler a chance to survey the scene from a distance. There was silence for a moment, then Kleist pointed to a large, flat, open area off to the right.

"There . . . that area will be used for gunfire testing."

But Otto Kessler was closely observing the scene directly in front of him. The outer shell of the factory was beginning to rise. Several hundred laborers moved about the work area in groups of ten and twenty, each group attending to a different task. Even from a distance Kessler was struck by the lack of energy displayed by these laborers, by a surrealistic aura which suffused the spectacle because of the laborers' slow, dreamlike motions. The men wore striped uniforms. Around the perimeter of the work area, defining it and marking it off from the world, stood armed SS guards — the men provided by Kurt Heiden in Berlin. A group of officers stood by and watched the laborers, the factory, the slow progress.

"Who are these people?"

"Polish laborers, Herr Kessler."

"Are these laborers, these people . . ."

"Slave labor."

Kessler wondered how long he would have to stay. He looked at his watch.

It had stopped.

"Shall we get closer, Herr Kessler?"

The two of them walked toward the construction site. Kessler could say nothing. He tried to distract himself by looking at the overcast sky, by examining the mud, the viscous slime beneath his feet, by glancing at the line of barren trees off to the left of the construction site.

Out of the corner of his eye he saw corpses lying near the edge of a narrow ditch. He turned and stared at them. He could not help it. A pair of vacant, dead eyes stared back. The bodies, ten, maybe twenty of them, lay in a heap. An arm, a leg, and another arm, each propped awkwardly against a neighboring corpse, pointed toward the sky. Ashen faces. Ripped uniforms. Skeletal limbs. Shaved heads. Death by exhaustion.

Two SS guards approached the ditch. They were carrying another body. With sovereign indifference, they tossed it among the others.

One of the officers in charge of the work saw Kleist and Kessler approaching and advanced to greet them. Kleist knew the man. Another introduction. Kleist and the man began an animated discussion.

Kessler heard nothing.

He was transfixed by the spectacle before his eyes. Where had Kleist brought him? Who were these striped marionettes who drifted in slow motion across this unearthly landscape? One of the laborers who was carrying a pile of bricks looked his way. A stolen, fleeting, illegal contact with the human world. Their eyes met for an instant. What knowledge was carved into this flesh, into these sunken cheeks? What knowledge lay concealed in the black depths of these eyes? Here was an obscene page already torn out of the book of history, a page already censored, a page not meant for human consumption. The guards stood by, observing closely, looking for infractions of the law. Kessler saw a group of laborers struggling with bags of cement. They were difficult to carry while walking on rough ground. The pitiful, lifeless shuffling of feet continued, this man here, that man there, struggling with tools, bricks, wheelbarrows. Exhausted teams of workers, suspended miraculously between life and death, labored across ground desolate enough to have been carved out of another planet. Everywhere the same expression, the same vacant eyes, met Otto Kessler's gaze.

"Herr Kessler," said a voice in the distance. Kessler stared, paralyzed by the spectacle.

"Herr Kessler . . ." — a voice calling him back from a dream.

"Kessler!" It was Gruppenführer Kleist. "Standartenführer Franz wants to know if you have a special request."

"Special request?"

"Yes . . . I mentioned to you only the other day . . ."

"No, there is nothing . . . there is nothing." The words tumbled out of his mouth, propelled by the force of suddenly unleashed, wild fear.

"Perhaps your own office in the factory? Would that be helpful?"

"Yes . . . yes . . . that's possible."

"You could not object, certainly."

"No . . . I wouldn't object."

Officer Franz heard this and immediately signaled to a colleague who was grasping a roll of papers in one hand.

"We will examine the blueprints," said Franz.

At precisely this moment a laborer slipped and fell into a

puddle, dropping several bricks on his own foot. Kessler saw it on the periphery of his vision.

Kleist and the other officers struggled with the rolled papers, trying to unfurl them.

A guard was walking toward the puddle. Kessler looked away.

There was Standartenführer Franz, pointing with an index finger at something on the blueprint. The other officers nodded.

A harsh voice, a bellowed command, reached Kessler's ears.

Now Franz was pointing to something on the construction site.

Kessler glanced back at the puddle.

The guard was abusing a drenched laborer who now stood, stoop-shouldered, before him. He struck the man with a closed fist.

Kessler turned away.

"Herr Kessler — a bit of lunch now? We can really do nothing here with these papers. Tomorrow we will return and make a decision on the exact location of your office — your own headquarters, so to speak."

They walked back to the barracks. Kessler said nothing other than that he wished to get more rest during the afternoon. Kleist urged him to do so. They could meet again for dinner. Kessler thanked him, explained that he felt no need for lunch, and returned to his room, where he collapsed onto his bed.

Otto Kessler stared at the ceiling, his mind numb and devoid of coherent thought, his body faint with shock. He craved sleep, the sheer escape of unconsciousness. Then he would know nothing. He closed his eyes, but the terrible images he had just seen, now forever stamped and burned into his brain, pursued him. They revolved uncontrollably before him, filling his consciousness, appearing on the walls, the ceiling, staring up at him from the floor. They would not depart. Fresh waves of terror swept through him. He looked again at his watch, thinking unconsciously that by defining his point in time he could discover the reference, the coordinate from the world of the living by which to orient himself in the world of the damned. He had forgotten to wind it. Before, the interior of his barrack's room, the iron bed frame, the wooden roof supports, the two unpainted wooden chairs and barren, knotted unfinished writing desk had seemed natural, necessarily functional accommodations for this undeveloped frontier setting. Now these objects receded from him. They became barely human, horrible furnishings in an antechamber to hell. The world fell away. His shoes, his pants, his shirt, his jacket became insanely arbitrary. They did not belong to him. His eyes darted about the room, a frantic search driven by the need to root the self to some benign corner of reality, but every object, every point of focus, repelled him and filled him with dread and loathing. And always, the fearsome images returned, pursuing him relentlessly, like some demented hound from the underworld.

Time passed, but he did not know how much. Outside it had become darker. Was it because of the clouds, or was the sun setting? He tried to regain control of himself by examining, scientifically, the state of his own feelings. Some of the shock was gone. Some of the terror had subsided.

But then, suddenly, Kessler was possessed by an unexpected desire, an urge that was indistinguishable from the passion of the voyeur. He was going to go back and look again. It was an uncontrollable, terrifying, compulsion. He had to see the living dead once more. He would confirm for himself the reality of these pornographic horrors.

Once again Kessler crossed the mist-shrouded ground — through the forest, stumbling over fallen branches, up the steep rise. The coldness of the winter night was setting in. Kessler reached the summit and once more looked down on the construction site. The laborers were lined up in even ranks. Evidently, it was the end of the working day. From a distance, the men resembled a mass of frozen, striped pillars. The guards stood on all sides of this immovable mass. The officers, those who had earlier in the day supervised the work, congregated in front of the ranks of laborers. One of these officers approached the front rank. Positioning himself directly before one of the men, he began to gesticulate wildly. He was shouting. Even from where he stood Kessler could intermittently discern individual words. The mass of pillars, whipped by a winter wind, remained motionless. The gesticulating officer concluded his tirade and walked back to consult with his fellow officers. All was still with the exception of the indifferent wind. It chilled Kessler's face. Several minutes passed. The officer approached the laborer and motioned to him. The man stepped out of the ranks. The officer reached for his pistol, and Kessler turned around and started down the incline. Neither distance nor the winter wind could conceal from him the explosion of the pistol shot.

"Gruppenführer Kleist, long railroad journeys are more taxing than I had thought. I'm sorry. Would it be an inconvenience if I took dinner at a later hour?"

"But of course not, Herr Kessler." Kleist stood just on the threshold of Kessler's barracks' quarters. "I will arrange everything."

Otto Kessler spent the night consumed by a flood of wildly oscillating and conflicting emotions. He knew that he would never again go back there, back to that mad spectacle of a nearly supernatural torment. They could try to force him to, but even if it meant his eternal damnation, he would not expose himself to these things . . . these horrors which threatened to destroy the foundations of his human existence. Who were they that they did such a thing to him? They had no right to do it. Kleist had no such right. The laborers, horrible creatures, had no right to exist, no right to be there staring at him, no right to corrupt his tortured memory, poison his heart, and humiliate his soul through the sheer force of their wretched existence. They had no right to ask anything of him. He silently raged at them, at these creatures, already less than human, already more than damned, who persisted in their miserable condition. From where had they come? How could there be any natural transition between human life and the existence of these cursed beings? They are the damned. Not for me, thought Kessler — not for human eyes.

But the monstrousness of these lies could not pass unnoticed. The spontaneous force of Otto Kessler's attempt to dissociate himself from reality did not make that effort any less transparent. He descended vertiginously into utter self-loathing. He lay in bed, paralyzed by the weight of self-hatred, wondering how he would live with the knowledge that was now his, despairing of any effort to rationalize away his former desperate wish to escape and know nothing. Gruppenführer Kleist would return in the morning. What would he do then? His colleagues would be pressing forward with the research. What would he say to them? He could resign his position . . . just resign and be done with everything. He could do it. But he knew immediately that that would never suffice. The intensity of his terror shattered every illusion. Otto Kessler could project for himself no image of the future that did not transform itself into the image of frozen laborers. Coherent thoughts would not come. The will to think, to decide, lay crushed beneath the enormity of a vision of hell.

Gruppenführer Kleist led him back. Early the next morning, they stood on top of the incline gazing down at the work. The laborers struggled on, actors in a film rerun by a diabolical projectionist.

Kessler decided to speak.

"Gruppenführer Kleist, it hardly seems probable that this factory can be efficiently built under these conditions." His voice wavered strangely as he tried to find the right tone for his words, an absolutely cold and indifferent tone. His heart raced. He hoped that Kleist would appreciate the emphasis on efficiency.

"What is your point, Herr Kessler?"

"These laborers are absolutely exhausted. They can barely walk. They can't perform these tasks adequately."

"Have no concern. The adequacy of the work is checked every day. Standartenführer Franz will not allow for inferior work. I can guarantee that."

Kessler could not press this further. He was in no position to judge the quality of the construction.

"And yet surely, Gruppenführer, the work could be done more rapidly if we used skilled German labor. The cost would be higher, I grant that, but the thing would be over and done with sooner."

"At the latest, Dr. Kessler, this construction program will be completed in six months. If there are unforeseen complications it can take but a brief while longer."

"Yes . . . I see . . . but you must realize that skilled German workers . . ."

"Herr Kessler." Kleist was using his most accommodating tone of voice. "Can you foresee a solution to our scientific problem? Something that you will be prepared to test in, let us say, four months' time?"

"No. I can't make predictions."

"Then your concern with the pace of the construction work puzzles me."

"It is always conceivable that an answer . . . a testable answer will be found."

"That is excellent. Then why don't we leave it at this. Should you find that you and your staff are close to a solution, and if, by that time, we have failed to finish here, then don't hesitate to apply whatever pressure you think is needed. I will immediately suggest to Standartenführer Franz that the labor force be tripled. There are more workers where these came from. Is that a satisfactory arrangement?"

For a moment, Kessler restrained himself. He experienced the compulsion to speak the truth, to say everything, to point out that the problem was the un-believable condition of the laborers, the poor clothing, the obviously inadequate food, the insanely cruel treatment by guards and officers. His heart began to pound wildly. The impulse to risk anything to effect a change, born of the shock and terror that still moved him, was balanced by the fear, by the intuition that a confrontation with Kleist might be too aggressive, too dramatic, that in the setting of this mad universe every humane impulse would function only to deepen the miserable fate of the laborers.

Gruppenführer Kleist started down the rise.

"Gruppenführer."

"Yes?" Kleist stopped, turned, and faced him.

"A man was shot here last night."

"Shot?"

"Yes . . . yes . . . shot. One of the laborers . . . shot down while standing in the ranks. I saw it myself."

"Ah . . . Franz did mention that to me after dinner."

"Is that really necessary . . . shooting these people? Is that necessary?"

"The man was caught stealing, Herr Kessler."

"Stealing? What could the man have been stealing?"

"The man was caught stealing bread from another

laborer. You understand? Standartenführer Franz is a good officer. He does not tolerate workers stealing from each other. He will not stand for it."

Karin Kessler prepared carefully for Otto's return. She asked Ingrid to buy some of his favorite foods. She determined that she would look her best when he came back. During Otto's absence Karin had thought extensively about what was happening between them. Wasn't part of the growing alienation her fault? Hadn't she surrendered too easily to the condition of secrecy, a condition for which Otto was not solely to blame? In retrospect she realized that she had all too readily indulged in a self-righteous bitterness, an ugly emotion which had affected all her subsequent behavior. Now she decided to adjust her attitude. She would be more flexible, more understanding, more prepared to work for the best within the status quo.

Otto returned. Ingrid served the special dinner complete with a good wine. Midway through the meal, Karin, wishing to formally mark the new beginning, apologized to Otto.

"It was very difficult for me at first," she said. "You've been so distant, so preoccupied. I'm not accustomed to secrets like this. But I see now that you have no choice. I've been ridiculously silly about it . . . just making things more complicated . . . more unpleasant. But now no more."

He said he understood. They could work things out together. She suggested that they go to a film, but he refused. He said he was exhausted.

But Karin Kessler detected something new in Otto's attitude. She did not see this at once, but within several hours of his homecoming the change could be discerned. A mad combination of resignation and despair permeated his expression. It was visible in his eyes. The substance and tone of what he said, even the subtly altered style of his walk, implied surrender. To what? Karin could not tell.

Was he resigned simply to the enormous difficulties implicit in the special thing he was working on? That would have been uncharacteristic of him. Was he resigned to the difficult relationship between them? But his pledge to cooperate with her in altering that relationship seemed sincere. It was the tone, the resonance, of his voice that was so unsettling. A faint tremor betrayed a profound fear and an equally deep desperation. Thus, Karin found herself torn apart by irreconcilable desires. She felt committed to her spoken resolution to act more reasonably, and that could only mean a willingness to accept, largely in silence, the reality of her husband's new situation, but she also felt, within hours of his arrival, a nearly uncontrollable urge to ask him but one penetrating question about this new and profoundly unsettling quality she observed in his behavior. But the pressure of the new resolution demanded that she say nothing. If she spoke immediately, the possibility of healing their strained relationship might be irremediably damaged.

Kessler returned to his office at the research center. His colleagues welcomed him warmly and asked if his journey had been successful. He answered them guardedly and changed the topic of conversation by making inquiries about the research. Gastner and Siemens thought they had something interesting and wished to present it at a full conference. Kessler arranged for a lecture presentation by the two men. This delighted him, not so much because he thought progress might be imminent, but because he realized that continuous deep involvement with the conceptual problems of the project might save him. The more he had to do the better off he would be. The reality of the factory and the reality of the scientific problem were totally incompatible. The latter could obliterate the former.

And so, Gastner spoke every morning for a week, and Siemens followed this with another three days of talks. Kessler listened patiently and offered his criticisms. He was forced to disagree with Gastner's analysis of non-dimensional R-M diagrams for aluminum alloys. A violent debate followed. Siemens suggested a test for confirming Gastner's conception. Kessler objected. They could not afford the time in which to empirically investigate every idea. The final session was long and enervating. Kessler succeeded in isolating a crucial conceptual flaw in Gastner's thinking. They had made "negative" progress. Another approach to the problem had been eliminated.

And Kessler continued to confer with his colleague Buchheim. They were still reviewing the findings summarized in Buchheim's massive report. Kessler lied to his friend. He told him that his findings would have relevance for a new electroplating technique.

But Otto Kessler enjoyed only four weeks' respite.

"Herr Kessler?"

"Yes."

"I have a request which I hope will not inconvenience you." It was Gruppenführer Kleist on the telephone.

"We must return to Poland."

It was impossible for Kessler to flatly refuse. In theory, he might have done so at that precise moment. Fear deprived him of the necessary courage.

"I thought we had settled everything."

"I must apologize, but the factory shell is nearing completion. There are last-minute decisions to be made about installing testing equipment."

Kessler tried to object. He claimed that he lacked expertise on those matters.

"Perhaps, Herr Kessler, but Standartenführer Franz insists. He is unyielding. He says that you are in command of this project. Final approval must come from you. He will not assume responsibility for . . ." and Kleist spoke at length.

Kessler yielded.

They left for the railroad station two days later. As

before, other officers from Kleist's headquarters were there. This time, however, Otto Kessler prepared himself psychically for the journey. Immediately after Kleist's call his reaction had been consuming dread, followed by a totally debilitating depression. But the instinct of self-preservation was present too, and it was that instinct which Otto Kessler knew he had to depend on. He would minimize the strain on his nervous system. No more shocks this time, he said to himself. Ruthlessly selfish calculation would save him. Otto Kessler secured his soul against experience. Deliberately cultivated madness would protect him against real insanity.

The SS dining car was the center of activity. The beer, the wine, the champagne, a lavishly served, gluttonous feast bathed in the ghostly blue glow of the gas lamps eased the passage to the underworld.

"I am pleased," said Kleist, "to see that you are loosening up, Herr Kessler. You need to relax more frequently."

Otto Kessler drank.

Four glasses of wine in one hour.

It was a quantity greater than he was accustomed to.

No partisans delayed their passage this time. At the station in Krakow, the traditional SS vehicle was waiting for them. Once again, Otto Kessler found himself quartered in the wooden barracks secluded away in the Polish countryside. There would be no shocks this time, he repeated to himself.

"Gruppenführer. I would like to meet with Herr Franz — here — in the barracks. Tell him to bring along the blueprints. I wish to discuss details with him."

So Kessler and Franz examined the documents in the barracks' dining room.

"When do the laborers arrive in the morning?" asked Kessler.

"At 7:00 A.M."

"Very good, Standartenführer. Then I will meet you at

the construction site at 6:00 A.M. — unless you can't manage to get up at that hour."

"You are fooling with me, Herr Kessler."

"Then it will be at 6:00. I'm sorry, but I find it impossible to think clearly while two hundred men are scrambling about falling over each other."

Franz was amused by this. He slapped his sides and laughed.

"And it is worse now, Kessler. We have speeded things up a bit . . . picked up the pace . . . r-rup, r-rup, r-rup," said Franz, rapping on the table as he rolled his *r*'s. "There's no slacking off now."

Kessler thought to himself that the man was a vicious swine.

"Right you are, Kessler. These laborers are a drain on the spirit."

Confidence swelled in Kessler's breast. It was like an interior flow of warm air that lifted his spirit. He had discovered the trick, the necessary strategy for surviving the journey. All he had to do was to act decisively, to demand without hesitation what was best for him, to outdo even his hosts in making unyielding requests — and all would go splendidly for him.

They met the following morning at the agreed-upon hour. Walking through the empty factory shell, Kessler gave Franz his ideas regarding the equipment. A specimen anchor here . . . oscillators there . . . testing rig to be suspended here. He did not do this too rapidly, for just as they were leaving the construction area, laborers began to arrive. There were even more of them this time. But Kessler was exuberant. He would get away with it. He would not be confronted by the wretched, cursed creatures.

"It is unfortunate," said Franz, "that we did not settle this business during your last trip."

"I make decisions when the time is ripe, Franz. During my last visit, your work had not progressed far enough."

He would let Franz know who was running the project. For an instant, Kessler began to enjoy his new posture.

But, upon returning from his early rendezvous with Franz, Kessler noticed that Kleist was standing just outside his own barracks.

He had some shocking news for Kessler.

"Do you remember Ludwig Ostmann?"

"Of course," said Kessler. Ostmann was a friend of Kessler's from the university.

"The Gestapo has arrested him. He has been giving aid to escaped political prisoners."

Kleist had just learned this from an officer who had come from Frankfurt. Kessler was about to express surprise, but it was too late. Kleist vanished into the barracks.

Thus, Otto Kessler's posture of calculated indifference collapsed completely. He did not believe in it. He knew it was a lie. When this collapse came, the vacuum created by it was filled by a new and more powerful hatred of self. He could not bear to remember his successful effort to manipulate Franz. Once back in Frankfurt, Kessler discovered that he could not work. The power of concentration deserted him. He sat in his office, lost in fantasies of escape, drowning in self-pity, consumed by anger and hatred directed alternately at himself, and at Kleist, Franz and the others who had ensnared him in an insupportable position. His mind recoiled from the thought of the laborers, retreating from moments in which he seemed to grasp a transcendental terror, into a more bearable sentimental pity. The climax came less than a week after he returned from the second journey.

On a Sunday night, Kessler had a terrifying dream.

He dreamed that he awoke in the middle of the night, lying flat on his back, fully dressed, in his own bed. A faint, ghostly, shimmering blue light pervaded the room. For a moment there was complete, uncanny silence, as if someone had removed the soundtrack from a film. Then, a single sound broke this stillness, the sound of human breathing. He knew, with absolute dream certainty, that the breathing did not come from the bedroom, although the sound had the presence it would have if its source were only inches from his ears. He glanced over at his wife's bed, but she was not lying on it. Instead, she was standing at a window beyond the bed, staring out, searching for something. He was just about to speak to her, to ask her a question, when she turned to face him. She executed the turn in slow motion, and when she had completed it, began to shake her head in a manner that let him know she could not help him. He rose from the bed and walked toward the staircase, intent on locating the source of the breathing sound. He looked down the staircase. The ghostly light illuminated everything. The walls were red. He descended the steps, turned to the right, passed through the corridor, and entered the kitchen. All was quiet. He stood in the center of the kitchen and waited. The door to the wine cellar opened. He went down the wooden steps. At the bottom he became conscious of activity off to the left. Turning in that direction he saw four SS officers sitting at a wooden table drinking wine and examining a large paper which lay on the table. The officers had pencils, T squares, rulers and dividers. They were busily making marks on the paper. One of the officers, it was Standartenführer Franz, motioned to him, indicating that he should approach the table and examine the document. He thought to himself that the paper was a blueprint, but when he looked at it, peering over the shoulders of one of the officers, he saw that it was a photograph of a man. The man stared out of the photograph with ghastly, pitlike eyes and sunken cheeks. The eyes were the pits of hell. They drew him toward them with magnetic force. He turned away. Standartenführer Franz, standing at his side, said, "I am sorry, but if you wish to install, there will be an entrance fee." Franz held out his hand as if awaiting something. He took two coins out of his pockets and gave them to Franz who, in turn, placed them over the two hellish eyes which stared out of the photograph. Then Franz motioned again, indicating that something was to be done on the other side of the cellar. He looked to the other side and saw, bathed in the intense white light of interrogation lamps, a large machine. The machine had three parts. A solid steel platform, three feet high, stood on the floor. A man lay on this platform. He was dressed in a striped uniform and was the source of the breathing sound. Another steel block hung from the ceiling. From it there protruded long, cylindrical steel bars. At the end of each bar there was a metal plate. Another block extended between one end of the platform and the end of the ceiling block directly above it. Dials were embedded in this block. He walked over to the machine and adjusted the steel bars so that the plates rested against the man's chest and skull. The machine started. The dials registered fifteen thousand pounds per square inch. The man spoke.

"A little more to the left, Herr Kessler, and you will have it . . . all you need do is adjust a bit more to the left . . . I can feel it in my heart . . . a trifle to the left . . ."

The man's eyes turned black.

He ran up the stairs, leaving behind the man, who continued to speak about "a little more to the left." When he arrived in the kitchen, Karin and Ingrid were there. Their faces were filled with pain and embarrassment. They knew everything. Ingrid was speaking: "A shameful guest . . . a shameful guest." He walked to the kitchen door and looked down the corridor, but instead of seeing the entrance vestibule, he saw, suspended in empty, black space, the disembodied head of Gruppenführer Kleist. He watched this head, and it grew larger. His fear increased, and the head came closer. His heart pounded, and the head grew closer and larger. In the last moments of the dream, he was staring directly into the cold eyes of this suspended, disembodied head.

Kessler woke up, terrified as he had never been before.

Late in the afternoon on the following day, Wolfgang Buchheim visited Kessler in his office at the research center. They discussed complex technical matters. Kessler argued convincingly on each scientific point, but he could not conceal from his observant friend the extent of his distress. His manner was distant, his eyes glazed over, his gestures strangely uncoordinated. Their consultation completed, Buchheim, standing at the office door, spoke.

"Otto?"

"Hmm?"

"Are you all right?"

"All right?"

"You don't seem to be quite yourself today."

"Yes, Wolfgang. I'm perfectly fine. There's nothing."

"I imagine all this is very tiring."

"It is . . . it is . . ."

"See you in a few days."

"Yes . . . the same hour."

"Take care of yourself, Otto."

Buchheim departed. Kessler turned in his swivel chair and looked out on the streets of Frankfurt. There were crowds outside, people on their way home from work. He did not know any of these people. Each of them worked at a different job, had a unique history and, no doubt, his own secrets. Kessler submerged himself in the faintly romantic aura of these simple truisms. These ideas possessed a force they had not possessed before. He envied these people because he was not one of them. History had not touched them in the way it had him. He was trapped. He wished to escape his situation. To be working for these others, men like Reinhard Kleist — he could do it no longer. But what could he do? The impulse, the desire to escape, could be given no substance. He could imagine no realistic alternative. An impotent world of daydreams and wish-fantasies constituted the only form of relief. A regression into sentimental, nearly magical ideas substituted itself for appraising real options. If he could be someone else, he would not be Otto Kessler. If he could be another, his fate would not be his.

«4»

Trevor Grey found a sealed envelope on his desk with his name on it. He opened it and removed a short note consisting of a simple and rather well-known verse.

> *Humpty Dumpty sat on a wall:*
> *Humpty Dumpty had a great fall.*
> *All the King's horses and all the King's men*
> *Couldn't put Humpty Dumpty in his place again.*

This note was signed by Harry Forsyth, Grey's colleague in espionage. Ostensibly nothing more than a literary quotation, this poem was part of a game, a fantastic two-level game which Grey and Forsyth had worked out during the summer of 1939, just prior to the German invasion of Poland. At the first level, it was nothing more than a game of chess, a game which Grey and Forsyth took great pleasure in. Complex strategic thinking excited both of them enormously. Both men possessed considerable skill. But chess thinking, complex as it is, lacked a dimension of strategy-game situations which Grey and Forsyth prized above everything else — the dimension of deception or "intelligence." True chess involves deception and intelligence, but not in the sense in which those terms apply to espionage work. Thus, these two men added another dimension to their ongoing games of chess. Each player would send his move to the opponent, not in the form of standard chess notation, but through some other medium which had to be correctly interpreted in order to yield the actual chess move. The medium for communicating the moves could be as broad as the deliberate, symbolic manipulation of seemingly real, spontaneous events. For example, in May of 1940, Forsyth suddenly began to accompany Grey each evening as the latter went home on the tube. Harry claimed he was going to visit a friend who had come to London and was staying at a hotel in Knightsbridge. Each evening, after getting off the tube, Forsyth insisted on the two of them buying a beer in a small pub called the Knightsbridge. On the third evening, while drinking in this pub, Forsyth launched unexpectedly into a lengthy monologue on the topic of religion. Grey waited no longer. He looked his colleague in the eye and said, "Very good Harry. Bishop to knight three. Am I right?" He was. The clues were all there. The talk about religion had symbolized the move by the bishop, while the name of the pub and the fact that the religious monologue had occurred on the third night symbolized the position to which the bishop moved.

So it was with the Humpty Dumpty poem. Grey knew that the reference to the "King's horses" could not symbolize a move by Forsyth's knight because the actual game situation precluded that possibility. Instead, he calculated that the significant thing had to be that Alice, in *Through the Looking Glass*, meets Humpty Dumpty while she is on the square Q6. This could only signify Forsyth's moving his queen pawn to that square. He was right.

Grey and Forsyth loved this strange game. Surely, it was

not simply the situation on the chess board that sustained their interest. Chess, with all its complexities, suffered from an excess of autonomy. Events in the world of human action were not influenced by it. But the amended game provided the participants with the experience of strategic thought with tremendously expanded significance. There was, theoretically, no aspect of their mutual interaction which Grey and Forsyth could not symbolically manipulate. Everything potentially contained hidden, special significance. Consequently, an interesting problem arose when they first started to play. They had set up a game without end. Grey and Forsyth discovered that even their discussions about real intelligence work, the real war, could function as ploys in the chess game. Therefore, they decided to agree, by fiat, that professional matters could not count as parts of their private game. This limitation was a minor restriction. The rest of experience was subject to strategic manipulation.

Grey penciled a note to Forsyth — "Dear Harry. P–Q6?" — and slipped it under Harry's office door. That done, he returned to the problems of real espionage work. One matter was foremost in his mind. After a long silence, Wolfgang Buchheim had been heard from once again.

In Frankfurt, Herr Buchheim had been compelled to resolve difficult problems. After he had informed his British controllers that he was leaving Essen, he had sent no word for a considerable period of time. His move had entailed the sundering of all underground contacts in Essen. Therefore, Buchheim had to resolve the problem of reestablishing communication with his British controllers. In addition to this, he had to contrive suitable means for obtaining and transferring valuable information. All of this had to be done in circumstances more dangerous than he had hitherto faced.

Now, how was Herr Buchheim going to obtain information from the Frankfurt research center? He knew he could not easily steal documents. The risks were too high. But Buchheim was a photographer; at least, he had slowly and deliberately cultivated photography as a hobby from the very moment he had become an Early Riser agent. He owned a great deal of equipment, including that necessary for developing film. He contributed regularly to photography and nature periodicals. In 1937, another Essen-based agent provided Wolfgang Buchheim with a British-manufactured miniature camera, an instrument measuring three inches by one inch by half an inch, and capable of producing photographs three-sixteenths of an inch square. Buchheim decided that photographing documents would be wiser than stealing them. But how was he to get this camera into the research center? The guards searched everyone. He could not risk carrying it on his person. So Buchheim disassembled the camera and, one by one, carried its small component parts into the research center concealed in the hollowed-out handle of his briefcase. It took him twelve days to complete this operation. Once this camera was inside he had to devise a way to leave it there safely. He could hardly afford to sneak the instrument in and out of the building given how time-consuming that was. Instead, Buchheim concealed the assembled camera in a wall behind the outer panel of a light switch. That too was a risky procedure, but he had surrendered a long time ago the notion that he could avoid all risks. If maintenance people, for whatever reason, ever removed the light switch panel, he was a dead man.

But there was a more complex matter to be settled. How could he get his information, his microphotographs, into the hands of the British? Wolfgang Buchheim was experienced enough to reduce this problem to a simple set of alternatives. Either he would go to the British, or they would come to him. He decided to wait for the British to come to him.

It was part of Trevor Grey's job, as a chief controller for Early Riser agents, to set up new contacts for Wolfgang Buchheim. For this purpose, he called upon the assistance of the four people who constituted the network that was known officially as the Dawn Group. These four individuals were absolutely reliable people who, living in Frankfurt, could be used as liaison between any source of important information and the one man responsible for channeling all information out of Frankfurt. This man's name was Herr Hanslick — a baker who operated a radio transmitter. Through him Trevor Grey let the Dawn Group know what the problem was.

First, the Dawn Group determined where Wolfgang Buchheim lived and worked. It took only days to do this. Chance had to play its part in the second phase of the Dawn Group's operation.

A woman named Grete Ohlendorff, code name Dawn Red, quit her job as a waitress in a downtown Frankfurt restaurant. This was not difficult for her. She had a volatile temper and deliberately cultivated the kind of strained relationship with her employers which could readily serve as a justification for leaving a job whenever it was necessary to do so. She took another job at a smaller restaurant-beer cellar located only five blocks from Otto Kessler's special research center. This move, in itself, could arouse no suspicion, for as far as the SS knew, no one was aware of the presence of the research project headquarters. Grete Ohlendorff calculated that the odds were on her side. She counted on only two things — the fact that Wolfgang Buchheim probably enjoyed his beer, and the more fundamental fact that he knew he had to make himself visible. An astute judgment. Buchheim discovered the beer cellar only seven days after he started working in the research center. Grete Ohlendorff recognized him the moment he walked in the door.

Buchheim ordered a stein of beer and a plate of sausages. She served him the beer first, taking her time clearing off the table and placing silverware and napkin in front of him.

"Thank you," he said.

"Hope you enjoy it," she responded, "but go easily. You know that too much of the stuff can be bad for you, especially if you're an early riser."

He laughed.

"I'm an early riser," he said.

"Dawn is a difficult time," she added.

"But not for the dedicated."

Buchheim knew that British Intelligence had found him.

Herr Buchheim began to display an embarrassing absentmindedness. On three consecutive days he had lunch in the beer cellar and departed without taking his pipe. Each day, upon returning, he would express relief at having recovered the pipe and would apologize for creating difficulties for the management. He didn't want others to think him incapable of looking after his own property. But, on the fourth day, returning again for sausages, Buchheim jokingly remarked that it would be far easier if he simply left one of his pipes at the beer cellar. He owned many pipes. With one at home, one in the office, and one in the restaurant, he would never have to worry about forgetting them. Grete Ohlendorff made a sarcastic remark about Buchheim's absentmindedness, and then agreed to the arrangement. The manager didn't care one way or the other. He couldn't be bothered with her whims. Grete placed Buchheim's pipe in a drawer next to the till.

"Clean it out for me a bit after I use it. Will you?" he said.

But there were two pipes — not one. Herr Buchheim

owned a second pipe which, to the naked eye, was indistinguishable from the first. Only very close inspection could have revealed differences in the grain of the wood. Now, when Herr Buchheim finished a roll of film, he carried it out of the research center in the handle of his briefcase. He developed the film at home. The final product consisted of a packet of twelve photographs, three-sixteenths of an inch square and an eighth of an inch thick. This tiny packet, concealed in a black paper pouch, fitted easily into the bowls of either of Buchheim's restaurant pipes. On days when he had material to transmit, he went to lunch with a prepared pipe. Grete brought him his other pipe. During the course of lunch, or a late afternoon beer, Buchheim would simply switch pipes. In turn, Grete would take the alternative pipe and, before returning it to its drawer, remove the packet of microphotographs. She left the restaurant with these taped to the inside of her shoe. Late every Friday afternoon, Fraulein Ohlendorff visited Herr Hanslick, the baker with whom she regularly did business. In payment of a whole week's bill, she would hand him a bunch of mark notes. The packet of photographs was always taped to one of the inside notes. Herr Hanslick, using a powerful magnifying glass, translated the contents of Buchheim's photographs into code. The radio transmitter in the rear of Hanslick's shop provided the link to London. No one ever suspected Grete Ohlendorff or Herr Hanslick, for both of them played to perfection the role of rabid anti-Semite.

But precisely how would Wolfgang Buchheim obtain access to the kind of information that the British wanted? That problem, unfortunately, could be solved only within the confines of the research center itself. Nothing of any interest ever left the building. Well — that was true with one exception. Of all the project personnel, Otto Kessler was the only man who left the building with a briefcase. He seemed to have a special privilege. Still, this was quite irrelevant. Buchheim recognized the impossibility of getting into that briefcase outside the confines of the research center. He could not seriously contemplate breaking into Kessler's home as the appropriate method for getting at the documents. Of course, it was conceivable that, while visiting the Kesslers on a social occasion, he could examine the contents of the briefcase. That was a widly unrealistic idea. Anyway, what guarantee was there that Kessler carried the most interesting materials in the case?

At first, Buchheim was content with letting London know what he alone was doing. He wrote out brief statements, photographed them, and passed them on to Grete. The first communication Grey received was one which read, "I am reviewing my old work on stress conditions and corrosion fatigue." Grey was furious. The message was not worth risking the entire Frankfurt underground communications network. But Buchheim was no more satisfied than Grey.

Initially, Buchheim assumed that, as time passed, he would learn more and more about the ultimate purpose of the project. He was wrong, and he knew that he was wrong. Weeks passed, and all he ever did was meet with Kessler and discuss the technical points of his report on past research. He noticed that Kessler displayed a certain discomfort during their conferences. Too often their eyes failed to meet. Kessler's voice lacked characteristic enthusiasm and conviction. The man seemed, in some way, to be unfocused and disoriented. From Buchheim's point of view, these symptoms could mean only that Otto Kessler was concealing something from him. He was not revealing the truth about the project.

Buchheim could not readily believe that he had been summoned to Frankfurt to write up reports about his past research. He understood his true capabilities as a chemical engineer. He knew that his work on acids and corrosion fatigue represented but a small part of his professional activities. It made no sense to him that Kessler would willingly waste his talents. Thus, one day, after six or seven of their meetings, Buchheim put a question to Kessler: "Tell me Otto, why do you want me here? We must stop this charade. Surely I can be of some genuine use to you." Kessler was taken by surprise. He could think of no immediate response. Since he wanted Buchheim's participation in the major work, he decided to speak the truth, at least indirectly. "Wolfgang," he said, "you are here because I specifically requested it. Tell me, when did you last attend a Party function?" That was all. Kessler broke off any further discussion on the issue by handing his friend a typed sheet filled with critical comments on one section of his report. The point was clear. Kessler valued him enough to appoint him to the staff, but someone else was unwilling to risk allowing him full access to project information. He was the object of an alarming compromise, one based on his political character. Someone thought him lacking in political zealousness. Herr Buchheim was a good agent, but not a perfect one. Playing a Nazi caused him great psychic discomfort. It was necessary to try harder. He would have to cultivate political passion. Nothing overdramatized, of course. Everything would have to seem natural and spontaneous, part of a real process of deepening of political conviction. He would have to be seen reading newspapers more frequently. He could make occasional remarks demonstrating enthusiasm, a scientist's academic variety of enthusiasm, for German successes. But that sort of character building takes time and patience. What could Buchheim do in the meantime? Kessler was the target. As project director, he had the important documents. Improvisations would be necessary.

116

Wolfgang Buchheim closely studied the security arrangements inside the research center. It did not take him long to realize that these arrangements were not so tight as they might have been. They contained a flaw. The SS had expended a great deal of time and energy tightening up security between the research center and the outside world. They had failed, however, to exercise equally methodical care in arranging for internal security. This did not surprise Buchheim, for he figured that the SS was not overly concerned about those who were part of the project staff. They had to worry about the wrong people getting inside, or about those more unreliable friends and associates of staff members. The research center occupied a total of four floors in the renovated office building. Two of these floors were above ground level, and two were beneath it. There were three additional floors located above the topmost floor of the project facilities. These had formerly housed the law-firm offices. The SS, in rendering the project secure against potential break-ins, had cleared out these top floors completely. No activity was permitted to go on above the research facility. It was just this precaution which provided Wolfgang Buchheim with the opportunity he was looking for.

An SS guard was stationed on every floor of the research center, but the SS, valuing efficiency and, to a small degree, the sanity of its men, did not place guards on permanent duty on the abandoned upper floors of the renovated building. Driven, just the same, by the professional impulse to check everything, the SS ordered that, periodically, each man on duty on the lower floors take a turn patrolling the abandoned floors. They could not risk someone's coming in through the roof of the building and concealing himself in an empty office. But the simple flaw in this scheme consisted, not in leaving each floor of the research center unguarded for a brief period of time each day, but in the fact that the upper floor patrols were organized on a routine, clockwork basis. Thus, Herr Buchheim knew that his own floor, for example, was unguarded between 7:00 A.M. and 7:15 A.M., 11:00 A.M. and 11:15 A.M., and finally between 3:00 P.M. and 3:15 P.M. He knew also that Kessler's floor was unpatrolled between 10:00 A.M. and 10:15 A.M., 2:00 P.M. and 2:15 P.M., and finally between 6:00 P.M. and 6:15 P.M. Buchheim told Kessler that a good conversation after lunch was both pleasant and productive. On the days of their meetings, he argued, the period between 1:00 P.M. and 3:00 P.M. would be conducive to good talk. Kessler agreed to this arrangement. Therefore, on days when one of these conferences was scheduled, Buchheim used the 11:00 to 11:15 A.M. period for removing his camera from the wall. It took him only four minutes to perform that operation.

Gruppenführer Kleist was not pleased by the internal security arrangements. He would have preferred a man on constant patrol on the abandoned floors. But the top-ranking officer on duty in the research center was unyielding. Kleist's criticisms hurt his professional pride. The Gruppenführer, true to his principles, decided not to pressure his colleague on this point.

But, for Buchheim, the greatest problem arose during the conferences with Kessler, for, obviously, Buchheim could take his pictures only if Kessler left the office. Everything had to be improvised. He could risk taking the photographs anytime Kessler stepped out, but only the 2:00 to 2:15 P.M. time period provided the safest conditions for assuming the risk. The chances, however, of Kessler's leaving his office during the maximally safe period were pitiably small. Buchheim tried to initiate a standard break in the discussion slightly before 2:00 P.M. in the hope that Kessler, for one reason or another, would leave the office. But Kessler resisted making this a standard practice. Consequently, out of the first seven post-lunch conferences, the longed-for coincidence occurred but once. Buchheim hurriedly snapped four photographs of materials lying on Kessler's desk, then he heard his colleague approaching down the corridor. The photographs, unfortunately, were next to useless. He simply had not had the time in which to go carefully through Kessler's desk, thus he had indiscriminately photographed scratch paper used by Kessler for mathematical computations. The Frankfurt baker painstakingly transmitted all the material. Trevor Grey was furious. It didn't take him long to learn that the material was unenlightening.

Wolfgang Buchheim knew that he would have to do better. He began by considering some melodramatic options. He could feign sickness while in Kessler's office, send Kessler back to his own office in order to get some medicine, and take pictures in his absence. But Buchheim knew that he wasn't that good an actor, and he could not believe that anyone would fall for such a transparent gambit. The idea was a product of desperation. Instead, he settled on something else. One day, during a conference, Buchheim managed to place a set of his own papers under a mail tray on Kessler's desk. He then suggested that, for a change, the two of them hold their next meeting at some outside location — perhaps a quiet restaurant. Kessler agreed. Several days later, when the two met outside the research center, Buchheim told Kessler that he had left papers in his office. Kessler, totally unsuspecting, gave him his office key, whereupon Buchheim ran back inside, entered Kessler's office, deliberately left the office door open, and, with the guard just outside in the corridor, took six photographs while making a great deal of noise shuffling papers around. It was outrageous, but it worked. It was also not to be risked again.

On yet another occasion, Buchheim managed to secure

more time for himself. He knew that Kessler held conferences with other members of the research staff in a subbasement room. These meetings were invariably held late in the afternoon — at around 4:45 P.M. They were called so that the inner staff could discuss lines of research, progress they felt they were making, and the like. Otto Kessler always went directly home after these conferences. Now, Herr Buchheim had observed something else about his friend. Kessler placed the key to his office in the left pocket of his overcoat. This was a foolish habit from a security point of view, but then, Otto Kessler had little appreciation for security matters. Buchheim also noted that Kessler hung his overcoat on a hook just to the left of the office door. There was no problem. One afternoon, Kessler stepped outside his office and Buchheim quickly took the key. That same day, Kessler went to one of the subbasement conferences. At 6:00 P.M., Buchheim let himself into Kessler's office and took twelve photographs. When he left the office, he placed the key on the floor directly under the coat hook. The following morning Kessler had to call upon the SS security people to let him into his office. When they did they found the key lying on the floor in plain view. Kessler was apologetic. He told the guards that he always put the key in an overcoat pocket and that it must have fallen out when he was leaving the office on the previous afternoon. They believed him. They did not associate the key on the floor with the sophisticated techniques which are supposedly the stock in trade of espionage agents. Buchheim realized that his plan had been ludicrously simpleminded. It was on this occasion too that he initiated a procedure for obtaining a copy of Kessler's key.

He wondered how long his luck would hold.

By the middle of April, 1941, Trevor Grey had received a considerable amount of information from Early Riser agent Buchheim. But quantity, in itself, was not important. The value of the information remained doubtful. It simply did not point, unequivocally, to the precise nature of the German project. Buchheim had sent mathematical computations. All these had been given to a team of Cambridge scientists who were asked to examine them with a view to inferring the type of project which could generate that kind of work. "Impossible," one of them remarked. "I'm not a mind reader, you know. You'll have to give us more than this." Nothing precise could be inferred from the information. Grey was frustrated by this. He knew that Buchheim and the others were risking their lives, and yet, nothing was coming of the risks. If Buchheim was limited to Kessler as a source of information, then the prospects were grim indeed, for Kessler was obviously concealing documents which referred explicitly to the nature of the project. Trevor Grey began to feel anxious for Wolfgang Buchheim, a man whom he had never met. In one communication, Herr Buchheim told his distant, invisible British controller that the SS did not fully trust him. Grey began to wonder how long Buchheim's luck would hold.

But there were four curious documents among those transmitted to London by Herr Hanslick. Two of them were memos, or rather, odd combinations of memo and private communication, sent to Kessler by a man whose name had never before appeared in British Intelligence dossiers — SS Gruppenführer Reinhard Kleist. From these communications Grey inferred that this man was responsible for security arrangements for the project. The general tone of the communications suggested that Gruppenführer Kleist and Otto Kessler were on friendly terms, and that beyond his role as security officer, Kleist fulfilled a general organizational function in the project bureaucracy.

The first of these documents was dated November 19, 1940, and read:

FROM: SS Gruppenführer Reinhard Kleist.
TO: Dr. Otto Kessler — Blocksberg.

Dear Herr Kessler: Welcome. I hope that you will find the new research facilities satisfactory. I apologize for the delay in completing the construction. Not everyone responds as you do to my idealism. Those involved in the construction work were told that it was a city government project. Any requests for changes in the facilities can, if you prefer, be addressed to me. I will suggest to the appropriate authorities that your desires be quickly realized. Good luck with your work.

The note was signed by Kleist. The substantive content of this communication was disappointing. Grey already knew the exact location of the research facility from Herr Buchheim. Still, it was interesting to observe Kleist's concern with misleading the construction crews. Of course, the note did contain the code designation for the project center — "Blocksberg." That piece of information would enable Grey to detect references to the project appearing in documents which, otherwise, might seem unrelated. Gruppenführer Kleist was evidently a helpful chap, quite willing to assist Kessler in any way he could.

The next document presented greater problems in interpretation. It was dated December 15, 1940, and read:

FROM: SS Gruppenführer Reinhard Kleist
TO: Dr. Otto Kessler — Blocksberg.

Dear Herr Kessler: Once again I apologize to you

for the long and difficult journey. Next time it will be shorter and easier. I have just received word from Horselberg informing me that all goes well with the construction of special quarters. Would it be advisable to provide space for additional staff members?

Again, signed by Kleist. This one was more intriguing and impressed Grey as the grounds for further investigation. The Germans were constructing something else related to the Blocksberg research center. This other structure was also worthy of a code designation. The idea of a factory readily suggested itself — a research center for working out novel conceptions, and a factory for translating these conceptions into material realities. Blocksberg and Horselberg were located at a considerable distance from each other. Horselberg suggested Eastern Europe, but France or Norway could not be ruled out.

Buchheim had also sent the texts of two other communications. One was a memo from Kleist to another SS officer named Franz. Kessler evidently received copies of all relevant communications. This one was dated December 16, 1940, and read:

FROM: SS Gruppenführer Reinhard Kleist.
TO: SS Standartenführer Paul Franz — Horselberg.

Dear Franz: It was extraordinarily good to see you. The work is going well. Kessler mentions the possibility of an early solution. That would be splendid — would it not? But I am concerned about the date of Horselberg completion. Let me recommend the procurement of a larger work force. This will be difficult, I know. If you can arrange it, good results shall come sooner. Please do not jeopardize other commitments. All of us have our job to do.

Followed by Herr Kleist's signature. It struck Grey as fascinating that the Gruppenführer took the space in which to state how "splendid" a successful completion of the project would be. This too implied that the Germans had something special going. Kleist's flexibility regarding Franz's other commitments indicated that he did not reserve a cooperative spirit just for civilian personnel. A good officer.

There was one other memo. Dated December 20, 1940, it was a copy of a document sent by Franz to yet another officer ordering the latter to do a survey of available labor resources. Franz wanted some of these "resources" placed at his disposal no later than January, 1941.

These documents fascinated Trevor Grey. He showed them to Harry Forsyth. The latter shared his colleague's feeling. There was something peculiar about the set of memos. What was it? Neither of them could say. It had something to do with the sensation of eavesdropping on the private talk of high-ranking SS personnel. Perhaps it was the cordial, friendly, nearly gossipy tone of the Kleist memos which lent them this indefinable extrapolitical, extramilitary dimension. This was the first time Grey had ever read SS documents. The style of the organization surely influenced the style of each member. But that wasn't it. Franz's memo differed radically in tone from Kleist's.

Forsyth and Grey agreed on one point. The contents of the documents were inconclusive. More information was required.

Now, this information had, in fact, become available. It was of consummate interest to Grey's partner in Early Riser operations — Douglas Trenchard.

"You see," said Grey to Trenchard, "this information is next to useless. The SS is not letting Buchheim in on the whole show."

"It's his fault, you know. The man hasn't done his job properly."

"Who? Buchheim?"

"Yes."

"You mean his political character?"

"I do. If they don't trust him, the fault is his. He hasn't been clicking his heels enough."

"That's easy enough for you to say. But then . . . you are right. They'll just keep him slaving away outside the main effort, and then dispense with his services."

Trenchard sat at his desk twirling a large magnifying glass in his right hand. Periodically, he picked up a piece of cloth and dusted the lens.

"At this point, Trenchard, the options open to us are simple. If he can do it, Buchheim has got to locate another source. We aren't going to get anywhere with this bloody business as long as he confines his attention to Kessler. He can tap Kleist's phone . . . find a way to listen in on staff conferences . . . something inventive."

"Until he gets himself shot."

"Oh right. Sooner or later I do have the feeling that they'll get him . . . poor bastard."

Grey arose from the solitary, lonely chair.

"He won't be the first they'll shoot," said Trenchard. Grey thought it was a rather bloodthirsty remark. He wandered toward the bookshelves.

"Well — what else can we do?"

He examined the titles of volumes. Trenchard said nothing.

"We could wait until Buchheim develops sufficient political character for everyone to trust him. That would be one possibility . . . would it not?"

He took down a volume on the problem of the theodicy and cursorily leafed through it.

". . . But that would take six months . . . a year . . . and then, why should they ever trust him? If the Germans can use our friend without increasing the risks to themselves, why shouldn't they settle for that?"

He placed the book back on the shelf.

". . . So we wait for all to turn out well in the end."

"Yes, but why wait?"

"Because it seems, Trenchard, as if we're at our wit's end."

"I've got something different in mind."

Grey turned from the bookshelves and faced his colleague.

"Indeed?"

"I believe we've been after the wrong thing."

"The wrong thing you say?"

"Hmm . . ."

"How so?"

"This entire matter with our friend Buchheim is a fraud."

Trenchard placed the magnifying glass on a corner of the desk.

"I am convinced of it," he added.

"Oh no . . . now really, Trenchard."

"Do you reject that hypothesis?"

"I'm not the sort who arbitrarily rejects any hypothesis."

"Then tell me," said Trenchard, pouring himself a glass of mineral water, "what's the reason for your initial response?"

Grey walked back to the chair. He forced himself to rethink what had nearly become an unquestioned assumption.

"The man has proven himself . . . hasn't he?" He sat down. "Buchheim's been our man for years."

"And most of those years were prewar years."

"You don't think the Germans have bought him off — do you? Personally I think this man is one whom we can trust."

"I think . . . Grey," said Trenchard with calculated deliberateness, "that Herr Buchheim is as honest, as touchingly trustworthy a fellow as one can hope to find in this line of work . . . but that's his problem — not ours."

"Of course they might have something on him." Grey was thinking out loud. "The SS may have picked up a relative, or they may be threatening him directly. It wouldn't be quite his fault if he hasn't withstood the pressure."

"Indeed, Grey, but let me suggest something else. They've found him out. The SS knows he's with us. Buchheim is straightforward as far as his motives are concerned, but he isn't exactly a skilled agent . . . is he? So they've found him out, only it isn't likely that he knows about it yet. The SS lets him go free so they can use a man who's in the right position. The right position, Grey, is one in which he sends us tempting, but utterly useless, information. That is rather a perfect description of what we have . . . tempting and useless."

"That's true . . . true enough."

"Perfectly cryptic references to a project which would be 'splendid' if completed, as our man Kleist puts it."

Grey stared at his colleague.

"Equally obscure references to a second location. A factory, you suggest?"

"Yes," said Grey.

". . . And it's all plausible, but to be candid, Grey, I don't believe a word of it."

"On what grounds? What are you getting at?" There was an impatient, anxious curiosity in Grey's voice.

"Consider these memos, the communications Buchheim

sent us. They are very odd . . . as you say yourself . . . odd and fascinating in an indefinable way. What's so peculiar about them is their indecisive quality. Why doesn't this Gruppenführer Kleist state his case. No — that's not it. Why doesn't he assert his authority more clearly? You see? Given the ostensible importance of this project, and the rank of the author, the tone of these communications is incorrect. It's rather as if the informality of the documents, the provocative references to secret locations . . . it's as though all of it were meant for our eyes only. The documents are secret. They travel through closely guarded channels. What's the purpose of their indirection? Their ambiguity? They've got Buchheim, Grey. They're using him to keep us occupied. There's nothing happening at this so-called research center. We'll be tracking down nothing for months on end."

"And the other location?" asked Grey.

"There's nothing there, or else, nothing out of the ordinary."

Grey remained silent for a moment, then began shaking his head.

"No," he said.

"My point is that —"

"No," interrupted Grey, "it hinges on Buchheim . . . on Buchheim, and I think you're wrong about him."

"You acknowledged —"

"I acknowledged nothing. You're wrong, Trenchard. I know it. Buchheim is too careful, and he cares too much . . . about everything. If he thought it even remotely possible that the SS knows he's our man, we'd not have heard from him. The fact that Kessler told him the authorities doubt his political character proves my point. Where did Kessler learn that? From the SS. If they wanted Buchheim, in all innocence, to maintain his contact with us, they would never have risked his finding out that they doubt him. I say they don't suspect him as an agent. We've got to stay with Buchheim. He's still our man."

"Really, Grey . . . how do you know?"

"He's too careful . . . too observant . . . too sensitive to everything."

"You've never met him."

"Since 1935, Trenchard, this man has sent us over thirty communications. I've read them and reread them. Buchheim is not a professional . . . you are right about that, but the crucial thing is that he's no fool. He has a sense for what's right . . . for what can and cannot be done. I know it."

"Grey," said Trenchard, his voice marked by sarcasm, "it sounds to me as if you actually care about this man."

Grey did not respond.

"We are like doctors, Grey — do you remember? It is suicidal, professionally speaking, to become too involved with the patient."

"Then let me rephrase my point, Trenchard. It is my intuition . . . my human intuition which tells me that Buchheim is still our man."

"The war effort, Grey, cannot be determined by your intuition."

For the first time, Trevor Grey felt tension between himself and Douglas Trenchard. He wondered if Green was the man behind Trenchard's new position. Was this the beginning of some interbranch rivalry, or were Trenchard's idiosyncrasies making themselves apparent?

"Very curious," Grey said. "A short while ago I was the first to suggest that Buchheim had been caught. You were more confident."

"Circumstances change, Grey."

"They do . . . they do."

"Or perhaps we are simply not destined to agree with one another."

"All right," said Grey. "I accept your position for the sake of argument. So, if there is a ruse, then where is the real show? Other than your doubts about Buchheim, what more positive evidence do you have?"

Trenchard did not arbitrarily suggest alternative interpretations. He was prepared to support his contention. He produced a thick file from the top right drawer of his desk. From this file he removed four aerial reconnaissance photographs taken over Essen.

"Courtesy of the RAF," remarked Trenchard.

These photographs, when examined closely, showed that between August and November of 1940, the Germans had been busy constructing a group of sizable buildings close to the center of the city. These structures were not dwellings of any kind, nor were they factories. They resembled a complex of university buildings and had been put up with remarkable speed.

Trenchard then produced a similar set of photographs which had been taken over Saarbrücken. A building complex of a similar nature was visible in these pictures too.

Last, Trenchard had received a set of reports from agents operating in Cologne, Düsseldorf and Hamburg. These documents confirmed that building projects similar to those visible in the aerial photographs were in progress in these other cities. The similarity in architectural styles shared by these separate projects argued that all of them formed part of a single, coordinated effort. These reports indicated that all of these building projects had been designated top-security areas, and that a minimum of six highly respected individuals involved in scientific research were unmistakably affiliated with these projects. In one case, rumors suggested that the projects were related to rocket research. This rumor, said Trenchard, had yet to be confirmed, but it was worth heeding.

These reports had reached London through the instrumentality of seven agent networks. Unfortunately, the Gestapo had picked up two of the agents who operated in Cologne. This too seemed to strengthen Trenchard's thesis, for it was clear that the Germans were guarding these projects closely.

"I will make this concession, Grey. If Buchheim sends us truly valuable information, then we'll know that the Frankfurt project is the real thing."

"I didn't know," remarked Grey, "that your position empowered you to make concessions to me."

He did not expect an answer. Trenchard ignored the remark.

"Can you believe that the Germans would locate a major research project in the center of a major city? That is too odd — is it not?"

Trenchard had another scheme in mind. Looking into Grey's eyes, he spoke softly, with condescending assurance, and with remarkable intensity.

"Grey, this afternoon I have an appointment with a Wing Commander Neill from Bomber Command. I'm going to suggest something to him, something in the way of a little experiment. If the bomber people will agree to it, I think it will be profitable to stage a series of air attacks against these building complexes I've shown you. Nothing really spectacular, mind you, but something impressive enough to get the Germans a bit unnerved. They surely will be unnerved, Grey, if there's any substance to my suspicions."

"Does Green know about this meeting?"

"Of course he does. He can see no harm in it."

"I see."

If the RAF found the idea practicable, said Trenchard, they would launch a series of selective, precision, daylight strikes against the locations in question. If these targets were as important as Trenchard thought they were, then one could reasonably anticipate an especially vigorous response on the part of the Germans. They would not idly sit by and watch the RAF annihilate a complex of top-priority targets.

"Of course, Grey, this operation will entail a high degree of risk for the participating crews."

When he said this, Trenchard broke off eye contact with Grey. Grey wondered if the man felt uneasy describing this admittedly dangerous operation. But Trenchard's voice did not display any of the discomfort or anxiety, if not the guilt, which one could expect even from a hardened professional contemplating a difficult engagement in which his countrymen will die. Grey's impression was that his colleague, gazing into the distance, was lost in an imaginative enactment of the prospective operation.

". . . But only a selective, precision attack can unequivocally communicate the identity of the targets to the enemy."

"Can you persuade them, Trenchard? You don't expect Bomber Command to seize willingly on this notion of yours — do you?"

"Assuredly not, but they shall see that the risk will not be an extended one. I'm not asking for another Verdun, you know," and Trenchard gave a fleeting smile just around the corners of his mouth. "The interesting results, Grey, the really telling results, will probably reach us through our agents. That's what we'll be waiting for. If I'm right, Grey, and these complexes are as crucial as I believe them to be, then the enemy will be compelled to respond dramatically to our initiative. They might immediately disperse the facilities, or strengthen the defenses by transferring fighter squadrons to the threatened areas . . . improve the camouflage . . . reinforce the flak units. But what we can expect is a coordinated effort, regardless of the substance of the effort. If all these locations constitute parts of a single project, then all of them should be under one command, and if they're under one command, then decisions regarding defense should affect them simultaneously. You see? If I'm wrong . . . which I doubt . . . then our attacks should fail to provoke a unified response. Presented in this manner, I don't see how the bomber people can refuse us the favor."

Trenchard peered through his large magnifying glass, subjecting the photographs to close scrutiny.

"Remarkable," he said, his manner and tone evidencing a profound concentration combined with equal admiration.

". . . The aerial reconnaissance people achieve astonishing results . . . clarity . . . definition . . . yes."

He was absorbed in the examination. Grey hesitated to speak, not wishing to interrupt this reverent diagnosis. He could not dispel the impression that for Trenchard, this examination had a ritualistic, sacred significance.

"Have you observed closely, Grey?"

"Yes . . . listen, Trenchard. There is, you know, an argument against your view."

Trenchard looked up.

"There is an argument against every view, Grey."

"Trenchard . . . if this entire setup, all these building complexes you've shown me — are part of the deception, and Frankfurt is the real show, then all the dramatic defensive gestures you expect will occur anyway as part of the deception."

Trenchard smiled at this piece of impeccable logic, the condescending and knowing smile of a master to a novice.

"A medieval theologian could not have done better, Grey."

"That's just your field too — isn't it?"

"Airy metaphysics, Grey . . . an exercise in speculative

metaphysics. I have my evidence here. Real photographs, taken by real cameras . . . real buildings. These are tangible . . . physical realities. You can see them, Grey . . . look. All you have on the other side, my good partner, is a set of completely useless memos and utterly worthless mathematical jottings . . . and one more thing . . . your intuitions."

"Yes. Well, in that case, perhaps we can meet again soon, Trenchard . . . some day when you are not quite so overstimulated. Right now I've got another matter to attend to." Grey headed for the door.

"Oh now . . . you aren't going to complain to Atkinson — are you?"

"Worried, Douglas?"

"Hardly."

"Don't flatter yourself. If it sets your mind at rest, Trenchard, I'm part of a committee interested in preserving historical monuments. We are being bombed, you know."

"Very moving, Grey. I like history."

"I thought you might." Grey left the office.

Grey could argue against the idea of Trenchard's air attacks, but he didn't believe the argument would carry much force. Trenchard had something on his side — his conception was dramatic and oriented toward vigorous action. In a time of war, that variety of idea had to appear more reasonable than Grey's willingness to await more promising information from Buchheim. And then there was always politics and flattery. Trenchard was not attached to the RAF in any formal sense, thus his suggestions would surely win him friends. Bomber Command aircraft could solve a Secret Service problem. The RAF would appreciate that.

Douglas Trenchard met with Neill and three other high-ranking officers at Bomber Command headquarters.

134

Essentially, they liked his idea. The rumor that the German project might involve rocket research proved extremely potent. There were questions from the assembled officers. For example, what would happen if losses were very high on the first day? For how long did Trenchard expect the RAF to sustain an insupportable operation?

"One day and no more," said Trenchard. "If it's that bloody, gentlemen, then I shall take that as sufficient proof of my case."

The officers winced at this idea, but then, during wartime a high-risk operation is justifiable if the potential benefits are great enough. Furthermore, there were still a number of RAF people who believed that daylight, precision attacks were possible in special circumstances. Trenchard's idea would serve as a further test case for these proponents.

"You might try something dashing," Trenchard said to the four as the meeting was ending. They were annoyed — a man in intelligence presuming to tell them how to conduct air operations. On the other hand, they were impressed by Trenchard's advocating so vigorous a use of air power.

The attacks were scheduled.

The first came on May 4 and consisted of eighty-six Wellington bombers in a low-level attack on the suspect building complex in Essen. They flew the mission at altitudes below one hundred feet. The crews reported that they had a terrific time all the way across France watching animals run and people wave at them. Things went splendidly until they reached a point thirty miles short of the target. Then, German fighters harassed them all the way to the target and back across the Channel. Nine aircraft were lost. The bombing was erratic because the fighters persisted in their attacks during the final approach to the target. Bomber Command was pleased with neither the results nor the losses, but agreed to give it another go on the following day. Even costly operations develop a momentum of their own.

On May 5, Essen and Cologne were placed on the target list. One hundred and sixty aircraft were dispatched, divided evenly between the two cities. Again a low-level assault was attempted, using a more circuitous route which would, hopefully, circumvent concentrated opposition. Limited success was achieved. Postmission photographs revealed a number of hits on both target complexes. But the defenses were stiff and exacted their toll. Fifteen aircraft did not return.

"Once more?" said Trenchard.

The RAF reluctantly agreed, but added one caveat. If the loss rate did not radically improve, the operation would be cancelled.

May 6 — one hundred and ten aircraft were dispatched to Essen, Cologne and Saarbrücken. The mission was a disaster. RAF officers decided on a high-level strike as a potentially surprising shift in tactics. The Luftwaffe was not fooled. Twenty-six aircraft were lost. The bomb-aimers reported that vastly improved camouflage made target identification more difficult.

"Fifty aircrews lost in three days. That's unacceptable," said Bomber Command. "No more."

But Trenchard was not dissatisfied. He called Grey and told him about the results.

"Increasingly strong fighter opposition . . . better camouflage . . . more flak in the target area."

"Damn it, Trenchard. You haven't shown anything," said Grey, and he hung up his phone in disgust.

Two hundred men lost. For what?

But two weeks later, they received news from an agent in Essen. The Germans were hastily abandoning the project locations. The word was that they were being moved to less visible quarters. Similar news came from agents in other cities.

Trenchard had evidently won his case. He was delighted. Here was the coordinated defense he had predicted.

Grey believed none of it. Here, he believed, was the coordinated deception he had anticipated from the start.

«5»

In the countryside east of Krakow, Otto Kessler had learned the limitations inherent in his world view, but those lessons were not easily translated into alternatives he could act upon. In deepening despair he continued to work on project I-P 9.

One afternoon, staring blankly at a page of equations, he decided that he would try to escape his situation. For him, such a decision was momentous. But again — what would he do? Each option, submitted to critical judgment, struck him as more unreasonable than his wildest scientific speculations. At first, the sheer existential fact of having decided on an attempt to escape provided Kessler with overwhelming moral relief. But this too soon proved to be an illusion. His protracted failure to conceive of courses of action soon became tantamount, in his view, to a lack of courage. Moral exhilaration gave way to renewed despair and hatred of self. The slave laborers called upon him to revolt. Contemplating their condition broke his will to act.

He went to his office and tried to be inconspicuously

nonproductive. He sat and did nothing while attempting to appear hard at work. This was improvisation. Kessler knew that he could sustain that posture for but a limited period. Each day he dreaded, more than anything else, the brief memo or the terrifyingly abrupt phone call from Kleist which would hurl him back to the edge of hell. Twice a week Wolfgang Buchheim came to his office. They discussed details in reports which one or the other had composed. These conferences grew more strained. Buchheim perceived his colleague's distress.

Otto Kessler decided that, as an interim solution, he would try setting the project off in a fruitless direction. He understood that such a solution — subtle, conceptual sabotage — could be risked once or twice at most. But Kessler was learning, as Buchheim had learned, that risks were unavoidable. His colleagues were not fools. Conceptual sabotage would have to be conducted at an extraordinarily high level of sophistication. He would have to think so far ahead of them that only a man of the highest intellectual caliber would be capable of detecting flaws in ostensibly perfect ideas. Kessler thought of how ironic it would be if, motivated by a desire to sabotage the project, he discovered the solution for the project. Gone forever was the "game" he played with Nature. He remembered, bitterly, Kleist quoting Himmler. No task existed for its own sake. The integrity of his work was destroyed. He smiled to himself as he contemplated the odds in favor of sabotage. He had himself chosen the members of the research staff. It was too bad they weren't less competent.

But it was at home that Kessler faced the severest trial. Within weeks of his return from the second trip, Karin Kessler understood that her husband was inhabiting a radically different universe, and she knew, with intuitive certainty, that that universe was alien and horrible. All semblance of normal communication between them broke down. Their conversation was confined to pointless clichés and useless pleasantries. The path of every dialogue moved carefully, as through a minefield, avoiding the "sacred" unmentionable things which filled their lives. It was in early June, 1941, when Karin Kessler decided that she could no longer accept this situation.

One night she found her husband standing at the window of the study, lost in thought. She entered the room and closed the door quietly behind her.

"Otto" she said, staring at his still turned back.

"Hmm..."

"This will not go on any longer. I want us to separate, or to get a divorce... something must be done. I am sorry to say it... but there's no other way."

He turned to face her. Despair was etched in the lines of his face. He said nothing. His mind struggled to absorb what he had just heard.

"Did you hear me, Otto? I've decided on this. There's no point in our continuing."

As he stood there in the study, facing his wife who had just said this hitherto unimaginable thing to him, Otto Kessler did not clearly think or articulate anything to himself. But, beneath the surface of consciousness, something was happening, something which manifested itself physiologically as a sharp pain behind his eyes, as a nearly explosive pressure against the inside of his skull. Invisible, silent processes of the soul reenacted, from the beginning through to the predestined present, the drama which had begun in the room where he now stood. Before the eye of the mind there passed a grotesque psychic montage — images of horror, highlights from the satanic odyssey. The inscrutable face of Gruppenführer Kleist, blackboards and equations, emaciated men, a supernatural landscape, the fiery reds of the dining car. And the momentum of this interior reenactment compelled Otto

Kessler to transcend the inertia and dread which weighed upon him so intolerably.

"Come with me," he said, and started to walk toward the study door.

"Where are you going, Otto?"

"You are to come with me," he repeated, and he spoke in a chilling whisper.

She began to speak again, but he wasn't listening to her. Kessler took his wife by the arm and led her down to the wine cellar. There, two dim light bulbs, hanging from the ceiling between wooden bottle racks, cast strange lattice-patterned shadows across walls and floor. In this under-world confessional Otto Kessler stood, only inches from his wife.

"Otto. What is happening to you?"

"You will listen to me. You must listen." He spoke as if the shadows themselves might overhear and betray his secret.

"Since December of 1939, since the night that the man from the SS was here, I have been working on a project . . . an absolutely secret project . . . one that I should speak of to no one. You understand? I've been under oath to remain silent. This project is called I-P 9 . . . Infernal Proteus nine. The aim of this project is the creation of an alloy . . . a metal . . . a fantastic substance . . . a lightweight, strong substance, something capable of use in ship construction, aircraft design, firearms manufacture . . . anywhere for almost any purpose. I was placed in charge of the research for this project. I was allowed to choose my own staff, request whatever I needed in the way of facilities. I was to have, I do have, total control of this research . . . total control. But there is one thing wrong with this project . . . one thing over which I have no control. It is for them . . . for them . . . it is for Gruppenführer Kleist."

"The man? The man —"

"Yes, the man who was here that night . . . this project is for them, for Standartenführer Franz, for Sturmbannführer Ritter . . . for all of them. They are mad . . . totally mad . . . they are Evil itself."

And he paused for a moment and looked away from her. He could not tolerate his wife's seeing his guilt. But then he was back, speaking as intensely as before.

". . . You think you know that, or at least you have suspected it . . . somewhere in your mind. But let me tell you something," he said, his voice aflame with boundless cynicism, "you do not know. You know nothing . . . nothing . . . I have seen."

And he was silent. His gaze once again fell away from Karin's eyes. She watched him, and suddenly, standing in the weird light cast by the naked bulbs, absorbing this dreadful confession, the past fell irretrievably away. It seemed to her now as if her request for a divorce, only minutes old, belonged to nearly forgotten history. Her right hand shot up in a spasmodic, uncontrolled gesture, the palm of the hand moving across the right cheek, distorting the eye and stretching the skin. But she could not remove the stain, could not obliterate the contamination that was now hers.

Silence was enough for Kessler. He knew he had reached his wife. A minute passed.

"So you believe me now," he said. "You believe."

"Yes." Her voice was barely audible.

"So you cannot have a divorce . . . or a separation . . . or anything of the kind. It is an outright impossibility. No one should even know that the idea crossed your mind. The instant they see something wrong between us, the instant they hear your request for a change, they'll suspect that you know about my work . . . or that you know what is not to be known. Or perhaps they'll think that I'm engaged in some illegal activity. It doesn't matter. If they suspect, that's all they need. Then, Karin, they will hound you to make certain you represent no threat to them. They'll watch me more closely because they'll believe I've told —"

She cut him off with unexpected fury.

"And now that you've told me, I'm trapped."

Kessler did not respond. He understood her perfectly.

". . . I'm sorry," she said. "I am . . . I shouldn't have —"

"Learn not to be a fool. My having told you makes no difference. If I had said nothing to you at all, if I had permitted you to leave, the SS would still assume that you're a risk. Do you think they require proof . . . statements . . . documents? They would take you away as a security measure. There's nothing that can't be done as a security measure."

"Then what will you do?"

"I don't know."

"Continue —"

"No. That's impossible. I cannot continue work on this project. I must find a way to stop it . . . delay its completion . . . sabotage. I cannot allow the successful completion of this thing."

Karin could only listen. He alone understood the logic of the choices.

"I can't quit the position. That too is out of the question. Someone else would take my place. If I did quit, they would ask for the reason. There is no answer that will satisfy them. And if they let me leave, do you know where we would be then? Watched — as no one has been watched before. I know too much. What rest, what peace could I know realizing that others might find a solution to the problem? It's a matter of time . . . time. All I can do now is try to slow up the work . . . steer the thing down a dead end . . . waste time on unprofitable approaches . . . but that can't be kept up indefinitely. If my mistakes become too obvious . . . my tactics transparent . . . if I'm too desperate, then I'm finished."

"Is that all? Are you confined to just that?"

"Am I confined? Yes. We are all confined. If you want to know what would be best . . . ideal . . . then it is simple. The British must learn about this."

"You'll be caught, Otto. They'll get you. They'll kill you. You can't attempt —"

"I didn't say I would try. I wouldn't know how to begin . . . where to go . . . whom to speak to. I'm not an idiot."

He walked away from her and stood on the spot where, in his dream, Standartenführer Franz and the others had crouched over the photograph.

"I am prepared," he said, "I am prepared to be a traitor, but I fear I am a coward."

So Kessler pursued his scheme of conceptual sabotage. On a Thursday, he scheduled a late afternoon conference in the subbasement lecture room. Graml said he wished to give a talk on the preparation of aluminum alloys. Even before the meeting Kessler knew, based on an outline of Graml's talk, that his conceptions would probably come to nothing. But he calculated that a minimum of one week could be wasted discussing the ideas.

At 5:10 P.M. Herr Graml began his discourse. Kessler and the others listened in silence. Perhaps it was the accumulated and largely repressed emotional strain that was responsible; that, and the fact that it was late in the day, but quite suddenly, after forty-odd minutes of Graml's lecture, Kessler began to feel weak and dizzy. The room reeled before his eyes. He began to sweat. His first impulse was to leave the room as quickly as possible, for he was seized immediately by the notion that his colleagues, gathering around him in concern, would see directly into his tortured state of mind. Everything would be revealed.

"A moment, gentlemen . . . please keep on."

"Are you ill, Otto?" asked Graml.

"Please . . . let the meeting continue. I have something for this in my office."

He left the room and rode the lift up to his office floor. Already he felt better because he had escaped the lecture, his colleagues, the pressure of the need to lie to them. Finding his key, Kessler opened the door to his office, but it had opened less than halfway when he became aware of light coming from his desk. Had he forgotten to switch off the desk lamp? In a second the door was fully open.

Wolfgang Buchheim was standing behind his desk.

Kessler closed the door behind him.

"Wolfgang."

There was no answer. Buchheim stood there, absolutely still. In his left hand he held a document. In his right hand Kessler could see a small camera. For seconds, the tableau was frozen. Then, Buchheim placed both camera and document on the desk. He sat down in Kessler's desk chair and waited. Daylight was visible through the blinds drawn over the window. Buchheim, knowing that there was nothing to be done, maintained his silence. With one hand he reached out and snapped off the desk lamp. He knew he was a dead man.

Kessler walked forward and picked up the miniature camera. Turning it slowly about in his hands, he subjected it to careful scrutiny — the scientist examining evidence in search of an answer to some theoretical question. But he stopped this pointless activity as abruptly as he had begun it and looked at his colleague uncomprehendingly.

"Spare me your expressions of patriotic disappointment, Otto. I work for British Intelligence."

Buchheim paused, then added, "I have done so for years."

He said this with astonishing equanimity. He was a man delivering a final statement before a jury of corrupt, ignorant men, unquestionably set on rendering a fatal judgment. He addressed the future itself, an invisible audience, not yet born, which would some day hear his words and understand them.

"What are you going to do, Otto? We haven't got all evening for staring at each other. Call a guard, or wait, if you prefer, for the one who's gone. He returns at 6:16."

Kessler looked at the wall clock. 6:03. Thirteen minutes.

"How did you get in here?" He asked this question because, for the moment, he could invent no way to deal with this ironic situation.

"Here," Buchheim pulled a key out of his pocket and tossed it on the desk. "It's a copy of yours — a little rough, but it works. You are unbelievably sloppy, Otto, when it comes to security. Your friend Kleist would be outraged. I stole your key out of your overcoat pocket and returned it without your noticing anything. I measured the key, photographed it from four angles, and from that information an adequate copy was made after six tries. It was simpler than I had anticipated. Don't ask me where the copy was made. The SS will be sure to get that out of me."

Otto Kessler had now discovered the way to reach British Intelligence. His contact man was sitting directly in front of him. The problem inherent in this unforeseen circumstance was both apparent and insurmountable. So near, yet so far. Kessler tried to calculate the wisest strategy for overcoming Buchheim's fear. He could think of nothing. There was nothing to do other than to speak the truth.

"Wolfgang. Time is short. Here, take your camera." He placed the device on the desk. "I am not going to call a guard. I have no intention of doing that . . . now or in the future."

Speaking required of Kessler a continued effort of the will. The anticipation of failure saturated speech with the feeling of the absurd.

"I must reach British Intelligence. I must reach London. You are the only way."

He paused between each sentence, feeling the need to add an exhortation, but he refrained from doing so. Wouldn't every overt expression of sincerity only confirm Buchheim's fears?

"Inform London that I'm prepared to tell them everything. The nature of the project, the location of the factory, the research findings. Anything I can find out for them. You can get this information through . . ." and he stopped, stared into silence by the incredulous expression on his colleague's face.

"Otto. In a matter of hours or days, I am going to disappear from the face of the earth. I pray for a quick death. I don't care to be treated as a fool at this moment."

"I am telling the truth."

"Kessler . . . Kessler. Do you expect me to believe this charade? You have just caught me spying in your office. You can turn me in and that will be the end of me. Frankly, I don't know how I will react under torture. I imagine that the SS will keep me alive long enough for me to tell them what they want to know. Suicide is also a reasonable idea. On the other hand, you can let me go. In that case, if I am fool enough to maintain my contacts, then I must do so knowing that I am being watched. I take the chance of destroying not only myself, but a great number of other people as well. How many I do not know, but there are others besides me. You see, there is no choice for me at all . . . none. My own life is already lost, Otto. I will not jeopardize the lives of others. All of this is simple . . . simple in the extreme. So your proposition is of no use to me."

"Buchheim — I am telling you the truth."

"Tell me, Otto. What story can you invent . . . what tale can you tell to improve your credibility? What can you say about it? I suppose that, at long last, you have discovered the less civilized aspects of your employers."

"Yes."

"Ah — I see. You have discovered that. Extraordinary. I am moved. It took you some time, didn't it, but it's really too much to expect that a man of your type will observe what's happening before his eyes. Very convenient too that your moral reawakening should coincide so nicely with our accidental meeting."

Kessler chose not to respond to this comment. He knew that Buchheim's trust could not be won through argument.

"Wolfgang. Project I-P 9 — remember it. Infernal Proteus nine. We are trying to develop a lightweight, strong alloy. It will be used in weapons production. The research facilities are referred to in code as Blocksberg. The factory producing test samples is located fifty miles east of Krakow. Code designation — Horselberg. They're constructing it with slave labor. I have seen it. You had better go now, Wolfgang. It's 6:12. If the guard returns, then I will have to explain your presence to him."

Kessler walked to the door, opened it, and checked the corridor.

"Leave now," he said.

Buchheim did not move.

"I am sorry, Wolfgang, if I've destroyed your usefulness as an agent. As your friend though, I insist on your leaving now."

Buchheim picked up his camera and left the office.

And now Otto Kessler and Wolfgang Buchheim commenced their waiting game.

Buchheim counted the days. Convinced that his colleague and the SS were merely playing with him, using him as an instrument in some broader scheme, the consciousness of time weighed upon him. How many days would pass before the SS, deciding on his uselessness,

148

picked him up? At his office, Buchheim sat at his desk and listened to footsteps pass his door. Papers lay in front of him, but nothing possessed the power to hold his attention. Anything could function as a distraction, for nearly everything became a sign that the SS was about to make its move. On the streets, where Buchheim felt especially vulnerable, he developed compulsive, fear-driven habits. He would walk down the sidewalk and wheel suddenly about, reversing his direction completely. This gross, uncontrolled effort to see if he was being followed was accompanied by overly broad facial expressions intended to broadcast to others the innocence of his motives.

Herr Buchheim did not go to his restaurant. Unused, his pipe sat in the drawer next to the till. He wondered if the manager, believing he would never return, might take the pipe as his own. Grete Ohlendorff served beer, made change, cleared tables, and waited. Buchheim did not come. He could not risk the lives of his contacts. But wherein lay the greatest risk? His resolve not to return to the restaurant soon became complicated by a precisely reverse consideration. Returning might be the wiser alternative. Was the SS observing him, waiting to see which previously habitual things he refrained from doing? This seemed highly probable, especially if Buchheim assumed that the SS, in league with Kessler from the start, had put him under surveillance a long time ago. He balanced the two alternatives in his mind. There were arguments on both sides. Buchheim felt paralyzed. The logic of a drama was beginning to play itself out, a drama he had envisioned before in dim outline. Discovery — isolation — paralysis — disappearance. These were the way stations on the path to destruction.

But the meetings with Kessler continued — after lunch, twice a week, in Kessler's office. Otto Kessler was waiting too. At first, he awaited his own imminent destruction. Immediately after the discovery it occurred to him that Kleist might have planted Buchheim in the office as a test of loyalty. This idea filled Kessler with unspeakable terror. He cursed himself for not having thought of this at the moment of discovery, for having permitted his spontaneously humane impulses to determine his actions. But after three days, when the SS failed to arrest him, Kessler dismissed this idea. Just the same, he understood that his failure to report Buchheim to the SS represented a fundamental decision. Every subsequent minute could only deepen his guilt by association.

What were Kessler's calculations concerning his meetings with Buchheim? He knew that he would be subject to intense interrogation if Buchheim was caught. Kleist would demand a detailed account of everything. He would have to review the contents of each conference with Buchheim. Kessler did not know if he could successfully hide his "guilt." But, if he broke off the meetings, then that too could only arouse the interest of the SS. Kessler hoped that Buchheim had managed to establish his "political character." Kleist had said nothing further about him. The guards did not pay him special attention. These were positive indications. Now, although the continuation of the conferences with Buchheim was both necessary and fraught with danger, Kessler could see that the sheer fact of their continuing to meet would not further his purpose. He knew that Buchheim had to deduce that if he, Kessler, was working with the SS, the meetings would continue anyway. But, from another perspective, Kessler understood that the encounters with Buchheim held out the only hope for success. He had to prove the sincerity of his desire to reach British Intelligence. Only the medium of ongoing personal contact with Buchheim would carry the persuasive weight necessary for surmounting deep suspicion. If Buchheim had become a thoroughly professionalized, dehumanized agent, then all was lost, for then nothing would transcend the embrace of his doubts. But there was no choice. Even radical suspicion could be overcome only by sustained human contact. At first, Kessler naïvely assumed that he could not fail, but then he began to see the implications of his position. Wasn't the opportunity for a spontaneous expression of his desire to reach London precluded by the need to strategically calculate every move? Could his authentic feelings survive these calculations?

And so, they met. They conversed about scientific conceptions, but the pretense involved, the charade that had to be maintained during such discussions, was intolerable. Eventually, Kessler would shift the conversation onto the only real problem that existed for both of them. He showed Buchheim every file, every report, every jotting down of every calculation he had in his possession. One problem was insurmountable. There was no official document containing an explicit statement of the purpose of the project. Another security measure. Kessler could not bring in the other members of the staff and have them confirm his description of the project. Dedicated Party members did not break security regulations. But Kessler explained to Buchheim the exact nature of the work each man was doing. He showed him reports composed by staff members. The goal of the project could be inferred from the documents. Kessler told Buchheim to photograph everything.

Bombarded by Kessler's unrelenting efforts to demonstrate his sincerity, Buchheim began to experience increasing discomfort. For how long could he tolerate the spectacle of a friend and colleague attempting to prove his honesty? For how long could he keep Kessler in this humiliating position? Buchheim's suspicions abated, but they would not completely disappear. One afternoon, seeming to give way, Buchheim agreed to photograph some documents, but even as he took the pictures, Kessler standing off to the side and placing papers in front of the camera, Buchheim knew that he was still unprepared to return to the restaurant.

"What are you waiting for, Wolfgang? Send the information. If you're lost either way, then send it."

But Buchheim held on. He would not risk it.

As the days passed, however, he began to believe in Kessler. One afternoon, during a meeting, Kessler described the scenes he had witnessed in Poland. Buchheim had never witnessed such events. He could not believe that Kessler was artificially manufacturing the horror, the dread, that animated his description. Still, Buchheim failed to act. His impulses conflicted. The strain of the meetings grew unbearable.

Then, on a Friday, late in July, weeks after the pivotal, accidental encounter that had changed everything, Kessler determined that one last, major effort might win his colleague's trust. He sensed that a critical moment had come.

"I can see, Wolfgang," he said, "that nothing I do can convince you that I am in good faith. The only real problem is your fear, not that that is a trivial matter. Your fear is understandable. Frankly, I share the feeling with you, even though you're unwilling to accept that. So, I will trouble you no more with this. My efforts have proved useless. I must try to reach London in some other way . . . only one last word with you on this difficult situation. Until now, I have admired your self-sacrificing attitude, your consideration for the others who might suffer with you, or because of you. To all appearances, you have acted in a way that minimizes the risks to everyone else. Excellent and admirable. But you have miscalculated. Your failure to do what I have persistently recommended will, in the end, bring about, more certainly than ever before, the destruction of yourself, your friends, and many others. Some weeks ago you set before me what you take to be the real options open to you in this situation — either to be hanged immediately, or to contact London and thereby risk the lives of your contacts. How many of them are involved, I don't know. To tell the truth, I don't care. You know, it has been quite interesting, Wolfgang, watching your transformation from a man struggling with great integrity in a morally difficult situation, into a man who is waiting to die. A sorrowful sight. But let me add another dimension to your already taxing problems. Within four to six months I expect that some testable concept will have been worked out by my staff. This must happen in spite of my efforts to prevent it. Now . . . what will happen if we are successful? Suppose that we find a way to produce a lightweight alloy, a quarter of an inch thick, capable of withstanding the impact of small cannon shells. Let's ignore anything more extravagant. Suppose that this metal enables us to produce aircraft which will give Germany air superiority for three months. That's all that's required. We will win the war, or rather, Germany will win the war. An interesting prospect, Wolfgang. So that is the dimension I ask you to contemplate carefully. Perhaps I'm telling the truth and you are wrong to withhold this information from London, even at the risk of endangering the lives of your contacts. If I am playing with you, if everything I say to you is a lie, and you act, then the lives of three or four, maybe a dozen agents, will be lost. There are more where they came from, I am certain. But if you keep silent, and I am telling the truth, then what will be the result? A German victory over the Soviets? Over England? Or the Americans, should they become involved. If that speculation strikes you as overwrought, then imagine only a war that drags on for two or three years more than it would otherwise. Add these considerations to your moral calculations."

Herr Buchheim returned to his restaurant. The pipes were switched. Herr Hanslick used his radio transmitter. Within five days of Otto Kessler's monologue, Trevor Grey had a message on his desk.

"Kessler discovered me in his office. He says he is one of us. Project I-P 9. Infernal Proteus nine. Factory — fifty miles east of Krakow."

That was all.

Buchheim told Kessler what he had done. When Kessler expressed his pleasure at this and confirmed his commitment to provide information, his colleague added a qualification.

"Good, Otto, but remember this. London knows you found me in your office. They're entitled to that information. You've overcome the problem of my belief in your honesty. The remaining problem is not subject to your control in the same way. Will London believe you?"

«6»

It was August, 1941, and Trevor Grey, Harry Forsyth, and many others fixed their attention on Germany's astonishingly rapid advance into the vast spaces of Soviet Russia. It was another demonstration, on a vast scale, of the military prowess that had impressed the world in 1939 and 1940. Gruppenführer Kleist was there too, accompanying the panzer units during the opening phase of the invasion, just as he had in Poland, Norway and France — observing, criticizing, suggesting. Each day brought news of territory gained by German forces, of courageous, suicidal resistance by the Russians. Grey and Forsyth understood that the problems of British Intelligence would dwindle into insignificance if the Russians did not hold.

The two British agents sat in a small pub just off Mansfield Road in Hampstead. Grey knew Will Sullivan, the owner of the place. The two men frequented the pub about once a month. There they discussed business in a relaxed, unhurried fashion. That morning Grey had met with Trenchard, and it had proven to be a frustrating encounter. The communication received from Buchheim was the subject of a difference in opinion not easy to reconcile. Trenchard refused to accept the message at face value.

". . . And why should he?" remarked Forsyth. "You've got to concede that the man has a point. Buchheim admits he was found out. Kessler discovered him in the office. He didn't come to Buchheim with the offer to work for us."

"But how could he have done that? Look at the circumstances around the event. Kessler is brought in as lead researcher on a project. He knows he is working on a top-security operation. He chooses all the people who work with him, and the SS clears each of them before admitting them to the staff. The project is absolute top security . . . they guard it day and night . . . no one unauthorized gets in. Now, in that situation, Harry, how can Kessler risk approaching anyone on the staff itself? He'd be mad to assume one of his own people is actually our man. He might try making a contact outside, but never on the inside."

Forsyth sipped his beer.

"All right," he said, "but what I fail to see is why you believe Kessler would be seeking a contact with us in the first place. He's achieved a high position. He's won the trust, the approval of the SS. Clean record and all. Not a blemish. What evidence do you have which makes his turning around plausible? What's he got that recommends him to us?"

"That's exactly what Trenchard says."

"For good reason."

"But I'll tell you, Harry. I'm not convinced."

"Now that's bloody crazy, Grey."

"You know me, Harry. I'm not just arbitrarily perverse."

Grey smiled, turned, and signaled for another beer.

"In this rotten business, Grey, the last thing you choose to believe is what someone just out and out tells you."

"I know . . . I know."

"Here you sit," said Forsyth, "a thousand miles from the scene of the crime, with one message in your hands, and just where do you place your money? On the least probable thing of all. You'd be better off betting on Hermann Göring as a British agent. It's plain mad to believe that one of their best scientific minds is on our side. Without further evidence, you can't make it stick. The objective facts force one to doubt Kessler."

"The objective facts?"

"Yes."

"Back at Oxford, we spent a lot of time discussing objective facts."

"Now look, Grey — don't bring your philosophical baggage into this thing."

"It isn't really a question of objective facts, Harry. It all hangs on how you decide to view the thing."

"Keep it reasonable."

"Imagination is everything."

"Flights . . . flights of imagination, Grey."

"So you think they've set up Buchheim?"

"Not unlikely — is it? In my view, the entire thing is transparent."

"One must give the enemy credit — you agree?"

"Yes . . . I do."

"This man Kleist can't be an utter fool. At least, we can't assume he is. Suppose he knew Buchheim is our man. Suppose, further, he wanted to set Buchheim up as a conduit for false information. If you were in his place, how would you do it?"

"There are several techniques."

"Correct . . . but surely one of them wouldn't be having Otto Kessler surprise Buchheim just as he happens to be committing an act punishable by death. One could hardly choose a worse moment. The SS would aim at misleading

Buchheim completely. What would be the point of inflaming his fears, increasing his suspicion?"

Grey paused and glanced at a customer entering the pub.

"You see," he said, still looking off to the side. "You're leaving out too much, Harry . . . too much. So is Trenchard."

"All right. What am I leaving out?"

For a moment, Grey traced a design in the foam of his fresh beer.

"It leaves out, Harry, what probably happened . . . what had to happen before that last message was sent to us. What you're saying is too simplistic . . . too purely rational . . . again like Trenchard."

"You can't expect us to run the war —"

"On the basis of my intuitions you were about to say?"

"Yes."

"Then you have been speaking to my good partner."

"Entirely independent judgments, Grey."

"Look. If you consider this case as a collection of bare facts, that's one thing, but I ask you to imagine the events themselves. Buchheim says he was discovered by Kessler in the office. That was hardly a confidence-inspiring situation. Thus, he could never have been foolish enough to believe Kessler right from the start. We know Buchheim isn't a professional agent. He's not playing at this type of work because he has a taste for danger . . . a perverse need to flirt with death and torture . . . that's not our man. He's a professional scientist who decided to work with us out of genuine conviction. His sensibilities must be rather finely tuned to the dangers implicit in his position, his imagination quite alive to the chances of being finished off in a slow, unattractive manner. Herr Buchheim is no hardened derelict who found himself a convenient wartime occupation."

"So . . . the man isn't a machine."

"Yes . . . and I emphasize it to make clear just what had to be overcome . . . the intensity of doubt . . . the depth of fear . . . the convolutions of judgment . . . before he was willing to assume the risk, the fantastic risk, of contacting us again."

Forsyth said nothing. He sipped his beer. Grey looked at his colleague, trying to assess the effects of his argument.

"Now you see, if that's the case, then something out of the ordinary had to convince Buchheim that sending his communication was a reasonable move. What convinced him? Who did it? Kessler had to be the man, Harry . . . only Kessler. He was the one who discovered Buchheim. He was the one who convinced him to go ahead with it. Our other people were out of the picture . . . offstage. They had to be. After the discovery in Kessler's office, Buchheim would never have contacted them until he judged it was safe."

"All right, Grey —"

"Suppose then I agree with you for a moment, Harry, and grant that there's a complex scheme, a fantastic conspiracy, going on here. Still, it had to be Kessler and Kessler alone who was the point of contact between the hypothetical conspirators and our man Buchheim. It's what happened between them that matters. Grant me that, Harry, that one simple fact, and the whole conspiracy idea collapses."

Forsyth was sitting back and listening. He knew that another piece of the argument was yet to come.

"Who is Kessler?" Grey continued. "In one sense he's not unlike Buchheim. A real research scientist. There's a biographical sketch of Kessler in a scientific journal in the British Museum. The man has spent a lifetime secluded away in laboratories, offices, university buildings. He's had his mind on mathematical equations, experiments, the heights and depths of metallurgical science. We all know that there are politicians, perfectly ruthless types, men capable of getting their own way, running about the universities, but Kessler isn't that sort. He's been blessed with special appointments, honored positions, university chairs occupied by only the best. He's been above the petty wrangling. The portrait that emerges from the biographical sketch was confirmed for me by someone else. I spoke to a chap named Basil Parks, the man who did the English translation of Kessler's major work. He found the idea of Kessler's being involved in secret service work absolutely laughable. He says that Kessler keeps to himself. Charming man, he said, although in a stumbling sort of way. I think that's the way he put it. Not a smooth type at all. It's rather hard to think of him as an agent. Of course, it depends on the sort of work the SS might ask him to do . . . doesn't it? The point is that taking photographs, or moving papers around on a desk, are different from lying perfectly to a man who doubts you . . . not a false word . . . not an expression which might give you away. Our Kessler has even less experience with people, with the control of his responses, his facial muscles, than most others. What does he know about systematic lying, prolonged deception, elaborate playacting? Those things constitute an art, Harry. Those things are not our man Kessler. The facts point to another breed of man, a type as far removed from the requirements of espionage work as I can imagine. And yet . . . and yet . . . this is the man who, through prolonged contact with Buchheim, convinced him to reestablish contact with us. I can't believe, given all this, that Kessler is lying. He hasn't got the talent for a protracted performance. Even if the SS tried to use him to mislead Buchheim, it wouldn't have worked. He'd have made a mess of it somewhere. Buchheim is in too dangerous a situation to have succumbed to a halfhearted, incompetent attempt at deception. And don't forget, Harry . . . these two men are old friends . . . colleagues . . . just like the two of us."

Grey paused and looked around the pub. It was a professional impulse.

"There's one other interpretation, Harry. Buchheim is knowingly working for the SS. Perhaps they've found him out and threatened him. But if that were true, they could control what he tells us, and in that case we would never have learned that Kessler discovered him accidentally. Why should they voluntarily maximize our doubts? It would be entirely senseless."

"You say," said Forsyth, "that Kessler could never be a professional agent. You claim that he doesn't have the necessary talent for deceiving Buchheim. Why, then, should we believe that now, quite suddenly, Kessler is willingly going to attempt deceiving the SS?"

"He'll try it if he's been driven to it."

"And you think he has been?"

"Yes . . . I do."

"How?"

"I don't know. We can't know."

"But surely you don't expect his skills will increase now that he's working for us."

"No, Harry. I never said Kessler would live long."

"You seem rather sure of yourself, old friend."

"I see no other way to understand this affair."

"And what does your partner Trenchard want?" asked Forsyth.

"Continue the air attacks on the other facilities. Keep track of the installations and strike at them."

"Then he wants to ignore the Frankfurt operation entirely?"

"Oh — he's quite willing to add Frankfurt to the target lists."

161

"The entire city?" asked Forsyth.

"His vision doesn't extend that far yet. But Trenchard is keen on bombing. A real enthusiast. And that's just the thing that's peculiar about all this."

"There is a war on, Grey."

"But what's the point? If we hit a real project now, it will be absurdly counterproductive. The Germans will disperse everything, as surely as they did the decoys. Every chance we'd have of finding out what they're up to will be sacrificed."

"So your solution is to keep Buchheim on the job?"

"We've got to stay with him . . . and with Kessler. As long as they operate, we're in splendid shape. Even if Kessler's team develops its special alloy, we'll learn about it the moment the German manufacturers do. Once they start manufacturing the product, then we also know what targets to hit."

"It's reasonable, Grey, but I don't see how you can bring Trenchard around to that view . . . or anyone else. And time is working against you."

"Yes . . . yes."

"You agree? If this state of affairs persists, then Trenchard will argue that not only are Buchheim and Kessler useless, but all of Buchheim's contacts have been compromised as well."

"I know."

"If he brings his case to military or government authorities, then his bombing solution, even if only an interim one, will appear the more reasonable option. Your view is too farfetched, too intuitive, too esoteric. It hinges on an interpretation of the characters involved. Your analysis can't prevail over Trenchard's methodical, forceful solution."

"So now I must go it on my own."

Forsyth was not expecting this. He looked surprised.

"What are you getting at?"

"Kessler and Buchheim must prove their credibility — that's what I'm getting at."

Grey insisted on paying the bill. It was a large one. He asked Will Sullivan if a personal check was acceptable.

"Of course," was the reply.

It didn't take Forsyth long to react.

"Transparent, Grey. Rook to bishop eight, check — I would say. Right?"

He was.

But Douglas Trenchard was intent on pressing his case. He requested a conference on August 10, 1941. He said, once again, that he wished to speak to members of Bomber Command. Trenchard's style disturbed Trevor Grey. The former was acting unilaterally, never asking Grey if he felt a need for conferences. Grey, on the other hand, did not object because he knew he lacked power in relation to Trenchard. He confined himself to sarcasm.

"Tell me, Douglas," he would say, "would you mind a guest at your conference?"

"Whom do you have in mind, Grey?"

"Myself."

Grey had his own designs in regard to the August 10 meeting. He wished to demonstrate the uselessness of air power in the current situation. Bombers could be put to better use. Trenchard was cool to the idea of Grey's presence. Grey was adamant. Trenchard did not offer further objection. Green thought the conference a good idea, and Atkinson, Grey's superior, expressed no interest one way or the other.

"These people must have their fun, Grey," he said.

"Yes — and I'm right in the middle of the entertainment."

"I'm sure you'll survive it all, Grey. I have every confidence in you."

Grey prepared for the meeting by writing up a summary

of his views. He distributed copies to the RAF officers on the day before the scheduled conference.

The meeting was held in Trenchard's office. Three RAF officers attended. Trenchard, sitting at his desk, looked officious. The others sat in chairs arranged in a semicircle.

Trenchard began by apologizing for the costly May air attacks.

"A disastrous experiment I realize, gentlemen, but not an unprofitable one. I want you to know that I appreciate the sacrifice . . . more than I can say."

Trenchard sipped slowly from his glass of mineral water.

"Well, Trenchard," responded Wing Commander Horton, "I speak for all of us when I say that we, in turn, appreciate your concern. Not everyone is so considerate of the other chap's problems."

Horton was a short, squat, pudgy-faced officer with a talent for wartime administration. Bomber Command valued him for his innovative ideas, those inspired conceptions which contributed to the effectiveness of the strategic air campaign. As he spoke his words of thanks, his fists planted on his thighs, his elbows jutting aggressively into space, the other two officers, Wing Commander Richardson and Group Captain Etherington, nodded their agreement.

"Still," interjected Richardson. "there are limits on sacrifice, even if the motive is reasonable."

He was prepared to forestall further costly suggestions.

"Oh — absolutely," chimed in Etherington.

"There are limits, gentlemen," remarked Trenchard, pouring himself more water. "After all. I don't want to dampen your enthusiasm . . . the collective enthusiasm. My colleague Grey, and myself, wish to present you with our problem. I have sent each of you a summary of the information obtained thus far by our operatives."

"Yes," said Horton, "we've all . . ."

But Grey did not let him finish.

"And I, gentlemen," he said, "have sent you a summary of my views . . . regarding this problem."

Horton was about to continue, but he stopped, emitting only an inarticulate sound. He had seen Trenchard, who, in turn, was glaring furiously at Grey. This was the first time Trenchard had heard about Grey's report.

"Trenchard," said Richardson, anxious to diffuse the accumulating tension.

"Yes."

"May I request tea?"

Trenchard turned to him.

"Excuse me," he said.

"Tea?" repeated Richardson.

Trenchard took them all in with a glance and announced, "Grey and I do not quite agree on what is to be done here . . . because we do not concur on what is actually going on."

Finding themselves thrust into the middle of a Secret Service dispute, this remark momentarily froze the RAF officers.

Trenchard summoned his secretary and ordered the tea.

"Grey," he said, while the officers shifted uncomfortably in their chairs, "please give us the pleasure of your views."

So Trevor Grey set forth his doctrine on the credibility of Wolfgang Buchheim and Otto Kessler. He expanded on his summary, filling in the outline with rich, imaginative detail. He felt the urge to dramatize his position, at several moments nearly inventing dialogue to put into the mouths of the invisible, distant protagonists, but instead he restrained himself. Grey had thought out his presentation in advance, seeking to express his case with consummate fluency. But as he spoke he knew he was failing. He was addressing the wrong audience, an audience selected by Douglas Trenchard. The postures and facial expressions of the three officers betrayed their mounting impatience, their lack of faith in Grey's hypothesis.

"No," he concluded, "Bomber Command must not waste its resources on the targets my colleague selects. Krupps of Essen is more important. Expend your energy on that. We all stand to benefit from successful raids on key targets. But I've seen no evidence which compels us to divert our forces to alleged enemy projects. Bomb factories, gentlemen. Our intelligence resources are capable of meeting the challenge of project I-P 9."

Grey fell silent, feeling unsatisfied with his concluding sentences. But there was no rectifying that. He knew he had spoken for too long.

Trenchard's secretary served the tea and then departed. For several moments the sole response to Grey's monologue consisted of the rattling of cups and spoons.

"I must say, Grey, that I cannot accept your analysis." It was Group Captain Etherington who spoke. "It leaves me unsatisfied. In any case . . . more specifically . . ." and Etherington groped for words, ". . . the unavoidable fact that this Kessler is in charge . . ."

". . . Cleared by the SS," said Richardson.

"Indeed, cleared by the SS," continued the Group Captain, "with no proof of a commitment to us . . . it seems hardly rational to base a policy on this man's word alone."

"No . . . I should think not." It was Horton, concurring with Etherington.

Trenchard sipped his tea.

Grey remained silent.

"Needless to say," remarked Richardson, fully conscious of jurisdictional boundaries, "it is not for Bomber Command to tell you what to do with your own people."

"And, on the other side," said Horton, "we have rather

weighty evidence. Trenchard points out the extent of the other facilities . . . in Hamburg . . . in Cologne . . . the coordinated effort the enemy has made to defend them. I don't believe we can ignore all this. These facts have significance . . . in my mind at least."

"And mine," said Richardson.

"In my view," continued Horton, "the peculiar location of the Frankfurt operation argues not that it is the real show, but that it was designed to attract attention, stimulate a misguided curiosity."

"No . . . no," said Grey. "It's wrong . . . you've got it wrong."

For a moment he could remember himself seated at a long, wooden table, under the imposing ceiling of an Oxford college dining room, debating with fellow students.

"In any case," said Horton, overlooking Grey's mounting excitement, "you must decide about your people, we decide about ours."

"My agents risk their lives, it seems to me, while you waste your damned time —"

"Oh now," said Etherington, "we must try to keep this civil."

"You can be bloody sure," said Grey, "that there'll be hell to pay if I'm right . . ."

"Grey!" shouted Trenchard.

Horton, seeking to avoid entanglement in this increasingly unpleasant argument, assumed the role of peacemaker.

"Mr. Grey. We understand your enthusiasm for your own point of view. We wish you luck should you continue to press your operatives for additional information. We, however, are not in a position to settle this problem. In the interim period I can see no loss involved in our pursuing the solution, the temporary solution if you prefer . . . offered by Douglas."

Even in the midst of this argument, Grey, always sensitive to details, was impressed by the fact that Horton referred to Trenchard by his first name.

"But I'll have nothing to do with organizing this bombing campaign."

Grey realized how pointless a remark this was. No one had asked for his participation in Bomber Command affairs.

Then Trenchard broke in, much as if Grey were not there at all.

"Our experiment in May pointed up the futility of daylight precision attacks. We agree on this."

"I should say so," remarked Etherington. "Both the Germans and ourselves have learned that lesson."

"Now," continued Trenchard, "neither the Secret Service nor myself . . ."

An egomaniacal distinction, thought Grey.

". . . have any wish to aggravate your losses, but we all know that night bombing is a different issue."

The officers nodded.

"The idea is already in the air . . . so to speak."

Etherington groaned at this atrocious pun.

"So, I shall leave it at this. Your goals and mine coincide," said Trenchard. "If, through your efforts, our disparate ends can be achieved, shall we not both be the happier for it?"

He paused and added, "I say that night area attacks are the solution."

"Bomber Command shall require precious little outside encouragement for that policy."

"I am aware of that, Group Captain . . . but then I have never considered myself a true innovator," said Trenchard. "I try to accomplish my tasks with the available means, utilizing the existing consensus. Through the gradual accumulation of small changes, revolutionary results can be achieved."

168

Grey remained silent. He wondered if Trenchard was simply going to encourage these officers to pursue a policy they were already intent on pursuing.

"We do enjoy encouragement," said Richardson.

"I'm certain you do," responded Trenchard, "and that encouragement is not without its value — is it?"

"No. I didn't mean to imply that it was," said Etherington.

"The public," said Trenchard, "does not yet fully realize the potential of the strategic bombing weapon."

"No," agreed Horton.

"When they do, there shall be objections. Area bombing is indistinguishable from mass murder."

Trenchard paused. The officers shifted in their seats. Grey felt the impulse to leave the room. The conference was taking a bizarre turn.

Etherington was about to respond to Trenchard's blunt remark, but the latter spoke first.

"For true professionals, the politics of destruction is an unpleasant, bothersome topic. It is nothing more than a hindrance. That's why I voice my support for your position. Each instance of what you, Group Captain Etherington, call 'outside encouragement' shall be valuable once your bombing campaign begins to achieve massive results."

"He is right," said Richardson, turning to Etherington.

"Very good," said Trenchard. "Whereas your campaign benefits from my political support, my ends stand to be furthered by your campaign. I ask only that the project locations I've shown you be used as aiming points by your night bombers."

"That would have to be cleared through Bomber Command headquarters," said Etherington.

"Of course," replied Trenchard, "but I trust you see the advantages of this solution."

"Indeed," said Richardson.

"Area attacks," continued Trenchard, "do not suffer from the disadvantage of warning the Germans we are on to their project. They will believe that they have successfully dispersed their facilities. Night operations reduce your losses while maximizing disruption in the target cities. We may even eliminate enemy project personnel, hit the facilities themselves, while we strike at the enemy's greatest population centers. By sacrificing precision attacks on these projects, we gain the advantage of demoralizing the enemy, sowing chaos everywhere. Surely, this is more promising than risky operations in daylight, or the reliance on intelligence networks which are" — and Trenchard looked at Grey, — "all too easily compromised."

"Yes," said Horton, "in this case you are right . . . not to mention the broader considerations. We shall pass on your recommendation to Bomber Command headquarters and to the Air Ministry."

"After all," said Trenchard, "consider only the advantage to yourselves, if not to me. Another important target means further opportunity for perfecting technique. Night navigation is in its infancy."

They agreed.

"Night bombing represents a challenge of the highest order. The enemy attacks on our capital were but ineffectual models calling for an infinitely expanded response."

Again they agreed, and Trenchard talked on: avoiding enemy fighters — jamming his radar — disrupting his ground control systems — overcoming the weather. Each challenge, said Trenchard, demanded a solution. He encouraged these officers, "talked shop" with them, expressed to them his interest in their professional problems. The officers, in turn, responded enthusiastically, seduced completely by this breadth of vision found so rarely among personnel belonging to competing service organizations. So the conversation went on. A second serving of tea was ordered. Grey excused himself, saying that he had another engagement. He left because he was bored, and disturbed.

Why had Douglas Trenchard called the meeting? What was its real purpose?

Although this conference with the RAF both puzzled and depressed Trevor Grey, its outcome did not surprise him. Having adapted perfectly to Bomber Command's mentality, could Douglas Trenchard have failed to secure its cooperation?

So Grey understood that he would have to proceed on his own. His case required a massive demonstration of credibility on the part of Buchheim and Kessler. The thought of these two men, men whom he had never met, never seen, never conversed with directly, never deserted him. For each of them Grey constructed imaginary faces, imaginary voices. They became characters in a living work of fiction, a "work" paradoxically dependent on modern modes of technology. Grey saw that his position was grounded completely in his intuitions about Kessler and Buchheim, and this recognition further compelled him to acknowledge the greater persuasiveness of Trenchard's case.

Bomber Command approved of Trenchard's idea — at least in part. Group Captain Etherington called him and told him so. Bomber Command would attempt placing its multicolored target markers in the vicinity of one of the project centers in Essen. "Splendid," said Trenchard. He appreciated even this limited cooperation. Etherington promised bigger efforts in the future.

But Douglas Trenchard had another request, one which surprised the group captain. Trenchard asked if it would be feasible for him to visit a bomber station. He wished to observe the men, attend a briefing, watch the ground crews, see the aircraft.

"I confess to a fascination with these things," he said.

Anyway, if a man was willing to advocate bombing policy, shouldn't he obtain an overview of the operations entailed by that policy?

"I see no harm in that," answered the Group Captain.

"Can you get a security clearance for me?" asked Trenchard.

"No problem at all."

And there was no problem. Trenchard was rapidly cleared for a visit to a four-engined-bomber station in East Anglia. An RAF officer assigned to the task drove him out to the station late in the afternoon on a hot August day. When they arrived, the bomb trolleys were already rolling out to the aircraft, the petrol bowsers were feeding the four-motored giants. In the long, low, functional watch office Trenchard met Group Captain Dwyer. Trenchard was just in time, said Dwyer, for an aircrew briefing was about to begin.

"Care to sit in?" asked Dwyer.

"Thanks," said Trenchard, "but actually I wouldn't mind a bit of a walk about the place."

The Group Captain told his guest he was free to go wherever he liked, ask whatever questions came to mind. More than anything else, said Trenchard, he wished to see the machines.

"By all means," said Dwyer, "out there, at their dispersal points. You can't miss them."

Trenchard left the watch office, crossed a patch of grass, and started his walk across the concrete field. The setting was peaceful, archetypally English pastoral. To the west there was a dense area of forest. To the north one could see, beyond verdant fields, the church spire of the nearest town. Occasionally, birds darted across the concrete field and then disappeared into bushes and trees. To the east, a flock of sheep grazed on the side of a gently rolling hill. Unnoticed by station personnel, Trenchard observed this part natural, part man-made spectacle. Eyes aglow, lips parted in a faint smile intended for no one, he saw a four-engined bomber, sitting in awesome silence at its dispersal point, basking in the English summer twilight, dwarfing both ground-crew hut and the human personnel who scurried about attending to its needs. Trenchard surrendered himself to the presence of this mammoth machine, sprung, as it were, from the collective mind of a thousand design engineers, product of ten thousand man-hours of labor, culmination of a million manufacturing processes. He knew intense satisfaction as his gaze followed the contours of this machine — this machine, the beginnings of a goal long sought after.

How foolish of Grey to have thought that the answer could lie anywhere but here, in these machines.

Other aircraft were visible, nestled safely away at a dozen other dispersal points on all sides of the concrete strip. Four-engined steel "kites," as the aircrew called them. They were silent, but they spoke to Trenchard. As surely as they had "souls" for their crews, they revealed their souls to him. Soon the silence of this ancient landscape would be shattered by the whistle and whine, the cacophonous roar of aircraft engines. He could hear it now. Distant, resonant peal of the spire bell obliterated, birds fleeing in terror, the grass waving and flattening out in the ferocious backwash of propellers. Defenseless nature bending before the power of pistons, cylinders, and the force of innumerable controlled explosions. The reverent silence of all human spectators enforced by this sublime thunder. Who could deny, thought Trenchard, the special beauty of these machines? Steel, copper, aluminum — molded, shaped, hammered and assembled into functional, yet aesthetic, form. Machines more than perfectly suited for an era, but rather part of the definition of an era. How pleasing the ratios between wings and fuselage, tail and stabilizers. The threat of monotonous symmetry surmounted by powered turrets protruding from nose, top, and tail — sleek black ventilated barrels silhouetted against the darkening sky. Trenchard could hear the rapid chatter of these weapons, he could see the flashes darting from muzzles, the arching parabolic lines etched by tracers in the night sky. Each aircraft, resting on mammoth undercarriages slung beneath wings and engines, sloping upward from tail to nose, seemed to strain toward the vault of the sky. Bomb-bay doors were closed now, but soon they would open, revealing steel casings wearing fins and countless cans of incendiaries.

Who could imagine that the solution might lie somewhere else?

Trenchard observed in silence. He saw the future. A vision passed before the eye of his imagination, the vision of a rehearsal — the preview for the apocalypse. Fleets of four-engined aircraft arrayed in the form of a stream, a virtually unstoppable phalanx of flying steel marching across hundreds of miles of black sky. His ears filled with the imagined thunder of this armada, a multisensory sensation transcending sound itself. For the organizers and participants, this achievement would demand the extreme of self-sacrificing mental and physical effort. Forecasting weather, routing the armada, deceiving the opposition, manufacturing and distributing supplies, briefing crews, finding targets in the black of night, marking target areas, dodging searchlight beams, avoiding flak. A collective, monumental effort — dedicated to the unrelenting pursuit of a vision. This airborne wave of machines, snaking through the blackness, would transform concrete into dust, brick into rubble, wood into ashes, living souls into charred corpses, alleys and sidewalks into raging infernos — it would convert man-made centers of life into the circles of hell. An inspired vision. Organization at the service of chaos. Specialists would combine their skills and act in the name of the principle that all material, flesh or concrete, may be understood in terms of a common denominator — combustibility. One hundred bomb blasts envisioned one hundred times over. The fires of ten thousand incendiaries joining into an ocean of flames. Mighty convection currents, cries of a tormented atmosphere, shrieking with hurricane ferocity through vaporizing canyons of steel and brick.

To imagine it was to admit the very possibility of it. To suggest that it could be done would be to half compel the conclusion that it should be done.

Trenchard understood the force of technological possibilities, he knew their potential for disrupting the faculty of judgment through the immensity of a hypnotic vision. But he also understood that he alone could never be the catalyst between potentiality and actuality. The paradoxical truth was that he could lead best only where he learned to follow.

And the vision? How could Grey contend with that?

Back in the watch office, Group Captain Dwyer asked Trenchard if he had enjoyed his walk. He had — immensely.

"Impressive machines," he said.

A pilot standing nearby was quick to respond.

"If you like the bloody things so much, you can go in my place one of these nights."

Trenchard laughed.

"Yes," said the Group Captain, "there are some people who think that Bomber Command provides us with an easy way to earn a living."

"You'll never find me subscribing to such an idea."

The pilot was unconvinced.

"Keep my offer in mind," he said.

And on the same day Douglas Trenchard was extolling the virtues of four-engined bomber machines, Grey made his first move.

He visited an ostensibly abandoned building in the West End, an old, boarded-up structure which contained radio transmitters used by the Secret Service. To his friend Desmond Crowden, Grey personally delivered the message he wanted sent to Frankfurt.

That night, Crowden beamed a coded message to Herr Hanslick.

«7»

The Frankfurt baker operated his receiver-transmitter on Tuesday and Friday mornings between midnight and 2:00 A.M. Herr Hanslick received and decoded messages directly, and then transcribed them onto a slip of paper two inches wide and four inches long. He then inserted this slip between others of precisely the same dimensions. To an innocent observer, there was nothing peculiar about these small bundles of papers. Herr Hanslick always kept a quantity of these slips on hand because he had a use for them in his business. On any one slip he noted the date, items purchased, and the cost of purchases for one customer on a single day. Now, Grete Ohlendorff made a point of buying goods on at least two days of every week. Therefore, on Friday, Herr Hanslick would hand her the week's accumulated bill on two or more slips of paper. The slip with a message on it was inserted between the others. Grete, in turn, handed him the mark notes on which she taped the crucial photographs Buchheim gave her in the restaurant.

This slip of paper technique was outrageously simple, as

simple as the restaurant-pipe method. A Gestapo agent, prepared to check everything, might have chosen to examine Buchheim's pipe or Hanslick's bundle of papers. But Herr Hanslick and the Dawn Group preferred to operate on the basis of a simple principle — the integration of espionage activities into the repeating patterns of daily life. They sensed that subtler, more elaborate procedures could prove self-defeating. True to this principle, Grete Ohlendorff chose an unobtrusive method for transmitting information to Buchheim. In her small apartment, she kept a supply of the restaurant's paper napkins. When she received a communication from Herr Hanslick, she transcribed it onto the inside of one of these napkins. At work, she kept this one isolated in the right-hand pocket of her apron. When Buchheim arrived, she brought him his pipe and place setting. She always placed down two napkins. If there was a message for him, the bottom one contained it. Buchheim always folded and pocketed the lower napkin. If there was no message for him, nothing was lost by taking it. Again, a simple procedure. The ease and openness with which Grete could integrate it into her work routine argued strongly in its favor.

On a day at the end of August, 1941, Buchheim pocketed one of these napkins. He did this with little or no sense of expectation because, for day after day, London had been silent. But this day brought something new. Buchheim drank his beer, ate his lunch, paid the bill, and returned to his office. He locked the door, sat down at his desk, and removed the napkin from his pocket. On it was written the following succinct message: "The authorities do not believe your man."

Buchheim burned the napkin immediately and then sat quite still in his chair, considering the import of the seven simple words he had just read. He had not been wrong. The problem was in London. He picked up the telephone receiver and dialed Kessler's office number.

"Otto? Wolfgang. I think I have something interesting here in the last paper. Yes. Can I see you? . . . Right away."

Whenever they conferred, they covered Kessler's desk with papers and documents for the benefit of whoever might walk in on them unannounced. Huddling over these papers, they assumed the postures of men hard at work on legitimate problems.

"I've received the answer, Otto. London doesn't believe you."

"I'm not surprised. It was too much to expect."

"But it isn't hopeless."

Kessler was puzzled.

"What do you mean?"

"You see, if they doubted us completely, we would have heard nothing."

"Yes . . . yes."

"But someone, the man responsible for contacting us, does believe you. I see no other way to understand it."

"What do we do?"

"You've got to find the way to obtain other information . . . things that are important . . . things London can confirm through other sources. There's no other way. Can you do it?"

Hitherto, Otto Kessler had refused to seriously consider this problem, but now that it was a reality, he saw the inevitability of it. Compelling Buchheim to believe him had constituted a small moral triumph. It had satisfied him deeply. Still, convincing Buchheim had been facilitated by the incalculable subtleties of face to face contact. He could not do the same with the authorities in London, people to whom he was connected by the airwaves alone.

Therefore, what options were available to Kessler?

Suppose, he thought, he completely ignored the communication Buchheim had received from London? What would that mean? He could persist in sending scientific information to the British regarding project research.

But that option was flawed. He knew that as long as no breakthrough occurred in the project, he could send only ambiguous, inconclusive information to London, and the very ambiguity of it could, in fact, only intensify the doubts of the Secret Service. The English surely understood how easy it is to generate the image of a project, whereas, in reality, nothing at all need exist. So Kessler asked himself whether his sheer persistence in sending information, rather than the substance of that information itself, might persuade London. Again — too risky. The Secret Service would be wary of long-range ploys. Furthermore, confronted by a stream of suspect information, London, entertaining doubts, would be forced to an ultimate decision. They might abandon Buchheim and deny him further contact with the underground communication network.

On the other hand, Kessler considered the alternative of remaining silent, waiting for the breakthrough in the project, and then letting London know the truth. Here too he could foresee unfortunate ramifications. The time lapse between the present and the unpredictable breakthrough had to be, in itself, necessarily unpredictable. To wait might mean a silence of six months, a year, or longer. Obviously, this silence, following upon London's last communication, would be easily subject to misinterpretation. It could be read as a tacit admission, on the part of German Intelligence, that an attempted ruse had failed in its purpose. If the British settled on that version of events, then the same irrevocable consequence might ensue as in the instance of pursuing the first option. The Secret Service, determined to excise a dangerous cancer from its underground network, would abandon Buchheim by depriving him of contacts. Total isolation would result.

But what if that did not happen? The prospects

remained depressing. Suppose, thought Kessler, that in one year his research staff discovered a potential solution. He would have to get the substance of that solution through to London. If he succeeded, then English scientists, exposed suddenly to what might be a radically new conception, would start to argue about its feasibility. That was inevitable. The British would not act precipitously on the basis of new and perhaps startling conceptions, especially if that would entail enormous costs and massive diversion of resources. Simultaneously, Gruppenführer Kleist would be ordering tests, and if these proved successful, full production. Therefore, Kessler concluded that a failure to win confidence early in the game could issue in fatal, irreversible delays at a critical time.

So Buchheim was right. Kessler understood that he had to demonstrate his credibility quickly and dramatically. It would be small comfort to anyone if that demonstration came on the battlefields in the east, or in the skies over Europe. But how was Kessler going to obtain the information London would appreciate?

Ever since the beginning of their relationship, Kleist had continually renewed his invitation to Kessler for luncheon in the SS headquarters' dining room. Kessler had accepted twice. After the second journey to Poland, he refused every invitation, claiming the pressures of work as an excuse. SS officers were intolerable to him. He had no efficient defense against the sense of dread, the feeling of degradation which overcame him in the presence of these men. But Otto Kessler now recognized that the SS dining hall, frequented by more fanatical members of the army, navy and Luftwaffe, was the one place where, through judicious questioning and attentive listening, he might gather valuable details concerning military matters. The officers spoke quite freely among themselves, trusting implicitly in the patriotism of those who dined with the élite.

The first problem would be this. How would Kessler be able to convince Kleist, without generating suspicion, that after this long period of abstinence from the headquarters luncheon, he was now willing to go back? Of course, Gruppenführer Kleist evidently trusted him without reservation. If he called Kleist and requested a late-morning conference about project-related matters, then an invitation to lunch would no doubt be extended. One splendid ironic possibility occurred to Kessler. He could talk to Kleist about security precautions at the research center. He could even recommend a tightening up of security. An ideal subject for a talk over an SS luncheon.

Kessler called Kleist and made his request.

"Absolutely, Herr Kessler, but let us lunch together first. Then we can talk. Come at noon tomorrow."

"Excellent. I shall try to make it a trifle earlier."

Kessler left his office at 10:00 A.M. the following day. He had arrived at the project center hours before that, intent on doing some work, but he had been utterly unable to concentrate. He knew that, for the first time, he was going to actively engage in espionage work demanding improvisatory skills. He walked to SS headquarters on B——strasse, but arrived there fifty minutes too early. He didn't want to be seen drifting about aimlessly, so, in search of distraction from his anxiety, he set off down a street lined with shops. He walked for twenty minutes in one direction, pausing occasionally to look at window displays, then he turned around and headed back. His pace was fast. He couldn't relax enough to slow down. At 11:50 A.M. he arrived in front of SS headquarters, a large three-story building constructed of dark stone. It was a massive, oppressive structure, exuding all the dread and terror associated with the organization it housed. Two enormous swastika banners hung down the walls of the building on each side of the entrance. Two SS troopers stood at the summit of the flight of steps which led up to the front doors. Inside, directly upon entering, there was a desk behind which there sat an SS Scharführer.

Kessler showed this man an identification card and asked for Gruppenführer Kleist. The Scharführer looked at a sheet of paper and ran his finger down a list of names.

"Room 107" he said. "Down that corridor on the right."

"Thank you," said Kessler, and he walked off down the hall.

Kleist was waiting for him.

"It is good to see you again, Herr Kessler," and Kleist walked forward to greet his guest. He was smiling faintly, that barely perceptible, enigmatic smile that was so distinctive a part of the Gruppenführer's narrow repertoire of facial expressions. Kessler was disgusted by the man's artificial affability. It had been some time since he had been in Kleist's office. He was impressed this time, more than last, by the weird inner-sanctum quality which permeated the room — the swastika banner, the dark wood desk conspicuously uncluttered, the photograph of Hitler, a single dark green file cabinet off in a corner, two chairs, the absence of really adequate lighting. The room was puritanical in its barrenness, Spartan in its orderliness.

"Today, Herr Kessler, we are having a small anniversary celebration. I assume you had this in mind when you called."

With his mind rigidly fixed on its subversive purpose, Kessler was inordinately disturbed by Kleist's celebration announcement.

"I don't know —" But Kleist interrupted.

"I can see you have forgotten. A man with your interests doesn't keep track of dates."

"No." Kessler was completely on the defensive.

"It is the first of September, Herr Kessler — the second anniversary of the invasion of Poland. We will be having champagne today, and more guests than usual. Army and Luftwaffe personnel, not to mention yourself."

Kessler said something about a "happy coincidence," but, in fact, he could not articulate a coherent response. His face was not behaving properly. He was conscious of his muscles as he tried to smile. He felt as confused as he had been on that first night in December, 1939. The act of contacting Kleist and coming to headquarters had presupposed a marshaling of courage, but now that Kessler found he was to be a participant in an SS celebration, his faith in his ability to survive the luncheon was shaken. But he could not turn back. He would be compelled to drink a toast to the idea of slave labor. Kessler tried to concentrate on the advantages of this celebration. Many officers would attend. This would provide many opportunities for overhearing interesting conversations. Champagne too. That would help loosen up tongues. The act of celebrating might also put everyone in an especially expansive mood. Memories of the train rides to Poland came back to him — the drinking, the jokes, the spirit of unchained, cynical brutality.

"Shall we go, Herr Kessler?" and Kleist ushered him into the corridor.

The weight of the memories oppressed Kessler and filled him again with loathing and self-hatred. He tried putting them out of his mind by concentrating on his immediate purpose. How was he going to play out his part? Wouldn't every act, each gesture, every word, betray the real intention which lay behind them? How many lies, how many false declarations of allegiance to SS ideals would he be forced to make in lending credibility to his part? Each lie would corrupt him. Each declaration would poison him. As he approached the dining hall, he felt as if stretched over the abyss which separated the reality of his intentions from the demands of performance. He could not dispel his fear.

They walked down a broad, carpeted, circular staircase and, at the bottom, directly ahead, was the spacious dining room containing large, round tables. Twenty or thirty officers were already seated, drinking and talking volubly with each other. Kleist stopped at the threshold and surveyed the room. He seemed to be looking for someone he knew. An officer spotted him and called out.

"Reinhard — are you going to join us today? Come over to see us."

"Later," replied Kleist, and stepped into the dining hall with Kessler directly behind him.

Waiters moved quickly to and fro, disappearing behind and emerging from white swinging doors which led to the kitchen. The officers were drinking their champagne. Bottles of it lay in the silver cooling buckets which stood next to each table. Kleist led Kessler to a still-unoccupied table.

"To begin with, Herr Kessler — some champagne?"

"Yes . . . splendid." The delivery was overexuberant.

"It's in the spirit of the occasion. We must maintain that."

"By all means." He held out his glass while Kleist poured.

Kessler decided to waste no time. He wished to appear motivated by a genuine, professional concern. Immediately he began by speaking about security measures at the research center. Had Kleist thought seriously about the problem of the rotating guards? Each floor at the center was left unprotected for brief periods of time each day. If that small flaw could be corrected, then the chance of someone's breaking into an office could be eliminated entirely.

"I have thought of that, Herr Kessler. Unfortunately, your idea encounters resistance in certain quarters."

So Kessler moved on to the topic of the project itself. He summarized each of the hypotheses his staff had already rejected and concluded by affirming his belief in the imminence of a solution. He apologized for the thing's taking so long, but qualified that with his usual emphasis on the unpredictability of scientific progress. Hesitantly, Kessler asked about the factory. It would be finished soon. Fortunately, said Kleist, due to the initiative and resourcefulness of Standartenführer Franz, a very large labor force had been assigned to the work. But suddenly, Kessler shifted his attention to a conversation coming from behind him. An army officer, presently on leave, was talking about the tremendous campaign in Russia. He spoke about Hoth's Third Panzer Group and the ferocious battle near Smolensk. Damned Russians. A tenacious people. Even in hopeless situations they refused to surrender. Two Russian vehicles senselessly challenging half a dozen antitank guns. Absolute suicide. But there was nothing to be done about it. German victory was inevitable. Just the same, three additional armored units were being sent to the Smolensk area.

Kessler repeated this piece of information to himself. That was the kind of thing he had to learn, memorize, and pass on to London. Or was it? With no military expertise, Otto Kessler was in an alien world. On what grounds was he going to decide which information was crucial, which trivial? Would the English be interested in those armored units? They could tell the Russians, but on the other hand, would the Russians learn about it through more direct channels? Perhaps it would be wiser to concentrate on things London would find immediately useful.

But Kleist was still speaking.

". . . remember, Herr Kessler, a solution to this problem . . ."

They were alone at the table. Kessler could not ignore Kleist completely. He had to be prepared to respond. Rapidly, his attention shifted back and forth, now to a remark by Kleist, then to a comment from the army officer, then back to the Gruppenführer. For brief seconds he could focus simultaneously on both conversations, but then he would lose the thread of one or the other. Otto Kessler, the scientist with two faces — Janus come to dine with the SS.

A waiter arrived and announced the menu. He recommended the chicken dish. At the same time, three other officers entered the dining room and sat down at the table with Kleist and Kessler. One SS and two Luftwaffe. Good, thought Kessler, and he emptied his glass. He was beginning to discover that a good performance would be possible. As he drank, the playacting would become easier. As on the train, drink made him light-headed and increased his sense of camaraderie with others. The gradual weakening of inhibitions would permit him to ask questions, enter freely into discussions, feel a surge of confidence.

"Brother officers," announced Gruppenführer Kleist, "I have the honor of introducing to you my good friend and trusted associate, Dr. Otto Kessler. Herr Kessler is personally in charge of a small, top-priority project. I shall say no more about it. The results he achieves . . . if you will permit me to say so, Herr Kessler . . . should be of significance for all of us."

The officers nodded and expressed their pleasure at meeting him.

"And this," continued Kleist, "is Oberst Volkmar of Luftflotte three." He pointed at the Luftwaffe officer across from Kessler.

"Ah," said Kessler, anxious to seize the initiative, "tell me, Volkmar, how are you faring against the English?"

Volkmar first sipped from his champagne glass and then launched into a long, rambling response. British daylight fighter sweeps, he said, were a damned nuisance. The night attacks were also difficult to cope with. Only two days before, two groups of Bf-110 night fighters had been transferred from northern Germany to the Ruhr.

"We are being forced to convert more and more of our twin-engined aircraft to the night-fighter role," said Volkmar.

"Finding the enemy in the dark is not simple," remarked the other Luftwaffe officer, Oberst Gottlob.

"Then new types of detection equipment must be developed," said Kessler.

"We shall have that soon," replied Volkmar.

"How soon?" asked Kessler. Was he being too aggressive?

"That is hard to say," said Gottlob. "We hope to have three groups of Junkers 88's equipped with new radar units within two months. More than that I cannot tell you."

"More than that we will not tell you," added Volkmar. He laughed.

"I understand," said Kessler. "I understand."

The food came. The portions were enormous. Kessler ate voraciously, partly because of anxiety, partly because the champagne was stimulating his appetite.

"I recall," remarked Gruppenführer Kleist, "a promise once made by Reichsmarschall Göring. He said we were never to be disturbed by enemy bombers." Kleist winked at his still-silent SS colleague. But the Luftwaffe officers were too drunk to be offended. They roared.

"One cannot depend on fat Hermann for prophesies," said Gottlob. "Anyway, perhaps Herr Kessler's project will solve our problem with the RAF. Am I right, Kessler?"

"I'm working on it . . . I'm working on it," said Kessler, and he finished off another glass of champagne. With mock solemnity, Volkmar and Gottlob applauded Kessler's remark. They were enjoying this civilian who could enter into military discussions in a humorous spirit.

The chicken was superb. As they ate and drank, empty

bottles were removed from the cooling buckets and replaced with fresh ones. It was Kessler of all people who, wishing to savor an irony, stood up and proposed a toast to the German military establishment on the occasion of the second anniversary of the invasion of Poland.

"A great victory," said Kessler, lifting his glass.

"And to future successes," added Kleist.

They all drank to it. The level of noise and merriment in the dining hall continued to increase. This distressed Kessler because it became difficult to overhear anything said at other tables. Over and over again he repeated to himself the interesting details he had picked up. The facts slowly accumulated. Night-fighter groups to be transferred. The installation of new radar units in Junkers 88's. An order sent to the Messerschmitt factory in Augsburg demanding an increase in monthly production figures for Bf-109 aircraft. The Russian front was putting a strain on Luftwaffe resources. Kessler listened closely, dropping questions into discussions whenever he sensed a chance to elicit a profitable answer. Occasionally, he and Kleist spoke on the side, in subdued tones, about the project. The Gruppenführer listened to the others too, proffering his usual suggestions about weapons, strategy and organization. He was the consummate politician. He watched, listened, and waited, and then broke into the flow of conversations in a manner that never failed to appeal to someone's interests. Unobtrusively, he could steer a conversation in the direction of his own choosing.

After a full two hours, they left the dining room. Kessler feared having to speak to Kleist alone in an office, so he asked if they could meet again on a less festive occasion.

"I am too far gone," said Kessler, and he gestured as if he were drinking from a champagne bottle. Kleist understood. They could meet again in three days.

When Otto Kessler returned to the research center, he

locked the door of his office and collapsed into the desk chair. Although he had been drunk throughout most of the luncheon meeting, the fantastic tension implicit in the situation had taken its toll on him. Now, locked away in his office, Kessler felt this tension transform itself into overpowering fatigue and weakness. The dizziness which had struck him during Herr Graml's lecture returned again. He put his head down on his desk and remained in that position for twenty minutes. But he could not rest. He had work to do. It occurred to him that he had better record the information he had so painfully gathered. Taking a sheet of paper from a desk drawer, he began to list facts. It was difficult. He was still drunk. His mind didn't want to function.

And then Kessler felt nauseated. It was a sickness induced by all the hatred, fear and revulsion he felt for his wretched, frightening situation. Here he was, a master scientist, capable of holding fantastically complex ideas in his mind without external aids of any kind — here he was, trying to accurately recall miserable, dumb facts about fighter squadrons and armored units. That he should be reduced to this, tormenting his memory, trying to compel an alcohol-saturated nervous system to function properly. That he should be reduced to drinking so that he could be a human being. It was intolerable. He forced himself to concentrate. He listed the facts. How humiliating it was that he, a man of hitherto unquestioned integrity, should be driven to a demonstration of his credibility for men whom he had never met.

Should he hold on to this piece of paper with the information written on it? He felt he had to so he could get everything right when the time came to tell Buchheim. He might easily forget everything before that, and any present attempt to memorize the list could come to nothing. He wasn't sober enough. But then, even Kessler, amateur spy, understood the risks entailed by keeping the list. No — it would be better to commit it to final memory now, regardless of the difficulties. So Kessler stared at the paper and concentrated, repeating the facts to himself over and over again, trying desperately to impress them forever on his brain. His eyes would not focus properly on the page. His mind rebelled against the effort. He wondered if he should call Buchheim. Call him right away. If he did, that would amount to a break in their established routine. "Do nothing unusual," Buchheim had said. It would be wiser to wait until the scheduled meeting.

Infernal calculations.

Kessler did wait. At the next scheduled conference he gave Buchheim all the information he had gathered.

"There will be more next time, Wolfgang, but it's going to be difficult getting it out of them. And tell London," he added, "that there's no progress on the project."

"Next time, Otto, don't write it down. Memorize it. You must."

Kessler told Buchheim nothing about the luncheon experience itself. The passage of time only aggravated his sense of shame. He chose not to think too much about all the champagne he had consumed, the champagne taken, no doubt, from the French — spoils of victory. And, in retrospect, he was shaken by the ease with which he had, under the influence of drink, toasted the war effort.

Once again, Herr Buchheim and the Dawn Group network performed their respective tasks. Buchheim photographed the paper on which Kessler had recorded his information. He did this in Kessler's office. Once developed, this photograph, nestled in its protective pouch, was placed securely in the bowl of the pipe. Grete Ohlendorff performed the switch. She took the photograph home with her taped to the inside of a shoe, and, by the end of the week, passed it innocently to Herr Hanslick. Hanslick read the material with his magnifying glass, converted it into code, and transmitted the text to London.

With his first ordeal at SS headquarters just concluded, Otto Kessler had now to prepare himself for another encounter with Kleist. As he did so, thereby becoming more preoccupied with his role as an agent, another frightening prospect began to haunt him. What would happen if Buchheim were caught, arrested, and taken away? That prospect could materialize at any time. Herr Buchheim's disappearance would isolate Kessler completely, for Buchheim, in strict obedience to the principles governing espionage work, had correctly refrained from informing Kessler about the system of contact and communication which linked him to the Dawn Group. Kessler obviously knew that Buchheim had contacts, but he knew neither who they were, nor how many there were. Buchheim, in turn, his perspective similarly circumscribed, knew only about Grete Ohlendorff's activities, although he had deliberately never asked for her name. Herr Hanslick had contact with several Dawn Group agents, but knew nothing about Kessler other than his name. Kessler, now initiated into the dangers of espionage work, could appreciate the paramount necessity for this principle of restricted knowledge, but since he was a major source of information, he wondered about the wisdom of an unqualified application of this principle to his own case. Thus, one day, Kessler, obsessed by the idea of total isolation, asked Buchheim for the location and identity of his immediate contact.

But Bucheim refused to give an unconsidered answer. He wanted to weigh carefully every relevant factor. First, he calculated that if the SS or Gestapo ever decided to arrest him, they would preface that action with an extended period of close surveillance. A methodical surveillance net, designed to ensnare all guilty associates, would surely include the restaurant waitress within its grasp. Any observant Gestapo man, following him to the restaurant, would be intrigued by the routine with the pipe. The waitress would be arrested too. What did this mean? A maximized pessimism forced Buchheim to conclude that he might just as well tell Kessler about the waitress. If he were picked up, she would go too, so what was there to lose? But there were other factors too. What would happen if they decided to remove him from the staff because Kessler and the others were more than adequate for the job? It was true that he might continue to see Kessler socially, but in addition to violating the principle of integrating espionage activities into daily routine, continued social contacts following his dismissal could arouse the suspicions of the SS. This too argued in favor of letting Kessler know immediately about the restaurant, the waitress, and the pipe.

And there was something else.

While grappling with this problem in his office, Buchheim began to contemplate the idea of his own death — a death from natural causes. This idea struck him as rather comic. A major war was being fought. This meant nothing other than that people were being offered a wide variety of ways in which to die. There was death by artillery fire, death by rifle and machine-gun fire, death by torture, death by drowning in sinking vessels, death by roasting in tanks and aircraft, death from wounds of all shapes, sizes and kinds. An astonishing variety of ways in which to meet one's end. Indeed, the world was so replete with these man-made methods for achieving personal oblivion that it was difficult not to think of them as part of Nature. Thus, when he thought of a heart attack, Buchheim laughed. For several minutes he could hardly control his laughter. It could happen to him, beyond a doubt. So that too argued in favor of telling Kessler what he knew. He couldn't see the wisdom of leaving Kessler devoid of means for reaching London. He told him about the waitress and the pipes.

"But you aren't a photographer — are you?"

"No," said Kessler.

"Then you'll probably have to work out something new. You can't risk the pipe business anyway. Two absentminded pipe smokers would be too much for anyone to believe."

"Yes . . . that's right."

"In any event, Otto, if they come for me, you'll have to decide for yourself whether contacting this woman is advisable. From a Gestapo or SS point of view, she would be perfect bait — you see?"

It was true enough. He did see. But Kessler chose not to worry about this. In addition to the tensions and difficulties involved in ferreting information out of Luftwaffe officers, the terrifying complications which would follow upon Buchheim's disappearance were too much to bear thinking about. Kessler looked at his colleague. "Maybe they'll have him carrying around sacks of concrete too." This is what he thought as he listened to Buchheim narrate the tale of the waitress and the pipes. They were all doomed. There could be no escape. For an instant he saw Buchheim standing before him, clad in tattered striped rags, shoulders stooped, eyes hollow, emaciated, already among the dead.

"Get as much information as you can," exhorted Buchheim. "Weapons, strategy, production . . . anything."

Buchheim could see that his friend and colleague, strained to the limit by his first visit to SS headquarters, was nearly paralyzed by a dread of the indefinite future.

And the strain that Otto Kessler had experienced during the first luncheon did not diminish. The nearly omnipresent need to perform, to assume a certain ruthlessly aggressive pose, to feign belief in an ideology now become repugnant to him — all this was a disease infecting his soul. He became possessed by the need to preserve a safe distance between himself and his Nazi persona. He was obligated to imitate the thing he wished to destroy. How could he survive this? Kessler could see that his prolonged performance for the benefit of the SS would drive him to deeper despair. The force of this despair threatened to immobilize him. It gave birth to a consuming hopelessness. Otto Kessler was a man thoroughly acclimated to the solitary pursuit of scientific knowledge. He understood the power, the force, of individual genius, and accordingly, he could not really believe in his efficacy as a member of a larger group. He began to doubt his ultimate usefulness as an agent. Could he, Buchheim and the Secret Service really effect a radical change in the monumental struggle consuming the world? Couldn't he make his greatest contribution by preparing university students for the world that would follow even this war? But even as he asked himself this question, Kessler already knew the answer. He could not avoid returning to SS headquarters.

He sought a strong motivation for overcoming his fear and depression. The image of the wretched laborers returned to him. Again he was possessed by rage and terror. But he could not afford preoccupation with these images. They too threatened to paralyze him utterly by obliterating the reality of the normal world in which actions are possible, consequences predictable. Kessler had to force himself, deliberately will himself, into action. Only an abstracted idea of his experience in Poland could serve as a reason, if not as the driving motive, for his espionage activity. His besieged self retreated from appalling memories, from the unbearable pressure of the present, from a vague and terrifying future.

He returned again to SS headquarters and lunched with

Kleist. They sat at the large, round tables. This time fewer officers attended. There was no celebration, no champagne. Just the SS and a few guests. Fortunately for Kessler, someone from the navy was present, so that in between exchanges with Kleist about the project, he could ask the man leading questions about naval affairs. He learned about an increase in the rate of U-boat construction. The officer mentioned that on the first day of October, one hundred and fifty new tanks would be shipped to North Africa, but he said nothing about a port of departure or arrival. Should he dare ask? He decided not to. The English could figure out a likely point of embarkation. Gruppenführer Kleist mentioned he was returning to Poland. There was another project demanding attention. Nothing extraordinary — only a resettlement problem involving minority populations in the occupied areas.

This luncheon was considerably shorter than the previous one. Preparing to leave SS headquarters, Kessler considered setting up yet another meeting. He decided against it. It would be a bad move. Kleist would surely wonder why he wished to return so frequently. After all, how much did they have to discuss? That was precisely the problem.

For Otto Kessler, this second foray into the SS dining room only further intensified his consuming anxiety. He was convinced that everyone could read his intentions. An infinite regress of calculations poisoned his existence, reducing his mental life to a series of obsessive-compulsive operations.

Should he make political comments more frequently?

Should he become an innovator and suggest new policies to Kleist and his comrades?

Or would that be "protesting too much"?

Should he exhort his research staff to even greater efforts?

Would his colleagues detect his changed attitude?

Every answer spawned new questions, every solution generated a fresh host of anxieties.

Were they following him each day?

Were they watching his home, his wife, his housekeeper?

Once, looking out of his study window, Kessler thought he saw Kleist in the distance, leaning against a lamp post, looking his way. In terror, he fled from the window. They were following him.

Or had he been imagining it?

Karin Kessler could not control her fears. Having tenaciously hounded and pursued the truth, she found that, having learned it, it was now exacting its own revenge. She wished that she were ignorant again. She felt utterly trapped, just as her husband did, only this mutual feeling did not unite them. Kessler's confession, complete in one respect, had still been imperfect enough to act as a further temptation. She was moved to learn more, to ask him what terrible things he had seen, but she could not do it. She wanted to know, but she did not want to know. Vague, nameless terrors filled her imagination.

And the truth? She did not really know it. No sooner did she learn it, than it receded from her. There were new secrets. After the accidental meeting with Buchheim, Kessler found himself driven back into the same position he had been in before. He told Karin nothing about his new role as agent, about Herr Buchheim and his pipes, about the visits to SS headquarters. Secrecy was even more imperative now than it had been before. But then Kessler asked himself — might it not be wiser to tell Karin everything? Why? So that if, for whatever reason, she were taken away, she might have something to tell them in order to forestall torture. That would make a better impression than remaining silent, even if she were genuinely ignorant. Mad alternatives. Condemn her to silence and leave her to imagine whatever version of the truth her feverish mind would invent? Or tell her everything, thereby making it easier for her in the event of her arrest? But the latter option endangered so many others. Infernal calculations.

Even if the merciless logic of circumstances placed Kessler in an untenable position, fear of the potential success of the project drove him on. There could be no return to the untroubled, serene past he had known prior to the fateful meeting with Kleist. His course was irreversible. So he would continue to subject himself to the spiritually debilitating journeys to SS headquarters.

But Kessler discovered that one pathetic form of salvation remained for him. Once he accepted the necessity, the inevitability of his entrapment, a limited freedom became possible for him. He could become a nihilist. Did it really matter that his sense of integrity had to suffer through his assuming a morally repugnant role? No one would care about his sense of integrity. Kessler thought back to the day he had convinced Buchheim of the wisdom of resuming contact with London. How had he argued on that day? He had assessed the moral weightings implicit in Buchheim's situation. You are indulging yourself in excessively refined, unrealistic calculations — your vision is too narrow, too confining — you are letting the sphere of personal experience, the agents you know, the people whom you meet, completely determine your actions. This is egomaniacal. Now, Otto Kessler realized that each of these arguments applied to himself, but in seeing this he also understood how distorted and inhuman these arguments really were. Here was the easy coexistence of the true and the insane, clear enough testimony to the perverseness of his reality. Accordingly, Kessler concluded that he would have to ignore his obsessions, put aside his concern with playacting and his preoccupation with the corruption he feared would devour his soul. All this would have to be put ruthlessly aside in deference to performing one simple function — obtaining information for London.

That was all that mattered. How best to do it? Be an actor, Herr Kessler said to himself. Concentrate all energy on the art of spying itself. Consider espionage as a technical problem, as a science. Become a virtuoso at deception. What would this mean for Otto Kessler?

When the answer occurred to him, he couldn't refrain from laughing. The solution was perfect — tragically perfect. He knew that the most perfect act, the one on which he could lavish the meticulous care of an artist, would consist of nothing other than his playing himself. Kessler — the devoted, dedicated scientist. That was the role which had won him everyone's trust in the first place. Why not maintain this image as a weapon in the game of espionage? He would parody himself. Kessler recognized something else which followed from this first realization. Since his decision to work for the British, he had relied solely on indirect methods for eliciting information from the unsuspecting. Why bother with such methods? They were far too complicated, far too convoluted and unproductive. Kessler suspected that he was playing an all or nothing game. Either the SS, relying on his past record and the importance of his position, would never dream of suspecting him, or everything would fall through at once. This meant that as long as he was trusted, he might just as well use his position with wild abandon. Indeed, the more outrageous his approach, the more successful he might be. The SS appreciated that principle fully, only it seemed they did not count on others' discovering its utility. Furthermore, Kessler saw that there was no other alternative open to him. He simply could not arrange for an indefinite number of appointments with Kleist and hope that knowledgeable military personnel would choose to lunch at tables within hearing distance. A more direct approach was imperative.

Kessler allowed three weeks to pass. Then he called Kleist and asked for a conference.

"More private than our last two," he said.

At the meeting, Kessler made his move.

"What I have in mind is this," he said. "I want to see drawings, as complete as possible, of the latest aircraft and tank designs. The staff has decided to concentrate on alloys used for specific weapons systems. If we could examine the structural characteristics of certain designs, it would be most helpful. Planning around the necessities of individual design constructs can, theoretically, lead to a testable solution much sooner. The solution will not represent the ideal, but it might give us a commanding margin of superiority in at least one design area."

Kleist raised objections to this, but Kessler was insistent. The Gruppenführer yielded.

"But you must understand, Herr Kessler, that I alone do not possess the authority for providing what you're asking for. I can only speak to the appropriate persons, state your case for you, and hope that they will honor the request."

That was good enough for Kessler. He was satisfied with himself for having made the request, and so carried away by his own audacity that his fear actually vanished, at least for a time. Furthermore, the results were favorable — beyond his wildest hopes. Ten days after the meeting with Kleist, Otto Kessler had on his desk the full drawings for the Focke-Wulf 190 fighter, and an equally detailed set of drawings for a new seventy-five-ton tank and its high-velocity eighty-eight millimeter gun. Simply incredible. Kessler could hardly believe his eyes. He put both hands over his mouth and tried to suppress the laugh that shook his whole body.

Two days later Buchheim came to see him.

"Somewhere in the Bible, Wolfgang, it says, Ask, and it shall be given unto you. You recall? Something to that effect. Look, my friend . . . look," and spread out the drawings for Buchheim to see.

"How did you do this?"

"I asked for them . . . that's all."

Buchheim photographed the documents and told Kessler that he too should learn how to use the camera.

"You keep the camera," said Buchheim, "and let me know when you need film or have something to pass on. Documents like this must be photographed as quickly as possible. They might want them back before we get a chance to meet. Do you have some place to hide the camera?"

Kessler copied Buchheim's technique and hid the device in the wall behind the light switch panel.

Thus, Herr Hanslick, through Grete Ohlendorff, received ten microphotographs of aircraft and tank designs. He could not transmit drawings to London. Instead, he passed them on to Oswald Bresch, code name Dawn Green, another of his regular bakery customers. The photographs were taped to one of the weekly bills. Herr Bresch was the first link in another network of agents which, stretching across Germany and France, and down through Spain and Gibraltar, would guarantee the arrival of these photographs on the desks of Douglas Trenchard and Trevor Grey.

«8»

And while these priceless photographs of German weapons were threading their way through the European underground, Trevor Grey, following his intuitions about the Kessler-Buchheim case, knew only continuing frustration. Independently, he sought out two Cambridge scientists and asked them what they thought of the possibility of the Germans' conducting research aimed at developing a radically new alloy. It was conceivable, they said, but unlikely. They argued that major research, especially during wartime, will tend to concentrate on perfecting new weapons systems, or on improving extant systems. If not these things, then maximizing production will be the goal. Numbers are everything. The side with more tanks, more planes, more ships, will win. It is a question of overwhelming the enemy.

"But it is possible," Grey said to each man.

"Of course it is."

"And yet you don't think they're working on it?"

"Look, Mr. Grey. The enemy is rampaging through Russia. They are expecting victory. Thus far, the Germans have yet to put their economy on a full wartime basis. I say that they needn't bother with long-term projects such as you are speaking of. Why should they trouble themselves with it?"

Grey encountered not only this skepticism toward his views, but literally exact repetitions of Trenchard's arguments.

"If, Mr. Grey, the enemy were engaged in that sort of work, we should certainly see more signs of it. No? Larger, well-coordinated efforts are the thing to watch for."

And Grey was slowly coming to grasp something else. Unconsciously applying his university-tutorial experience as a model, he naïvely assumed that a position clearly articulated and cogently argued would carry everything before it. Idealistically stated, he believed that "truth" would speak for itself. It was not that he placed excessive faith in bare, dry facts — the empirical data. As a humanist, he could appreciate Trenchard's and Forsyth's reluctance to conclude anything on the grounds of a few secret documents, a batch of mathematical calculations, and a set of code words. But when, to these facts, one added strong insight into the human agents operating behind the "dry facts," when one argued about the human logic of a total situation, then Grey ceased to understand his colleagues' failure to be persuaded. His frustration was further aggravated by the curious way in which both Trenchard and Forsyth appeared to understand and even accept the internal logic of his argument about Buchheim and Kessler, and then proceeded to dismiss the entire thing as a species of argument. They didn't see how decisions could be based on distant intuitions about two men.

Grey also began to grasp his defenselessness in the face of still other factors. He began to understand the force inherent in Trenchard's advocacy of the night-bombing "solution." That solution, general though it was, possessed enormous appeal. In this case, Trenchard's superiors accepted it. Grey's superiors, also recognizing the popularity, the "necessity," of the idea, were hardly prepared to argue against it, nor were they about to allow Grey to combat it. It was not, then, that Grey was losing in the Kessler-Buchheim affair, it was rather as if the whole thing were slipping away from him. The shocking generality of the bombing solution baffled him and paralyzed all attempts to argue the other side of the case. He could hardly argue against the bombing offensive in its entirety since the RAF was interested in objectives other than those recommended by Trenchard, but when he argued against bombing as a solution to this one problem, then miraculously, the positive aura of the bombing campaign embraced and supported Trenchard's position. Obliterating the enemy from the air would end the war all the sooner, and the end would resolve every other problem. A magical conversion principle dominated every discussion of project I-P 9. The more vehemently Grey posited that the Frankfurt project was the real thing, the easier it became for Trenchard to convert that argument into further endorsement for bombing. Every time, with infuriating, reductionist simplicity, Trenchard emphasized the importance of bringing the enemy to his knees through massive strategic destruction.

Grey saw that the organizational and technical aspects of the bombing campaign were developing a complex, autonomous life of their own, a life which absorbed the energies of thousands of RAF personnel and completely fascinated Douglas Trenchard. It wasn't precisely true, therefore, that Trenchard's arguments refuted Grey's. Instead, what Grey came to realize was that his partner's position, especially his preoccupation with Bomber Command operations, subsumed his own position and reduced it to sheer insignificance. Grey was not being refuted. He was being ignored.

This is what puzzled him, and one morning, sitting in

his office thinking about these bizarre circumstances, a shattering idea occurred to Trevor Grey. He had been doing nothing more than running through a list of alternative interpretations when this idea, rising into consciousness, seized him viscerally.

Trenchard was a German agent. He was certain of it.

But why?

This visceral certainty was not arrived at through rational deduction. No. It was rather that this new hypothesis, thrown in among half-forgotten facts and dimly remembered observations, magnetically aligned all evidence into a striking and undeniable pattern.

Four days before receiving the new series of photographs from Frankfurt, Grey took Forsyth to the pub in Hampstead. Will Sullivan, fulfilling one of Grey's special requests, showed the two agents into the claustrophobic, wood-paneled room that served as Sullivan's business office. Only there, thought Grey, could they be sufficiently alone.

"Do you know what I learned the other day, Harry?"

"What?"

"Trenchard requested permission to visit a bomber station in East Anglia."

"And they let him, of course."

"Indeed they did. Are you surprised? A refusal would have been indecent of them. Trenchard must spend half his time at RAF headquarters."

"You don't know that for a fact — do you?"

"No."

"I thought not."

"The details of RAF operations are no part of Trenchard's job — are they?"

"I suppose not. But the man is entitled to some curiosity."

"He's got his own work to do. Why is he spending his time with them?"

"Look, Grey," said Forsyth, "let's have out what you've come to say. Why are we sitting here, secreted away? Your taste for melodrama is offensive."

"I think Trenchard is working for the other side."

Forsyth was speechless. He was sitting behind Will Sullivan's desk, cramped into a corner. Following Grey's statement, he let his head incline backwards, his eyes glancing upward and playing over the low ceiling of the small chamber.

"Consider it . . . just for a moment . . . before you reject it flatly."

Grey was pleading with him.

Forsyth silently puffed out his cheeks for just a second — a fleeting expression of exasperation.

"Well . . ." he said, but could say no more because Will Sullivan entered the room carrying two pints. It was on the house, he said. So poorly timed and incongruous was this event that the two agents could barely bring themselves to express their thanks.

When Sullivan departed, Grey, rather than let his colleague complete his interrupted remark, began the explication of his view.

"Trenchard decides to win the confidence of the RAF. Correct?"

"Hmm . . ."

"He talks to them extensively. He flatters them. The RAF can do anything. He tells them that their aerial bombardment campaign can solve his problem. An absurd . . . positively ridiculous idea in the first place."

"Yes . . . I'm with you on that."

". . . But bloody good politics just the same. Strategic bombing is in its infancy. Within two years or less, the RAF will be able to raze entire cities to the ground. As this program gathers momentum, the planners incur the risk of exciting public opposition. Bomber Command can

hardly mind a bit of political support from another service
. . . a thing hard enough to come by at any time.
Comparatively, Bomber Command is a new, unproven
organization. So Trenchard helps them out in that respect."

Forsyth was unresponsive, but his silence was more than
a product of curiosity. Grey sensed his colleague's
impatience.

"Trenchard, winning this confidence, more than earns a
reciprocal gesture. They permit him to visit one of their
stations. He observes the equipment, participates in
briefings, learns the locations and operating procedures of
the station. No doubt, they are prepared to have him visit
other stations."

Grey paused and drank some of his beer.

"He might even learn something about target selection — you see? It depends on what he requests."

But now Forsyth had to respond. It had gone too far.

"No . . . never," he said.

"It hangs together —"

"As you said of your interpretation of the Buchheim-
Kessler business."

"Then explain Trenchard's behavior."

"There's nothing to explain, Grey, nothing. That's the
difference between us. You see a riddle. I see nothing.
Sometimes, Grey, there's absolutely bloody nothing to be
seen."

He got up and crossed to the opposite corner of the
room, just a few feet away. He felt confined by the room,
by what he was hearing. He wanted to escape.

"Just how," he added, "do any of Trenchard's actions
serve the Germans?"

"The Germans are roughed up a bit for a while, here
and there, but they get a man in a position in preparation
for a single, devastating blow against Bomber Command.

You've got to admit that it would serve their purposes admirably. What trouble are we giving them other than mounting harassment from the air? They've got a major show on in Russia, one for which they need every tank, every gun, every plane. Bomber Command diverts resources from the eastern front. It endangers their industry, depresses civilian morale. Crippling Bomber Command would be a major achievement. So, they buy off one British agent, bide their time, accumulate the necessary information, and then strike. At the very least, Trenchard can get target selection data back to the Luftwaffe. That alone would double our nightly losses."

"That's good, Grey . . . very good. I asked a foolish question." Forsyth was searching for the one question that would demolish his colleague's idea.

"You are maddeningly consistent, Grey . . . as always . . . not that I accept this notion. No, not for a moment. It's arbitrary. There must be scores of individuals who have secured clearance for visiting bomber stations . . . individuals not formally affiliated with the RAF. I don't understand you, Grey. What sets Trenchard apart from the others?"

"It's his manner, his strange, impenetrable style . . . everything about him . . . right from the start of this whole affair . . . it strikes me as wrong . . . it's out of joint . . . it doesn't make sense. I don't understand him."

"He doesn't agree with you."

"It's more than that."

"A personality difference . . . that's all."

"No, that isn't it. It's that, almost imperceptibly, he's come to dismiss the Frankfurt project as a problem unworthy of consideration. And it's not a matter of his thinking me right or wrong. It's of no account to him one way or the other. That's the odd thing. Take the information we've been getting from Kessler. He examines it, passes it on to interested parties, and then considers it no further. The bombing offensive absorbs all his energy, all his time. It engulfs everything else. Even when he agrees with me, the agreement is converted into a further warrant for bombing. Why didn't he join Bomber Command? They'd have taken him. But no — you see, I think he's right where he wants to be. He's perfectly positioned for obtaining information about a multiplicity of Bomber Command operations, and, at the same time, Secret Service channels give him a link back to Germany. His enthusiasm for bombing is the thing that makes him legitimate in the eyes of the RAF."

Forsyth was back at Sullivan's desk, his elbows on the arms of the chair, his hands over his face. Reason told him Grey's idea was untenable, but now that it had been released into a paranoid universe where "reality" itself was the fundamental problem, the very unreality of the idea lent it an uncanny, magical force. Forsyth dropped his hands and looked at his colleague. Suddenly, he looked quite tired.

"Grey — you've got to make your decision."

"I know, Harry."

"Just how seriously do you take this idea?"

"I'm certain of it."

"I'm not, you know . . . I'm not."

"Right . . . I know that."

"So you have to make the decision. I won't tell you what to do."

"You don't want the responsibility."

"That's right. I don't want to lose my job."

"No — I'm sure you don't."

"If Trenchard is a German agent, Grey, then nothing else should matter to either of us. That would be too serious to ignore. You'll have to try to get him, or to use him to our advantage. Are you prepared to watch him?"

"It might have to be done," said Grey.

"Are you prepared to bring this to Atkinson's attention?"

"No — not yet."

"I didn't think so. Because you haven't got hard evidence yet — have you?"

"No."

"If, Grey, you bring this matter to Atkinson, and you're wrong, or if you move too soon in any way — they'll break you fast. They'll break you."

His tone was ice. It was without mercy.

"I say this to you as a professional . . . not as a friend."

"Because as a professional you're unprepared to support me."

"Quite right, Grey."

"You think Trenchard is innocent?"

"You've got nothing on him . . . nothing at all."

"I suppose not."

"I don't deny, Grey, that your idea is . . . what shall I say? . . . frightening. But I withhold my assent to it. I deliberately withhold it. You need to know more before you move. I need to know more before I support you. You let your imagination play with the facts. I restrain my imagination and keep to the facts."

"And yet, my idea frightens you."

"Yes — but why? Because it is true, and now I am compelled to face the truth? Because your own personal style creates the impression of truth? Because Trenchard, even though innocent, is an admittedly strange chap? Which of these is the explanation?"

Grey said nothing.

"Or is all this a question of Kessler and Buchheim — a question of your attachment . . . is that the word? . . . to these two men?"

But Grey did not answer any of these questions. For the moment, he was thinking only of Otto Kessler and

Wolfgang Buchheim, and remarked, "I wonder if I shall ever meet them?"

But Trevor Grey had no intention of ignoring what were still unsubstantiated suspicions. Forsyth had said there was no clear evidence, nothing to show to Atkinson, and yet the idea retained its hold on Grey's mind. It haunted him. On the night following his talk with Forsyth, Grey walked home alone. He passed piles of rubble, demolished homes — products of the Blitz. He returned to his flat, a small, one-room accommodation with bathroom and stove. Grey lay down for a while and allowed his mind to wander. Then he picked up a novel which lay open on a table next to his bed. He couldn't concentrate on it. He lay still for half an hour. Then, rising from the bed, he switched off the lights, pulled aside the blackout curtains which still covered the one window, and looked out on the street below. He found that this idle gazing relaxed and cleared his mind, preparing him for some more directed intellectual effort. He stood at the window for nearly half an hour. Thoughts of Trenchard came to mind. Where was he now? Visiting an RAF bomber station? Perhaps riding in the night sky over Germany as a guest of Bomber Command? The tone of Trenchard's voice filled Grey's memory, that cool, offhand way of dismissing what he considered irrelevant. He could hear it. That bizarre man, devoted to his RAF friends, twirling the magnifying glass in his hands, ordering tea, keeper of the strange book collection. What was he doing now? "Because you haven't got hard evidence yet — have you?" Forsyth's words. His friend's surprisingly merciless tone came back to him too.

Then, four days later, the photographs arrived. Grey stared at them. "Fantastic," he said under his breath.

"I assume you've received a copy of what I've just received." He was on the phone with Trenchard.

"Yes, Grey."

"I'm coming over to see you right away."

Half an hour later he burst into Trenchard's office without waiting for the secretary to announce him.

"All right, what do you think of that?" he said, trying to conceal his excitement, but pointing vigorously with the forefinger of his right hand at the group of small photographs which lay in clear view on top of Trenchard's desk.

"What do you think of that? There's what I've been waiting for. Kessler is with us. He's with us. There's no doubt of that now. I knew it. I knew it all along. Now we must give him the support he needs."

Grey turned from Trenchard and headed for the maroon chair.

"No bombing attacks," he said, and sat down, punctuating his judgment, "certainly not directly on that part of the city where Kessler is working. We must not drive off that research staff to some other location. Kessler and Buchheim must remain in touch with Dawn Group. We must, if anything, increase the number of contacts, give Buchheim an emergency channel he can use, just in case. Things might get a bit tighter over there. We can't tell. Above all Trenchard, I think we can go to the top of the government with this. They can be persuaded to follow this closely. We can commit some of our own people to research. At least, we shall test out anything Kessler sends us. That's imperative."

Trenchard kept silent during Grey's self-satisfied monologue. As always, he sat behind his desk, betraying nothing of his immediate reactions.

Now that Grey was finished, there was silence. In a characteristic gesture, Trenchard reached for his glass and the bottle of mineral water. Grey wondered if the man relied on the liquid for some magical form of sustenance.

"Grey," said Trenchard, breaking the silence, "I am forced to say what is unpleasant."

He poured from the bottle.

"This entire matter has unbalanced you."

He said this with a trace of condescending concern in his tone and manner. He replaced the stopper in the bottle.

For one instant it occurred to Grey that Forsyth and Trenchard could be working together. He rejected the idea. It was mad. No — Trenchard was playing his own game.

"What are you saying to me, Trenchard?"

Again, the silence was excessively long.

"I am saying to you, Grey, that you are losing perspective . . . losing distance on the events . . . losing precious objectivity. Professionally suicidal."

"You see what Kessler has sent us?"

"I do."

"Then perhaps you have failed to examine the documents closely."

"I have not failed to do so, Grey. As a lover of machines, I have just spent several hours enraptured by these materials."

Grey had to stop for a moment. Was this really happening to him? Was he going mad? Even a German agent wouldn't pretend to this astonishing indifference toward the photographs.

"It's you, Trenchard . . . you . . . who have lost perspective . . . lost touch with reality."

"I see no need for this kind of display, Grey."

"Trenchard, are you trying to argue that the Germans would willingly part with this information, with these drawings?"

"I am not trying to argue that point, Grey. I *am* arguing it."

"No . . . no . . . that's absurd . . . that's too bloody ridiculous."

"Now tell me, my good partner, what are we going to do with these drawings? Hmm? I am certain that the RAF will find them interesting. They will be appreciative. So will the tank officers at Sandhurst. But what difference will these pictures really make? We shall design a new, faster Spitfire, which, I dare say, we are doing anyway. And the army will improve its armored vehicles and antitank guns which it, need I point out, would be doing anyway."

"But these documents, Trenchard, these documents are top secret."

"My congratulations then to the genius on the other side who discovered that they need not be."

Grey rose from the chair and, seeking distance from Trenchard, headed for the bookshelves, shaking his head with frustration.

". . . it's mad . . . senseless . . . absurd . . ."

"Optimizing the mechanical factor is every nation's first priority, Grey, at least during wartime. We hardly need the other side's thinking as an impetus."

"Trenchard. That doesn't imply that the Germans are anxious to help us out."

"They will — if the benefits outweigh the price."

"What benefits?"

"The gaining of our confidence in preparation for a greater strategic deception. The war will be won on the battlefield, Grey, as a result of strategic decision. The human factor — you know? The thing you understand so well."

"Damn, Trenchard. That's not what this thing is about."

"Then you tell me, Grey, what it is about."

Grey walked back to the desk and stood directly in front of it, looking down at his colleague.

"The point of these documents is that they prove Kessler is our man. He's ours. You yourself approved my staying with this problem so we could confirm Kessler's position one way or the other. We've got the proof we need."

"I approved, Grey, because I was in no position to stop you."

"I see now. It would have taken a transcript of a General Staff conference to convince you."

"That would have been something, Grey."

"Stop your damn games, Trenchard."

"Yes, my friend. It would have taken a transcript of a General Staff conference to convince me. Nothing less. But you'll never see it. Not from Kessler. He's a true German, Grey — a bloody Nazi. And as for you, Grey, I can hardly prevent you from pursuing a fantasy. That's Atkinson's problem."

Grey took his seat again, back in the maroon chair. Defeat was written on his face. The expression was intended for Trenchard.

"I was a fool," he said, "to have accepted this arrangement in the first place."

"You've been wrong from the start, Grey . . . utterly wrong."

"Then nothing would have convinced you . . . absolutely nothing."

"It costs the Germans nothing to surrender these drawings. These weapons are in production, or near production . . ."

But Grey did not object further. He listened to his colleague continue to discourse on the supposed enemy ruse. While Trenchard spoke, Grey reached two decisions.

First, he was going to bring the details of the Kessler-Buchheim affair to the attention of higher-ranking Secret Service personnel. Upon leaving the depressing meeting with Trenchard, he returned to his own office. He immediately began the preparation of a report which he intended to submit first to Atkinson. Atkinson knew nothing of the growing tension between Grey and Trenchard. So, Grey opened this report with a detailed chronological account of the events comprising the Kessler-Buchheim Early Riser case. He defended the credibility of both men. He followed this with a discussion of Trenchard's position, carefully explaining what he believed to be the principal errors in judgment. Grey concluded this report with a series of arguments designed to show that the government could no longer choose to ignore the potential import of the enemy's project, and that, at the worst, there was nothing to lose by assuming the reality of that project.

Grey wrote several drafts of this report. Everything would count. The strength of the arguments, the power of the style, the judicious use of available evidence. Three hours after he had begun the work, when he was deep into the second draft of the report, the telephone on Grey's desk rang. The harshness, the unexpectedness of the sound alarmed him and filled him with anxiety.

He knew immediately what the call was about, even before lifting the receiver.

"Grey?"

"Right."

"Atkinson here. Had a call from Green. Could you squeeze in a bit of a chat this afternoon?"

Thus, later that day, Grey listened to the realization of his accurate premonition.

"I'm taking you off Early Riser altogether, Grey."

Atkinson expected an immediate response. There was none.

"I suppose you want to know my reasons."

"An explanation would be appropriate."

"Early Riser is not proving especially productive."

"That depends on your point of view."

"Not rewarding enough, at any rate, to justify two men, full time."

"Ah."

"One can handle it."

"This is Green's work."

"See here, Grey. That's quite enough."

"Yes, sir."

"I'll not be put up to anything . . . not by anybody."

Atkinson paused, no doubt in order to emphasize this affirmation of his independence. He shifted about in his squeaking swivel chair and nervously arranged some papers lying on top of his desk.

"Now, if you'll give me a moment, I shall gladly explain this action to you. Green, your bête noire, says you seem rather an extravagantly competent, industrious chap. He tells me Trenchard is the source of that rumor."

"How charming of him to have put in a good word for me."

"I thought so myself. Must be the habits you picked up at Oxford." Atkinson smiled. "Agreeing entirely with Green, I see no reason to squander your talents, Grey, on such an unproductive operation. You see. Secret Service always has your interests in mind."

"I didn't think my friend Douglas was quite so greedy."

"Is he now?"

"Hmm . . ."

"Well then, good. Let him indulge himself. These petty political maneuvers are of no interest to me — not in this case at least. If Green really wants to secure glory for his people, then I wish him luck."

Grey was going to be assigned to an equally important operation — the underground networks in Holland and Belgium aiding British airmen who had been shot down.

"That is fitting," said Grey, "helping to clean up after the mess Trenchard leaves behind."

"The Dutch are also giving us information, Grey, on German early warning radar. You wouldn't want to miss that — would you?"

"No."

"Then you have no objection, I presume?"

"None, sir."

Grey revealed nothing about his report on the Kessler-Buchheim affair. He figured that Atkinson would be prone to discount it anyway, choosing to interpret it as the gesture of an embittered man. But this encounter with Atkinson forced Grey to reassess his report from another point of view. In writing it, his sole motive had been the desire to alert the government concerning the importance of the German project. He had kept this motive apart from his suspicions regarding Trenchard. But now that he had been removed from the Early Riser operation, Grey saw that if word of his report got back to Trenchard, the latter would be certain to read it as a piece of personal revenge. This would put Trenchard on his guard, an unfortunate consequence if one assumed that he was working for the Germans. This bore on the second decision Grey had made during the conference with Trenchard. He decided to look for further evidence of Trenchard's being a double agent. For Grey, Trenchard's reaction to the drawings had only confirmed his suspicions. Now that Trenchard had arranged for his removal from Early Riser, Grey could understand it only as a move designed both to protect the Frankfurt project, and to further secure Trenchard's relationship to the RAF. Therefore, he would pursue Trenchard, pursue him without mercy; not only because he found him strange and repellent, but because he knew that if Trenchard was a double agent, then Otto Kessler and Wolfgang Buchheim were lost.

On December 5, 1941, Trevor Grey inaugurated a new practice, one which puzzled Harry Forsyth. He started to leave his office earlier in the afternoon than was his custom. By 4:45 P.M. Grey wanted to be sitting next to a window in a small fish and chips shop located on the side of the street opposite the building in which Trenchard's office was housed. This building was not directly across from the shop, but by leaning forward slightly and glancing thirty yards down the block, Grey could observe the entrance to the building. He waited at a window counter, sitting on a stool, sipping tea.

On December 5, Trenchard did not appear. Nor did he on the sixth, the eighth, or the ninth. He was away. Or had he been moved to a new office, perhaps at his own request, just to make it difficult for certain others to find him?

But Grey did not give up. He returned to the shop on the tenth. Nothing happened. He entertained himself by listening to other customers express their relief and excitement over the fact that the Americans had finally entered the war. Then, at long last, at 5:15 P.M., on the eleventh, Douglas Trenchard stepped out of the entrance of his office building and stood for a while on the sidewalk, adjusting his coat and observing passing automobiles. The cold, damp December wind blew hair into his face. Grey walked out into the street just in time to see Trenchard place the bowler hat on his head and start off in the opposite direction. His pace was slow. Grey knew that Trenchard operated a Secret Service automobile. Had he brought it with him? It was unlikely. The rationing of petrol saw to it that even government personnel used automobiles only for important trips.

Grey followed Trenchard down the street, keeping a distance of thirty or forty yards between them and hoping that the large number of people on the street would make concealment easy. Trenchard reached a corner and turned left. This forced Grey to quicken his pace. He crossed the street and turned the corner so that now he would be following on the same side of the block. This must have been a mistake. Grey lost sight of his man behind other people, once, then again, then for good. He reached the next corner, looked in every direction, but could not locate his quarry.

For three days in succession, Grey lost his man. He would be behind Trenchard, the latter would turn a corner, and by the time he could round that same corner, Trenchard would be gone. Into a tube station? Or a building? Or disappeared into a crowd? Grey didn't know.

He decided to abandon for a while these attempts to follow Trenchard. Some other strategy was necessary. Then, but one week after his last attempt, he succeeded. It was like a belated reward for his hard efforts.

It was early in the evening, December 17. Grey and Forsyth were in a pub in Knightsbridge drinking beer. They were discussing an event they had attended the previous Sunday. Grey had a group of friends from his university days who played together as a string quartet. They were excellent amateurs. Once a month, on Sunday evenings, they met and worked at the quartet literature. Although he was not a practicing musician, Grey attended many of these sessions. He had invited Forsyth to the last meeting because Harry, although professing ignorance of music, expressed an interest in it.

Sitting near a window at the pub, Grey was trying to explain his liking for chamber music.

"You must have heard how remarkably intense it is. There's no mistaking that. Of course, listening to amateurs, even good ones, hack away at Beethoven opus 130 isn't precisely an ideal first exposure to the literature. It musn't have made much sense at first, but if you attend a few more of these sessions, you'll begin to hear the sense in it. You asked me what is so special, what is so appealing about this kind of music. I could speak of individual works, but let me put it in more sweeping terms. It's the nature of the artistic effort that's so fascinating. The quartet itself. Four players, each, ideally, a master of his instrument, combining their skills on an equal basis, and in the absence of a leader or conductor. Four voices, independently beautiful, yet dependent on a thorough understanding of one another for achieving the greatest aesthetic effect. You see? It is democracy in music."

But, having said this, Grey stopped quite suddenly. Forsyth was expecting more, but Grey was staring out the window.

"Go on," said Forsyth.

"Look," responded Grey. "It's our friend."

Forsyth had to move behind Grey and look over his shoulder.

"Where?"

"Two blocks down . . . on the corner . . . opposite side."

It was Trenchard, clearly illuminated by the headlights of a passing automobile.

"What's he doing here?" asked Grey.

"Why shouldn't he be here?"

"I'm going to see for myself."

And Grey left Forsyth in the pub. He stood in a doorway and waited for Trenchard's next move. But what was the point? What did he expect to see? Soon Trenchard was joined by another man and the two set off down the street. Grey followed them until they turned into Beaufort Gardens — a dead-end street. Trenchard lived there. What was Grey to do? Sit on the steps of one of the houses and wait for Trenchard's guest to depart? Should he follow Trenchard's friends too?

Instead, Grey walked home. His success had been a hollow one. When he arrived home he found Forsyth waiting in the corridor of the ground floor. The landlady had let him in.

"I thought you would have been home by now, Harry."

Grey started up the staircase.

"This thing has driven you half crazy — hasn't it?"

Forsyth was following him up the steps.

"Go home and get some sleep, Harry."

They reached the top, turned, and walked toward the next flight.

"How far are you going to go with this thing?"

Grey was already halfway up the second staircase.

"I don't know, Harry . . . I don't know."

"What's the point, Grey? It's senseless."

Grey stopped climbing and stood on the steps, his back facing Forsyth. Forsyth, still on the first landing, looked up at his friend.

"If Trenchard is a double agent, then, even if you get him, Kessler and Buchheim are dead. They'll wait until they think they've got a whole network identified, then the Gestapo will pick them up. And if Trenchard is really one of ours, then your position is no better. He's had you taken off Early Riser. He's got everyone convinced he's right."

"That's right, Harry."

"You've got nothing on Trenchard."

Grey finally turned and looked at his colleague.

"You think I ought to give it all up?"

"Yes — I do."

"See you in the morning, Harry."

And Grey climbed the remainder of the steps and vanished into his flat.

Following Trenchard on foot had proven unproductive, so Grey decided on something new. If Trenchard was going to lead him to something interesting, then it was probable that an automobile journey might be involved. He would, then, be especially interesting to observe on those days when he took his car to work. Grey altered his procedure.

On the morning of December 22, 1941, he awoke early and walked to Beaufort Gardens. He stationed himself in a doorway so located that Trenchard, pulling out of the street, would be visible. If he simply went to work on the tube, then Grey would proceed ahead to his own office. If Trenchard used his automobile, then Grey, upon arriving at his office, would put in a requisition for an automobile. The Service did not permanently provide him with one, but when he claimed a need for an automobile, he usually got it.

For two days nothing happened. Trenchard did not show at all. Was he out of the city? Was he doing some work in his flat?

Then, on the twenty-fourth, he showed. His automobile pulled out of Beaufort Gardens. Grey went to his office and put in his requisition. By 11:00 A.M. Mrs. Phillips informed him that his car was ready at the Secret Service depot. Grey lunched quickly, picked up his machine, and drove to W____ Street, the location of Trenchard's office. He parked fifty yards down the street from the entrance, turned off the motor, sat back, and began to wait. It was 12:22 P.M. He was risking nothing. Trenchard could leave early if he was going to drive somewhere.

An hour passed. Trenchard did not appear. Grey started to read a newspaper. Out of the corner of his eye he could see people when they emerged from Trenchard's building.

At 1:45 P.M., a police officer, puzzled by his long wait, approached Grey.

"What are you doing here, mate?"

Grey showed him his Secret Service identification card and said, "Waiting for a friend."

The officer walked away.

At 2:35 P.M. Trenchard appeared. He was accompanied by an RAF officer. They walked toward Grey's machine, but then turned right into a narrow driveway. There was a parking area behind Trenchard's building. Five minutes later, Trenchard's automobile pulled out into the street and turned left. Grey began to follow him.

Within ten minutes it was apparent that Trenchard and the RAF officer were leaving the city. Grey followed at several hundred yards' distance.

He tailed them for over an hour. Fifty miles north of London, Trenchard pulled over to the left lane and shot onto an exit road. Grey followed. On the subsidiary road there was only one automobile between Grey and Trenchard's machine. He would have to rely on his quarry's suspecting nothing. Trenchard turned off again, this time to the right. Grey turned onto this smaller road, but stopped almost immediately. He wanted to increase the following distance, but no sooner had he come to a halt than he could see, nearly two hundred yards in the distance, Trenchard turn off once again to the left. Grey drove to the point where the two roads joined and decided immediately that he could go no farther. These were country roads. He did not want to be caught driving down a dead end. He pulled off to the side and left his machine parked between two thick clumps of bushes. Getting out, he started to walk down the narrow dirt path onto which he had seen Trenchard turn. It was broad enough for just one automobile. He would walk down this path for twenty minutes. If he found nothing, he would have to assume that Trenchard and the officer had left him far behind. It was cold. Barren trees, grotesquely deformed skeletons in the fading winter light, lined both sides of the road. The sky was absolutely clear. It would be a good night for the bombers. Grey walked on, keeping to the side of the road. He covered a mile. Nothing. What should he do now? He could return to his automobile and wait for Trenchard to return. But then he would be caught on an unlighted country road at night. His lights would give him away. He considered passing through the trees and investigating the surrounding countryside.

But Grey received the answer to his problem. The

silence of this icy country setting was broken by aircraft engines exploding into life. He had suspected it all along. This was but another of Trenchard's visits to the bomber stations. The sound came from beyond the trees on the right side of the road.

Grey walked into the woods, confident that the continuous roar of engines would drown out the insignificant sounds of footsteps and the snapping of twigs and branches. The forest area was not wide. After covering a hundred yards, Grey reached the far edge of the woods, and from there he could easily observe the twilight spectacle. A dozen four-engined bombers were taxiing slowly on a concrete strip. Grey understood why Trenchard had come. Even from a distance of over half a mile, Grey could see that these were a new type of bomber aircraft. They came from the left and formed into a line. The head of the line pointed directly toward the woods from which Grey observed everything. Upon reaching the head of the line, each machine turned ninety degrees to the right and waited until a flare, propelled into the darkening sky, signaled the moment for taking off.

And there, standing in the field, halfway between the edge of the woods and the concrete strip, was the solitary figure of Douglas Trenchard, his escort no longer with him — come to worship the new bomber machines. He was silhouetted against the combined light of the day fading in the west, the exhaust flames of aircraft engines, and the flickering incandescent blaze of the starting flares.

«9»

Could Otto Kessler have realized that Reinhard Kleist knew everything? Sturmbannführer Wolf, an officer on Kleist's staff, said of Herr Kessler, "He has worked for us long enough. He is a traitor."

Only the expression in Kleist's eyes revealed that he had known this for a long time. Otto Kessler's months of torment had been a gift granted to him by Gruppenführer Kleist.

And what did Reinhard Kleist think of Otto Kessler — the "traitor"? He thought of him as but another example of an often repeated experience. Kessler was weak. He was, like countless others, incapable of fidelity to his word. Having signed a contract, he now sought to escape his commitment. Herr Kessler suffered from a pronounced narrowness of vision. Willing, at first, to dedicate himself to a cause, Kessler, like the others, was unable to remain true to a commitment once the implications of that commitment became clear. He wished to avoid his obligations, to deny the remorseless logic of circumstances. Herr Kessler was guilty of bad faith, of monstrous ingratitude. Reinhard Kleist was disappointed by Otto Kessler. No matter how many times he encountered it, this human shortsightedness distressed him. And, in this case, Kleist's disappointment was twofold. Observing Otto Kessler's response to the spectacle in Poland, he had anticipated his being too weak to do anything, but this had not turned out to be the case at all. Kessler had become a traitor. That had been the second disappointment, the one compounding Kessler's "internal" disloyalty. In his own way, then, Reinhard Kleist was saddened by Otto Kessler. For him, Kessler's status as a traitor had a significance it did not possess for his colleagues. It was the tragedy of Kessler's personal revolt, his failure to honor a bargain offered in good faith, that affected Kleist most deeply. Otto Kessler had underestimated his opponent.

Technically, Kessler was an enemy of the state. This fact normally implied an immediate arrest. The staff officer who had doubted Wolfgang Buchheim's loyalty recommended Kessler's incarceration in a concentration camp. But that was not Gruppenführer Kleist's style. He left that approach to his less imaginative colleagues. He would not suggest Kessler's removal from the project. In his view, the use of a massive, impersonal system of punishment was good only as the final resort. To each his own, said Reinhard Kleist, by which he meant that each individual, and each criminal act, merited its peculiar form of punishment. For holding this view, Reinhard Kleist's brother officers considered him a reactionary.

On January 20, 1942, fulfilling his sense of symmetry, Gruppenführer Kleist called upon Otto Kessler at his home. Ingrid was away visiting relatives. Karin Kessler had gone out to pass the evening with friends.

"How much longer before we have results, Herr Kessler?"

Kleist stood in the center of the study. Kessler was at his

worktable. He knew that something had gone wrong. Had Buchheim been caught?

"I am expecting something soon. A month, maybe two, Herr Graml has come upon something highly promising."

"Excellent, Herr Kessler," and Kleist paused.

Was that all he had come to say?

"I have not been in this room in a long time, Herr Kessler."

He glanced around. He was a tourist visiting a historical monument.

"You were not expecting me here at this hour, Herr Kessler. Am I correct?"

Kessler nodded.

"I hope, quite sincerely, that Herr Graml's idea, the one you speak of, will prove fruitful. I have grown weary all this while, waiting for results."

This sarcasm unnerved Kessler. He didn't know what to say. Stalling for time, he got up from behind his worktable.

"Where are you going, Herr Kessler?"

"I was about to suggest that we move —"

"This room is to my liking."

"Very good."

"You are trying to avoid the issue, Herr Kessler."

"No."

"I do not wish to be further entertained by your views on the nature of scientific progress."

Kessler sat down again.

"I have grown weary of that too," added Kleist.

"Those views represent the truth, Gruppenführer Kleist — the truth. I have never sought to mislead you."

"So you wish to speak about truth, Herr Kessler. Then allow me to make matters more compelling for you. Let me provide you with another motivation in this already complex situation. I state one thing unequivocally. You are working for British Intelligence, Herr Kessler."

This sentence tore through him with the force of a dagger. Kessler was paralyzed with fear. He leaned forward and put his clenched fists on the worktable. His face turned ashen gray. He was sweating. He was ice cold. A knot of terror convulsed his stomach.

"I do not guess this, Herr Kessler. I know it."

And Kessler collapsed backwards in his chair. The heavy sound of his accelerated breathing filled the room.

"You thought you had worked out safe espionage techniques. Perhaps you have. The details are of no interest to me. More important, Herr Kessler, you have believed that you could conceal from me the true nature of your feelings. In that, you have been a fool. I know everything. You are an amateur, Kessler, an amateur. You haven't the skills with which to deceive me. I have seen into your heart since our first journey to the east. You were doomed from the start, Herr Kessler, from the very beginning."

Kessler put his hands up to his face. He was shaking.

"So, Herr Kessler. You do not approve of my colleagues. You do not like Standartenführer Franz. These men are repugnant to you. The Party and what it represents repels you. Now, therefore, you are seeking to escape from your obligations to me, from our bargain, from the terms of our contract . . ."

With his hands still over his face, Kessler muttered something. It was incomprehensible. His voice was quivering.

"What, Kessler? Speak."

"No," he said, "no obligations . . . not to you . . . not to you."

"I am not concerned with your personal feelings."

But then Kessler slammed his fist on the table.

"Murderer."

The word was a shrill scream. He rose and pounded the table again and again.

"You are scum . . . the gutter . . . filth . . . all of you."

229

"You will work for me."

"Never . . . never."

"Yes . . . you shall. I am going to take hostages."

Kessler fell silent. He was leaning forward on the table, supporting himself. He was still trembling.

"Hostages . . ." he said in a hoarse whisper.

"Yes, Herr Kessler," replied Kleist. "That is my colleague's, Sturmbannführer Wolf's, idea — not mine. He insists on it. Your wife shall be the first."

Kessler fell back into his chair. His brow was covered with perspiration.

"My wife . . . my wife . . ."

"If you succeed, Herr Kessler, in coming up with a solution, a possible solution . . ."

"By when . . ."

"You leave that to my judgment. I shall decide it. You work. If you are successful, then no harm shall come to either you or your wife. If, however, you delay this project, if you persist in your dilatory tactics, then it shall be a simple matter to mention your unpatriotic activities to those who will see that they are punished. Both of you shall disappear."

Kleist paused. Kessler kept silent. There was no response to this threat.

"Now," continued Kleist, "I do not recommend that you attempt seeking the help of your friend Herr Buchheim."

"Where is Buchheim?"

"Do not try to contact him. That would be senseless."

"You've killed him . . ."

"Herr Buchheim has been removed from the project. The mercy I argued for in your case did not influence my colleagues in his."

"Then he is dead."

"That is not your problem, Herr Kessler. He is beyond your help."

"You've killed him. He's gone . . "

And Kessler was lost in grief over his friend. His hands covered his face once again. His attention was barely focused on the last things Gruppenführer Kleist had to say to him.

"I have been fascinated by your reactions during these past months, Herr Kessler. You are the same, all of you . . . agents . . . spies . . . espionage personnel, It is astonishing. Did you actually expect that the information you sent to the other side would be put to productive use? You believe that you are serving the Good, Herr Kessler? Do geographical demarcations have a significant role in a universal morality play? An interesting, but naïve, assumption. What significant difference will your pathetic gestures make? Sending drawings of tanks and aircraft to the English, sending your mathematical computations for Cambridge scientists to puzzle over. You have congratulated yourself for these gestures, but they are absurd. Your vision is confined, Herr Kessler. It is sadly limited to immediate necessities. But you are not without courage. You could not have believed that the Secret Service would take you at your word — a man with your apolitical reputation, trusted by the SS. It was unfortunate, from your point of view, that you had to rely on the elaborate mechanisms of the underground. It must have been painful for you to realize that the sincerity of your new convictions was reduced to insignificance by the machinery of deception. Even the better side could not afford to trust you, and yet you proceeded. Splendid courage, Herr Kessler. My compliments. But no one will remember you for it. Your vision is short, as I have said. You have contacted London, Herr Kessler, because you wish to place your findings in English hands. You would prefer that this weapon serve English purposes. And yet, once your idea achieves reality, once it is practical, the question of who finds immediate use for it will make little difference, for as an idea, it will possess a life of its own, a life which will achieve its peculiar ends divorced from any other consideration. Is your knowledge, Herr Kessler, a substitute for moral order? No. I think not. Good luck to you, Herr Kessler."

And Gruppenführer Kleist left as abruptly as he had come.

That night, Otto Kessler went upstairs to the bedroom before Karin came home. He did not expect to sleep. He wanted only to avoid speaking to his wife. He dreaded her reaction to what had happened. When she finally returned, he lay in bed pretending to be asleep. For hours he tossed and turned, possessed by uncontrollable fears, wracked by grief over Buchheim's fate. His terror was pure and unreasoning. His end, he knew, was only days away. Karin called to him in the middle of the night, thinking he was having a nightmare. He did not respond. Later, he got up, unable to lie there any longer, and returned to the study. The image of Reinhard Kleist seemed to hang in the air. He paced along the sides of the room. His heart would not stop pounding. Dizziness overcame him, so he sat down. His mind, overwrought from the shock of the interview, returned obsessively to the horrible moment when Kleist had said he knew everything. When daylight came, Kessler was still in his study.

He went to his office. Exhausted and distracted, he could not work. Out of sheer fatigue, his fever pitch of emotion had subsided to a state of dull numbness. He sent a memo to his staff telling them that Kleist was dissatisfied with the lack of progress. He mentioned that Buchheim had been removed from the project. Sitting at his desk, staring blankly out of the window, the ghosts of former responses returned to plague him. He blamed the slave laborers in Poland for his miserable fate. He cursed the day he had met Reinhard Kleist. The images of contemptible SS officers momentarily enflamed his hatred and fear. But these were but the futile rehearsals of old feelings — feelings that contained only part of the truth. More than ever before, Kessler recognized the ineluctable logic that had brought him to where he now was. In retrospect, the trajectory of his recent history appeared to have moved with the predictability of the stars. This realization did a peculiar thing to Kessler. Gradually, his fear became abstract. His ultimate fate was completely out of his own hands. He could not affect it in any way. He understood that Kleist could do terrible things to him. He had seen some of those things. Even Kessler's resignation to fate could not entirely defuse his terror at the thought of these possibilities. But there was one way in which to transcend even that fear. For the first time it occurred to Kessler that he could take his own life.

It was not until three days after the terrifying interview that Kessler, beginning to coherently recall and piece together Reinhard Kleist's statements, began to ask himself questions about what Kleist had meant.

During the interview, his fear had been so great that he had failed to react to Kleist's apparent indifference toward his contact with London. It had been his fellow officers who had argued for immediate arrest, not Kleist. He had said something about arguing for mercy, for keeping him in his position as project director. What did this mean?

It occurred to Kessler that Kleist's indifference could be explained by a German agent in London, a man short-circuiting British Intelligence activities in Frankfurt. Perhaps this German agent guaranteed that important information did not reach British authorities. But if the SS had permitted Buchheim to operate for so long because he was, in fact, harmless, why had they suddenly decided to take him away? Had the German agent in London been discovered?

But these speculations, believable as they were, had to

assume a secondary place for Kessler. In retrospect, he was haunted by Reinhard Kleist's strange "philosophy." This too seemed to explain his indifference to British Intelligence activities. Kleist did not think that the outcome of the war would make much difference if seen from a broad perspective. Why was this? Did he believe that a German victory was inevitable? In that case, it would have cost him nothing to pretend indifference toward the outcome. Did he believe, perhaps, that the Allies would win and that, therefore, sending London bits of information was an absurdly unnecessary gesture? But, as Kessler tried to reconstruct Kleist's final monologue, something even more abstract held his attention.

Gruppenführer Kleist had spoken about the independent life of the project idea, and of the potential force of that idea in a moral vacuum. Kessler wondered whether Kleist actually dismissed the outcome of the war as having less significance than the destructive potential inherent in a new alloy. That view would certainly entail an indifference toward the question of which nation developed the alloy first. Was Gruppenführer Kleist truly apolitical? But Kessler could not believe this. A high-ranking SS officer indifferent to Germany's fortunes on the battlefield was inconceivable. If Kleist's statements, then, could not be read as honest expressions of his attitudes, how could they best be understood?

So Otto Kessler had to return to the fundamental fact that Reinhard Kleist was an intelligence officer. One had to understand his statements in reference to underlying strategic purposes. Kessler could see that Kleist had easily grasped, right from the start, the extent of his moral anguish. That had been simple. Kleist knew him as a thoroughly bourgeois individual, a man unaccustomed to making decisions involving the lives of others. It had been easy enough for the SS to apply force, whether or not

Kleist claimed responsibility for doing it. They calculated that by "taking hostages," by increasing the pressure, they could force the desired result. Kessler figured that Kleist was not anticipating his suicide as a means of escape. But, if the strategic point of Gruppenführer Kleist's monologue had been to force him to complete the project, then Kessler could still not understand either the emphasis on the irrelevance of the war's outcome, or the discussion of the special alloy's universal potential for destruction. Indeed, given Kleist's apparent purpose, these points seemed self-defeating. Kessler could feel their force only as a motive for refusing, in despair, any further work on the project. How could that result be to Kleist's advantage? Thus, Kessler was compelled to return again to the hypothesis that Kleist had been indulging in honest self-revelation. But why?

Thus, Kessler could make no unified sense out of Gruppenführer Kleist's speech. There were other puzzling things too. Why had Kleist said that it had been Sturmbannführer Wolf's idea to take hostages? Why had he emphasized the mercilessness of his brother officers? Why did he disclaim responsibility for SS actions? Was all this nothing more than a bizarre penchant for historical accuracy? Surely it was mad of Kleist to believe that a victim would be interested in the exact source of his fate. The SS, as an organization, was acting in this case. That was all that mattered. Then why all the unnecessary details about final responsibility? In the context of the interview they had sounded completely out of place.

One week after the interview, Kessler told his wife everything — everything but the fact that she was a hostage. He did not expect her to help him, but he could no longer live alone with the secret of his fate. He told her in the study, the one place which possessed a nearly magical attraction for him.

"Buchheim was an agent," he said to her. "I would never have guessed it. The opportunity was there. I found I could do nothing else."

"Why are you telling me this?" was her response. "If they know everything, then you are finished . . . dead . . . there's no way out."

"Kleist says no harm will come to me if —"

She didn't allow him to finish.

"And you believe him?"

He paused, wounded by her desperate impatience.

"No," he said. "I don't believe him."

"I see," she responded. "And what is to happen to me . . . to me?" She was screaming at him. "I am the wife of a traitor."

He didn't answer. She didn't expect an answer. Karin Kessler had been frightened enough by his first confession to believe that, in this special case, her actions would make no difference. Even if she left him, she knew she would be placed under surveillance. She was too close to him, too close to his project.

"Tell me no more. I want nothing to do with this. Nothing. Tell me nothing. Tell your friend Kleist that I know nothing. I've had nothing to do with this business, with Buchheim. I never met him. I don't know him —"

"I know," he said, and left the room.

What would Kessler do? He knew he was trapped completely. Buchheim's disappearance meant isolation. Buchheim had also been right about the significance of the event. Kessler sensed that going to Buchheim's restaurant was impossible. This judgment was correct. A journey to Buchheim's restaurant would have been senseless. Grete Ohlendorff was already dead. The police net had consumed her. Herr Hanslick had been more fortunate.

And what of the project? It was beginning to demonstrate progress. Herr Graml had indeed come up with a potential solution — a method for producing steel alloys that would lead to an increase in strength. There would have to be tests. At the very least, even if the conception was sound, Kessler figured that several months would have to be spent eliminating unforeseen problems. Of course, an initial failure would delay success indefinitely. In spite of Gruppenführer Kleist's threat, Kessler found he could only hope for that failure. All he desired was more and more time, for only time would give him the leeway in which to determine the best way out of his entrapment.

Kessler wondered if he could establish new contacts. But how? Could he escape? But to where? There were violent alternatives too. He thought of killing every member of the research staff and burning every document pertaining to the project. The idea was absurd. Kessler knew that he was not a killer. In any event, in spite of their political attitudes, Kessler liked the members of his research staff. He could not transform his hatred for Kleist and the SS into real dislike for the staff members. Could he talk to them? Was it conceivable that their political attitudes, maintained in a state of ignorance, might dissolve once exposed to the true nature of the cause they were working for? That was something to wish for, but Kessler knew that if he tried this once and failed, his final destruction might follow immediately. So, what could he do?

Since the SS would be watching him more closely than ever, Kessler judged that trying to reach British Intelligence would be unspeakably foolish. Only one solution was feasible, the easiest of all. He would wait. He would wait and hope that, first, the British were interested in what he had to tell them and that, next, they would try to reach him once they realized that Buchheim was gone.

This decision had to be based on one view of Gruppenführer Kleist's peculiar monologue. It had occurred to Kessler that Kleist's indifference toward his espionage activities implied the existence of a German agent in London. If that were true, then waiting for British Intelligence to contact him would be senseless. But Kessler concluded that there was no such agent in London. Kleist had tried to deceive him by tempting him to infer the existence of such an agent. Why would the SS willingly jeopardize an operative in London by revealing his existence to a man who had worked for the Secret Service? The wrong people might still find out about it. But, from a strategic point of view, Kleist's suggesting, however indirectly, the presence of a German agent in London made sense. Kessler calculated that if Kleist wanted to keep him working on the project and, at the same time, allow for the possibility of the Secret Service successfully reaching him, then a hypothetical German agent in London might forestall any further underground operations in Frankfurt. Why should anyone risk his life sending information across the Channel with the full knowledge that his efforts were being sabotaged at the other end? That had been the point of Reinhard Kleist's speech. There was no German agent in London. Kessler would wait. From this calculation, Kessler drew one further inference. Did Kleist really know that he had been working for the British, or had he only assumed this on the basis of Buchheim's guilt? Kleist, operating on the basis of this assumption, might have come that night only to frighten the truth out of him. It was too late. He had succeeded.

For Trevor Grey, there was only one alternative. Denied any official connection with the Early Riser operation, convinced, furthermore, that Douglas Trenchard was a German agent, Grey knew that he would have to maintain contact with Buchheim and Kessler while keeping his superiors in ignorance regarding his actions. He continued to follow Trenchard, even after the experience at the bomber station. Trenchard returned to the station several times, only further confirming Grey's notion that this man was obtaining information about RAF operations for the enemy. And yet, it was undeniable that Trenchard had official clearance for these visits, for he made each of them in the company of an RAF officer.

Only one person could help Grey, Desmond Crowden, the man who operated one of the Secret Service transmitters. He was responsible for communicating with all European-based agents who were run by Grey's main office. If Grey could get Crowden to work with him by impressing upon him the gravity of the circumstances, then Kessler would not have to be abandoned.

On January 22, 1942, Grey called Crowden in the transmitter room and asked to see him. Crowden suggested Grey's office, but Grey turned this down. He wanted to avoid all interruptions. Crowden must have been surprised by this because the two men never met outside the sphere of their professional activities. So Crowden asked Grey to come to his flat in Brentford. Grey agreed. On the evening of the twenty-third their meeting took place.

Grey started by telling Crowden that he had been taken off the Early Riser operation.

"I know. Atkinson informed me."

"What's the word from Frankfurt?"

"Why do you want to know that?"

"It's important," said Grey.

"That's no longer your concern — now is it?"

"Let's say Desmond, between the two of us, that I have been the victim of political ambitions."

"Ah — aren't we all."

"Yes."

"So now you want to win the war all by yourself?"

"I must . . . I must. Everybody else is enjoying it."

"But now, Grey, you really are not entitled to information from Frankfurt."

"That is a pity."

"But you say it is important . . . so very important."

"I would never lie to you, Desmond."

"Then what I say to you is strictly between the two of us."

"Agreed."

"Just a favor between friends."

"I am moved, Desmond."

"Frankfurt says that your man Buchheim is gone — disappeared."

Grey had been expecting this. He was shocked anyway.

"And something else. Dawn Red has disappeared too."

Grey sipped the tea Crowden had made for him.

"These people can't last forever, you know."

"Kessler . . . what about him?"

"Frankfurt says he's still with the project."

"They've contacted him?"

"No. They've only seen him. The official word to Frankfurt is that they should forget him."

"That's Trenchard's work . . ."

"That message was authorized by Atkinson."

Grey got up and walked across Crowden's dingy flat. He felt trapped by this latest piece of information. A light, cold rain fell against the window in the living room. From where he stood, Grey could see the overcast hanging over the city. Nature itself was conspiring against him.

He was certain that Trenchard and Green had convinced Atkinson that Kessler could be forgotten. The Frankfurt project had been secured against British Intelligence. Trenchard was protecting German operations as well as sabotaging English ones. Grey rejoined Crowden at the kitchen table.

"Here's what I want, Desmond," and he proceeded to

tell Crowden everything. His monologue lasted nearly two hours.

"But you've got to understand, Grey, that you're asking me to violate a cardinal regulation. Every communication I send out has got to be seen and approved by a section head. I can't send the material you give me. It's my neck if anyone finds out."

Grey was asking Crowden to participate in unauthorized espionage activities. He was unrelenting in his demand. He described what he thought to be the inevitable ramifications of a failure to stop the German project. He spared Trenchard nothing. His description and interpretation of Trenchard's activities proved to be the turning point in the conversation. Crowden had to concede that Grey's version of the events was plausible. Late in the evening, he succumbed to the sheer force of Grey's convictions. He agreed to send unauthorized messages directly to the Dawn Group.

On January 25, 1942, Herr Hanslick received a coded communication from London.

Otto Kessler's home was located on a long block in a solidly middle-class district of Frankfurt. On Kessler's side of the street there were six other private homes. A large public park formed the backdrop for these houses. A row of four- and five-story apartment buildings lined the block on the opposite side of the street. The only exception to this was a nine-floor hotel located fifty yards down the block from a position directly opposite Kessler's house. This hotel, the Europa, was a relatively luxurious one. It catered to upper-class businessmen and high-ranking government officials.

On January 26, a young man named Werner Kempe arrived at this hotel and told the head porter that he was looking for a job. Kempe, age twenty-eight, was a short man, no more than five foot six, with a stocky body and angular face. He suffered from a pronounced limp, the result of an automobile accident at age fifteen. This limp had disqualified Kempe from any form of military service.

The head porter sent Kempe to the manager, Herr Rathmann.

"What can you do?" asked Rathmann.

"Anything you want me to do."

"And your leg. What about that?"

"It won't bother me if it doesn't bother you."

"There are others around without your disability."

Kempe reached into his jacket pocket and pulled out an N.S.D.A.P. party card. He waved it in front of the manager.

"It is wartime, Herr Rathmann. I wish to serve the public."

"Can you carry bags . . . spend the day on your feet?"

"I am not a malingerer, Herr Rathmann."

"That's the only position available."

"I like it."

"Then you start tomorrow — the 7:00 A.M. to 6:00 P.M. shift. One hour for lunch. We will work you hard. Pick up your uniform downstairs and report to Herr Dopfer in the morning. Three marks an hour salary. Good day to you, Kempe."

The following day, Werner Kempe spent his time receiving instructions from head porter Dopfer and carrying guests' luggage between the lobby and the rooms of the hotel.

At 3:10 P.M., a blond-haired gentleman wearing a heavy, blue winter coat and carrying a camera slung over his right shoulder entered the hotel and seated himself in an opulent, high-backed chair in the lobby. He took a magazine off a table to his right, opened it, and began to read.

This man's name was Josef Gotz.

Five minutes later, a new guest entered the lobby

carrying two valises. He placed them down on the thick green carpet near the registration desk. While this man was giving his name to the head desk clerk, Werner Kempe approached Josef Gotz.

"Pardon me," he said to him. "May I help you?"

Gotz looked up from his magazine.

"No. I am just waiting for someone."

"Very good, sir."

At this moment, head porter Dopfer, standing at the registration desk, summoned Kempe.

"Kempe," he said, "you are to take Herr Zuckriegel to room 310."

Room keys were hung on hooks fixed to a wooden board mounted behind the registration desk. While the desk clerk completed the signing in of Herr Zuckriegel, Werner Kempe removed two keys from their respective hooks — one for room 310, one for room 618. He then picked up the two valises and asked the new guest to follow him to the lift.

Herr Gotz now left his chair and followed the two men. All three boarded the lift.

To the lift operator Werner Kempe announced, "Six please."

"Pardon," said Herr Zuckriegel, "I thought I was to be in room 310."

"Ah yes . . . my apologies . . . third floor."

The lift operator turned to Herr Gotz.

"Your floor, sir."

"Seven," said Gotz.

Werner Kempe brought Herr Zuckriegel to his room. At the same time, Gotz got off the lift at seven, located the stairway, and descended to the sixth floor. Four minutes later Kempe came up the staircase, let Gotz into room 618, walked back down to the third floor, and then rode the lift to the lobby. Within ten minutes of its being removed, the key to room 618 was back on its hook.

For nearly an hour, Josef Gotz, sitting at the window of room 618, studied the home of Otto Kessler. This study did not reward him with an answer to his problem, but in surveying the areas surrounding Kessler's home, two things caught his attention.

First, an automobile was parked at the end of the block nearest the hotel. Two men sat in this automobile. Herr Gotz figured that they were Gestapo. He was right.

Second, while surveying the paths winding through the park behind Kessler's home, Herr Gotz saw a street cleaner going about his business. This man was equipped with the standard paraphernalia of the trade — a barrel, about four feet high, mounted on wheels, and a long wooden pole with a nail protruding from one end. The man wore a winter coat which did not appear to be part of an official uniform. Slowly, this man went about his job, spearing scraps of paper and depositing them in his mobile barrel.

At 7:15 A.M., the following day, Herr Josef Gotz made his first appearance as a Frankfurt street cleaner. He carried a pole in one hand, and with the other pushed a barrel mounted on a four-wheel dolly. He approached Otto Kessler's home from the corner at which the two Gestapo agents, different ones this time, sat in their automobile. Gotz could see these two men sitting in the front seat talking. The one in the right-hand seat was smoking a cigarette. As Gotz rolled his barrel past the automobile, this man opened his window and threw out the cigarette. It rebounded off an iron lamp post and came to rest on the sidewalk. Gotz approached this still-smoldering butt, made an exaggerated show out of picking it up, and deposited it in his barrel. Then he turned to the two agents, clenched his left fist, and snarled, "Filthy swine." It was a good display of lower-class resentment. The man in the car made an obscene gesture and shouted something. It was unintelligible. Gotz moved on. With pole pointed toward the ground, spearing occasional pieces of paper, he began to make his way toward Kessler's house. The day was bright and cold. Gotz stopped and buttoned the collar of his coat. On this particular day, his coat was old and worn. Several men on their way to work passed him. Gotz gestured to them as if he knew them. One of these nodded back. At 7:22 A.M., Gotz was ten yards from Kessler's house. He was working down the block at a leisurely pace. He stabbed at some papers lying near the edge of the curb and deposited them in his barrel. At 7:25 A.M. Herr Gotz increased his pace, walked past the front steps of Kessler's home, and headed for a bunch of papers lying at the foot of a tree set back thirty feet from the curb. He speared the papers and then moved on. Gotz was now rolling his barrel near the tree line that marked the periphery of the park. Twenty yards beyond Kessler's home, Herr Gotz stopped and looked around as if in search of litter which he had failed to attend to. It was 7:32 A.M.

Otto Kessler was walking down the front steps of his home.

Ten feet away, directly in the middle of the sidewalk, Gotz spotted a cigarette butt. He moved toward it. He could hear Kessler approaching from behind. Reaching the cigarette butt, Gotz bent over to pick it up. He turned his head slightly so that he could catch Kessler as he moved into the periphery of his vision. Gotz began to rise. Kessler passed him, and just as he did, Gotz rose to his full height and spoke softly, barely above the tone of a whisper.

"Greetings from London, Herr Kessler."

That was all. Gotz pushed his barrel. Otto Kessler walked on as if nothing had happened. But he had heard everything.

British Intelligence had reached him.

Now Otto Kessler planned to make it easier for this street cleaner to contact him a second time. He would make certain that he passed him again on the following morning. They could not stop and talk, but obviously, thought Kessler, this man had something else to tell him.

The next morning Kessler sat in his study and waited. From the study window he could observe the sidewalk down to the end of the street. At 7:30 A.M. the street cleaner appeared again. Kessler left, walked down the front steps, turned right, and started down the street at his customary pace. At the moment when he passed the man, he heard the voice whisper just one word.

"Europa."

What did they expect him to do? Kessler knew that a Gestapo car, no doubt on Kleist's orders, trailed him to and from work each day. Had he not spotted this car, he would have assumed anyway that he was being observed constantly. This situation meant that he could not deviate from his well-established routine. Kessler now knew that the hotel Europa had some connection with British Intelligence activity. He calculated that if the underground agents had observed him closely enough to determine the need for inventing the complicated and melodramatic means of contact they had used, then they surely realized that he could not easily initiate contact on his own. He could not walk into the Europa lobby and wait for an agent to speak to him. He knew that he had to get information to London's agents without leaving his home or his office, and without departing from the standard route he used to get from one to the other.

On the third morning Herr Gotz appeared at the far corner once again, pushing his barrel. But this time his appearance was intended for the Gestapo alone. Kempe and he had decided that he should go off in some new direction so that the police would get the impression that his route had been altered by the authorities. This would minimize suspicions once Gotz failed to appear altogether. There was a second reason for this strategy. Otto Kessler had to be left without further aid from the initial contact man, and with nothing more to go on than the last word that man had spoken to him. Kessler had to be forced to look to the Europa hotel for the solution to this problem.

Thus, on the third morning, while Herr Gotz pushed his barrel down the street away from Kessler's home, Kessler sat in his study and waited. He had his coat on. His briefcase was closed and ready to go. By 7:35 A.M. the street cleaner had failed to appear. He grew impatient. Five more minutes passed. Kessler left the study and entered the living room. He drew aside the curtains on one of the windows and looked down the street to the left. No street cleaner. Had he been abandoned already? Had they closed in on these people in so little time? The man on the street had said only one substantive thing to him. Europa.

Kessler climbed the stairs to the second floor, turned right, and entered Ingrid's room, where there were two windows, one looking out onto the street, the other on the side of the house. From the latter, one could obtain a clear view of the Europa. Kessler pulled aside the curtains, opened the window, and looked out at the hotel. He was barely conscious of the cold air flooding into the room. Kessler began to examine the building closely, hoping to find the answer to his dilemma. A doorman stood in front of the building, under the awning, moving about in an effort to keep warm. Kessler examined each floor of the hotel. He ran his eye across the rows of windows. All of them seemed to be closed — at least at first glance. Then Kessler noticed that one window was open on the top floor at the far side of the building. It was unusually wide open considering the time of year. The hotel windows were two-piece units. Each half was framed in wrought iron and pivoted open in an outward direction. In this one odd case, the window half farthest from Kessler was open at right angles to the building, and the nearest half was swung completely out so that it was parallel to the building wall. A man was at this window. He was clearly visible, and it was apparent to Kessler, even at a distance, that this man was looking directly at him. The man did not move for nearly half a minute, then he raised an object to his face. It was a camera. Kessler raised his right hand. The man at the window lowered the camera, raised his own hand in a gesture that was not quite a wave, and then reached out and closed the window.

The sign had been given. They would be watching closely.

Kempe and Gotz knew that it would be best to observe Kessler's home in the evening. On most days, he arrived home somewhere between 4:45 and 5:15 P.M. The exceptions to this were the days when Kessler did not appear until 7:00 P.M. or later. On that third morning, Kempe, using Gotz's camera, had given Kessler the signal, but from that point on it had to be Gotz who did the watching. The two men worked out a simple arrangement. Gotz planned to arrive at the hotel at 5:00 P.M. or before, depending on what his own schedule would permit. Werner Kempe would get him into the building through a service entrance at the back. They could not afford to repeat the strategy they had used on the first day. Before Gotz's arrival, Kempe would check the hotel's reservation book. In this way, he could determine which rooms would be unoccupied. It would be a simple matter to let Gotz into one of these rooms and leave him there with the camera. He could wait and watch Kessler's house. But what would happen if a guest without a reservation was assigned to the room in which Gotz was stationed? There was only one solution. Using the house phone, Kempe would ring Gotz's room telephone once. They had to hope that Kessler, upon arriving home, would get to work quickly. Kempe's shift ended at 6:00 P.M. Gotz could not remain in a hotel room beyond that hour.

At the beginning of February, Gotz began his vigil. He waited two nights at an eighth-floor window. Nothing happened. Kessler was taking his time.

It was on the third night that Kessler initiated his first communication. He arrived home at 5:05 P.M. and went directly to his study. He took six twenty-four-inch by twenty-inch sheets of drawing paper, the kind on which he liked to work out mathematical computations, and taped them together. This gave him a single, enormous sheet on which he could write out a verbal message. In large, thick, black letters he inscribed his first communication. Kessler took this sheet to Ingrid's room. There, he positioned a bureau two feet from the window, draped the sheet over the front of the bureau and secured it in place with a jewelry box, and then moved aside the window curtains. Kessler switched on the lights for two seconds, turned them off for ten seconds, and then switched them on again for ten more seconds. Herr Gotz was prepared. With a thirty-five-millimeter camera and telephoto lens he took two pictures.

On the following evening, Kessler repeated the same procedure. He filled another large sheet with mathematical equations and a single statement of the project's current goals. He signaled with the lights in Ingrid's room. Herr Gotz snapped two more photographs.

But that was to be the end of all contact with Otto Kessler.

One would imagine that the SS or Gestapo caught Kempe or Gotz. Both men knew that their luck would not hold out indefinitely. An underground agent could expect to survive for a year, maybe two, but no more. The security organizations were too persistent, too methodical, too brutal. Eventually, they caught you. But, in fact, Kempe survived until 1944, and Gotz, miraculously, survived the war, although he did so only because a serious illness prevented his participation in the underground after December of 1943. The Kessler affair did not end because of the destruction of either of these two men.

On the day after Gotz had taken the photographs of Kessler's equation sheet, Kessler arrived home earlier than usual. Gotz had not yet come to the hotel, so it was Kempe, standing on the sidewalk under the awning, who first spotted Kessler. He sensed at once that something had gone wrong. The irregular rhythm and slow pace of Kessler's walk suggested imminent disaster. Twenty minutes later Gotz showed up. Kempe let him into a sixth-floor room. Only five minutes after assuming his position at the window, Gotz saw a black Mercedes pull up in front of Kessler's house. An SS officer got out of the car, walked quickly up the steps of Kessler's house, and knocked at the door. He was admitted.

Gotz waited. It was already dark. The street lights had been turned on. The Mercedes stood, double-parked, its engine silent. From the hotel window Gotz could see the arm of the driver.

Who was the man who had come to visit Otto Kessler? Gotz decided that he would try to photograph him when he came out. Perhaps British Intelligence could determine his identity and, from that, deduce something interesting.

Fifteen minutes later, the officer appeared again. He emerged suddenly from the house and walked rapidly down the steps. Herr Gotz snapped his picture. The Mercedes drove off.

Gotz shifted his attention to the second-floor window. He was prepared for Kessler's signal.

He heard a sound behind him. The door opened. It was Kempe. He had a minute to spare and wanted to see what was happening. The two men stood at the window.

Otto Kessler walked out onto the porch of his home.

"What's he doing?" said Kempe.

Kessler moved down the front steps, turned to his left, and seemed to drift aimlessly for ten or fifteen yards. Then he stopped and stood motionless for nearly a minute.

Gotz took another picture.

Kessler walked to the curb, stepped off it, and stood between two parked automobiles.

"My God," said Kempe, "he's coming over here . . . to the hotel."

Off to the right an automobile rounded the corner and headed down the street toward the Europa.

Otto Kessler threw himself in front of it.

«10»

Trevor Grey could see that if he played quite accurately it would be possible to break Harry Forsyth's queen-side defenses by a clever combination of bishop and rook. After several hours of concentrated study, the wisdom of this strategy struck him with special force. That, too, was one of the things Grey loved about the game — the astonishing way in which the truth could lie, in the open, right before one's eyes, and yet remain undetected. It was all a question of the player's strategic intelligence. The pieces did not conspire to hide the truth.

Grey sat up into the early morning hours considering the state of his game with Forsyth, considering the efforts of the Dutch underground and its attempts to aid British airmen, and, as always, considering the ongoing case of Otto Kessler and Douglas Trenchard. That problem was still with him. It would not leave him in peace. There were bad days, at least he thought them so, when Grey could feel the strength with which he had held convictions about the Kessler case begin to drain away from him. But how could he maintain such convictions in the absence of any form of support? Grey began to believe that he might lose this special struggle.

He continued to visit Sullivan's pub with Forsyth. Their friendship had not suffered in spite of the tensions implicit in the Kessler-Buchheim-Trenchard case. That subtle point had passed at which both men had recognized that there was nothing to be gained, and perhaps something to be lost, by further arguments about the matter. They drank beer, ate dinner together, enjoyed each other's company, and talked animatedly of other things — military strategy, other cases, the role of America in the war, politics internal to the Secret Service, Atkinson. But Grey's preoccupation with the Frankfurt project did not cease.

One afternoon, then, as the two men were leaving work, Forsyth suggested that they return to his flat. He said that they could have a beer, play a fast game of chess, a different one from the more elaborate game that was forever in progress. Grey accepted the invitation, but the drink, the game of chess, the additional conversation were not the chief motives underlying Forsyth's invitation. When he arrived at the flat, a sparsely furnished two-room affair on Stanley Road in Richmond, Forsyth asked his colleague to make himself comfortable on the single, dark brown sofa. "I'll get the beer," he said, and set off for the second room, but ·as he passed the dining table near the doorway he stopped for a moment, walked over to the table, and picked up a folder which had been lying there. He brought this folder to Grey and said, "Here, have a look at these while I have a go at the drinks. Quite fascinating."

He then retraced his steps and entered the second room which contained a small, nearly closet-size kitchen area. Grey heard him rattling around with glasses and bottles. Forsyth called in, "I got those from Atkinson. He got them from Green."

The folder contained at least thirty photographs taken by RAF reconnaissance aircraft. Each day, following a Bomber Command strike on a German city, reconnaissance planes recorded the extent of the damage. These photographs allowed Bomber Command analysts to determine the concentration of explosives dropped in the target areas. Each picture was marked with the name of the city and the date of the attack. Grey examined these photographs. Bomber Command still had a great deal to learn. Rarely did these pictures reveal massive destruction concentrated in one area. He found one exception to this in a photograph of Düsseldorf. One could clearly discern several rows of buildings destroyed by concentrated hits from high-explosive bombs. It was easy to distinguish the decimated zones from the intact ones. There were houses and buildings with roofs, and those without roofs. Some structures had walls, others did not. An arbitrary sledgehammer had descended on one block, but not on another. What impressed Grey was that from the vantage point of Bomber Command reconnaissance, all cities looked the same. Here was a perspective on human centers of civilization that was unique to the century. Photography as a technical medium, combined with the methods of an artist, can capture the traditions and characteristic atmosphere of a city. It was fitting, thought Grey, that in these aerial photographs, remarkable products of an abstracted technical skill, every city was reduced to nothing more than a set of objects waiting to be destroyed. Forsyth did not need to say anything about these photographs. Grey understood why he was being permitted to examine them. Trenchard was one of the many people who were advocating the raids the results of which were recorded in these pictures. What conclusion, then, was Grey to draw from this impressive evidence? How could he rationally persist in maintaining that a man who stood firmly behind a policy aimed at killing, wounding and rendering homeless tens of thousands of the enemy's civilian population was, in reality, a German agent? And the air attacks whose results were recorded in these photographs would, no doubt, appear insignificant in the light of future Bomber Command operations.

"Bomber Command has its opponents," said Forsyth, reentering the room with glasses of beer, "those who believe it's doing an inefficient job. But I'm told, by informed sources, that there are bigger, more spectacular raids to come in the near future."

Grey could imagine what they would be like. Square miles of city reduced to ashes. Tens of thousands annihilated by concentrated showers of high-explosive bombs and incendiaries. And surely, didn't there come a point in the very imagining of such destruction when the suggestion that an advocate of massive area bombing was a German agent had to be judged as wildly absurd? The photographs were achieving the effect Forsyth intended. Grey's convictions about Trenchard were suffering a further erosion.

Trenchard was a strange man. Unquestionably.

He was inscrutable. No doubt. These things had to be granted.

"But look," said Forsyth. "Look at what he's doing. These are the acts he wishes us to commit against the enemy."

Could this man be a German agent?

Grey did not remain at Forsyth's flat for long. He could not concentrate on chess. The photographs disturbed him because the implications were so unavoidable. He had known all along that Trenchard advocated heavy bombing strikes against German population centers, but it was an entirely different thing to actually see the results of these attacks.

But still, thought Grey, as he lay in bed that night staring at the ceiling, even if Forsyth was right about Trenchard,

Trenchard could be wrong about the Frankfurt project. He was quite capable of an innocent error in judgment. Grey was not yet prepared to surrender all his convictions. He still thought that Kessler was telling the truth. But why, he wondered, had he begun to doubt Trenchard in the first place? Those suspicions had had their origins in theoretical speculations about Kessler and Buchheim. It was true that the double-agent hypothesis had struck him with great force, but what had he had to go on other than the internal coherence of an intuition grounded in meager evidence? Was Trenchard's infuriating, cool stubbornness a sufficient basis on which to accuse him of being in league with the enemy? And what of his visits to the bomber stations? Trenchard was a Secret Service agent. It was probable that his activities were related to entirely legitimate, official cases. Grey asked himself what an active imagination might construe out of his own activities. What about his monthly trips to Sullivan's pub with Forsyth? Did those meetings have to be interpreted as nothing other than informal, friendly encounters? Subjected to dispassionate analysis, Trenchard's actions did not unequivocally condemn him.

Grey thought through these considerations time and time again. As he did, the notion of Trenchard's guilt lost some of its objective probability.

Why, then, Grey asked himself, couldn't he dispel completely the feeling that something was wrong?

On the day following his visit to Forsyth's flat, Grey received a note from Desmond Crowden. He asked for a meeting. They had lunch in a pub. As they were about to part, Crowden handed Grey a sealed envelope

"Something from your friends," he said, and walked off.

Grey returned to his office, locked his door, and ripped open the envelope. It contained a set of photographs, all of which had been channeled through Crowden's office, and a single verbal message.

"5-2-42. Kessler dead. Suicide observed. Following visit from SS officer."

Grey was shocked by this simple communication. He walked the city streets for several hours after reading it. He had known Otto Kessler in only the most indirect way, but he could not maintain the professional's attitude toward the death of this man.

Late in the afternoon, he made a telephone call.

"Parks? . . . Basil Parks?"

"Yes."

"This is Trevor Grey . . . from Secret Service."

"Ah yes. Good to hear from you."

"There's something you should know."

"Yes . . ."

"Kessler is dead."

There was a long silence. When Parks spoke again, the nervous exuberance was gone from his voice.

"When, Grey? What happened?"

"I learned of it today. It happened last week. Suicide."

Another silence.

"Do you know why?"

"We can only guess."

"Yes . . . of course."

There was nothing more for the two of them to say. Each was lost in his own reactions to the event.

"Thanks for letting me know, Grey."

"It's too bad . . . that's all."

"Yes."

"Good luck to you, Parks" — and he hung up.

Grey went through the photographs. He found the one of an SS officer striding across a sidewalk toward an automobile. That man, figured Grey, was probably Gruppenführer Kleist, the man whose name had appeared on the memos Buchheim had sent so long ago. He looked at this photograph in a cursory manner. In itself, it could reveal nothing. The Frankfurt agents must have thought that London would be interested in the identity of Otto Kessler's SS acquaintances.

What had this man told Kessler? What words had been spoken during the final moments of the drama?

And there was a photograph of another man. It had to be Kessler. Had it been taken just before his death, or had the agents taken it at a random moment? It made no difference. Only someone interested in the history of the man would bother to ask the question.

And the other photographs? At first glance they appeared to be nothing more than pictures of a house. Grey examined them with a powerful magnifying glass. He found out why these pictures had been sent. The second-floor window. Kessler had placed a large sheet of paper directly behind it. In the first photograph, a simple message appeared: "Test 4-42." In the second photograph, Kessler had written "Current Solution" on the top of his sheet. This was followed by a series of technical terms and a set of equations. Grey decided that, once again, he would go to Cambridge.

Could there be any doubt now about Kessler's legitimacy? Did a man commit suicide as part of an espionage scheme? Even Trenchard would be capable of seeing that point.

That night, when Trevor Grey returned to his flat, he was still disturbed by the death of Otto Kessler. He had not expected his position to be confirmed in such a tragic manner.

He examined his ongoing chess game with Forsyth, looking for the hidden strategic options. At 10:30 P.M., feeling exhausted, Grey turned out the lights, got into bed, and fell asleep quickly.

He had a terrifying dream.

He rode in the night sky over Germany. The light of an enormous bomber's moon illuminated the scene. It was as if he were capable of flight himself, for he was suspended in the sky, moving among a stream of heavy bombers. The four-engined machines were everywhere. The roar of the engines was deafening. It obliterated everything else from consciousness. The flames of ten thousand engine exhausts lent the sky an orange glow. This locust swarm of bombers marched through the freezing night atmosphere. He saw into the cockpits of these machines. They were without pilots, without crews. They flew themselves, gently rocking from side to side, maneuvering about in space, each machine a conscious, living organism. Then the steel jaws of death opened out. The cannisters and cylinders tumbled earthward. But then he was on the ground, walking the streets of a city, ears still filled with the thunder of engines. Explosions erupted, blossoming out everywhere. Dragon tongues of flame lashed out into the night heavens. Brick, steel and concrete shattered under the blows of invisible demonic hammers. The wall of fire, the ocean of flame, a contagion imported from hell, tore at the atmosphere, devouring oxygen, sucking life itself out of the planet. Flaming timbers, hurled through space by the savage breath of the fire-beast, flew past him. Then people filled the streets. They walked, wandered, and ran about — living human torches bathed in white phosphorous. The inhabitants of the inferno streamed past him. And Douglas Trenchard was there too, off in the distance, standing near a mass of human torches. He was the circus director, the ringmaster, cracking a whip, signaling to the miserable victims.

But then Grey woke up, his heart pounding with a fear he had not known since childhood. He lay still, looking at the wall near his bed, the vivid dream images passing before his mind's eye.

He could not sleep at all after this dream. It stayed with

him, speaking to him, telling him something, something private and intended for him alone. Getting out of bed, Grey began to pace around his flat, occasionally stopping to look out the window at nearly deserted streets. He looked at his watch. It was only 11:55 P.M. He was still unsettled and restless. What was the point of remaining in the flat, walking to and fro like a caged animal? He decided on an unusual course of action. He would go back to his office. As a Secret Service agent, his identification papers would clear up any problems if he were questioned by the police. Once in his office, he would reexamine the material in the Kessler file which was still in his possession. He could even consider preparing another confrontation with Trenchard. Perhaps the man could now be convinced that the German project deserved close observation, that Otto Kessler, now dead, had been telling the truth.

So, locked away in his office in the middle of the night, Trevor Grey examined the material in his Kessler folder.

What could he reasonably deduce from this information?

There were the memos — from Gruppenführer Kleist to Otto Kessler, from Kleist to Standartenführer Franz, from Franz to Oberführer Kohler. There were the code words. Grey already knew what they referred to. There was the familiar, friendly tone of Gruppenführer Kleist's communications. Nothing irrefutably substantive.

And the mathematical calculations? What of them? The Cambridge people had been unwilling to infer any unifying scheme on the grounds of such incoherent scientific information. Would the new material give them something more conclusive?

The military information? Trenchard could not deny that it had been accurate.

Was it simply the fact of the suicide alone which would lend all the other material its persuasive force?

The photographs? One contained the additional scientific data, and the other a date for a test. These things would surely appear significant in the light of Kessler's death.

Had that death itself been a message? The suicide had been committed in a manner that permitted the underground agents to observe it. Had Kessler grown so fearful of even the remotest possibility of successful completion of the project, or of the idea that the British might still choose to doubt him, that he had used a staged suicide as a method for sabotaging the project and demonstrating his honesty?

And there was the photograph of the SS officer, the man who was, no doubt, Gruppenführer Reinhard Kleist. There he was, captured on film, striding toward his automobile across the uneven stone sidewalk, the scene illuminated by light cast from iron lamp posts. Trees were visible in the upper part of the photograph, as well as the figure of a man who happened to be passing by at the moment the picture was taken.

Grey studied this photograph. He wondered if he could discern any of the features of this man's face. He lifted a magnifying glass out of a desk drawer and moved it over the surface of the picture. The officer's high peaked cap concealed the upper part of his face.

The details of this picture fascinated Grey. This moment from history, arrested, frozen, saved for all time, elicited his most intense curiosity, a curiosity that sought to understand, to fill in, the missing parts of the arrested events. This photograph, the most concrete representation of the past imaginable, was filled with mystery. He examined each detail of this picture, seeking to locate the truth that was locked away in the patterns of light and shade. The roof of the waiting car (what had the driver been doing?), the trees (utterly indifferent to everything), the bottom of the porch steps of Kessler's home (used only moments later by Kessler himself), the man passing by (what had he been thinking?) the shadows cast in several directions by the street lamps — he observed these things closely.

And then, something caught his attention. It happened when he realized that his investigation had been misdirected. One would not discover the truth by scrutinizing molecular physical facts. It was not a question of what was in the picture.

Something was missing from this photograph. Trevor Grey knew that the answer to the problem of the Buchheim-Kessler case lay before his eyes.

Trevor Grey spent several days in the British Museum. He had gone there before, at the very beginning of the case, to research the man Otto Kessler. Now he returned there again to research the strange and disturbing thing he had seen in the photograph of Reinhard Kleist.

It was a Thursday, late in February of 1942. Grey passed the day in his office looking after matters pertaining to the Dutch underground. Late in the afternoon, he quit his office, rode the tube back to his flat, had a small dinner, and then got on the telephone. He dialed Harry Forsyth's number.

"Forsyth? Grey. I want to see you. Yes . . . tonight. Come over here. Good. See you in a while."

Forsyth was surprised by this call. He couldn't understand why his colleague had used the telephone for this contact. Why hadn't he requested a dinner meeting or a trip to Sullivan's pub? Why had Grey failed to mention this need for a special conference while the two of them had been at work? Their offices were, after all, directly across the hall from each other. This indirectness was unusual, out of order. Forsyth had tried putting off the meeting. Grey had been insistent.

From the moment when Grey opened the door of his flat, Forsyth sensed that something was disturbing his friend. The signs of this disturbance, whatever the cause, were written on Grey's face. The eyes betrayed a distractedness. A lack of color in the cheeks seemed to indicate a nervous exhaustion. An odd hesitancy in Grey's pattern of speech suggested that although he had demanded the meeting, he was participating in it reluctantly. Forsyth knew immediately that the Kessler affair had to be the source of his friend's distress. Nothing else was quite so replete with the potential to unsettle Trevor Grey. But, for Forsyth, this situation was becoming intolerable. He saw that, theoretically, there might be no limit to Grey's speculations on the significance of the Frankfurt project. Therefore, he had been in Grey's flat only a few minutes when he decided that he would try to terminate any discussion of the Kessler affair before it attained to levels of undemonstrable speculation. He would have to tell his friend precisely how he felt about these discussions.

Grey offered Forsyth a drink. Forsyth accepted. Grey poured two beers into glasses, gave one to his colleague, and invited him to sit on the faded couch. For several minutes Grey stood in the middle of the room, glass of beer in hand. He looked confused, as if he were trying to figure out just where he was. He was, in fact, attempting to decide on where to begin his story. Finally, he sat on one of the collapsible chairs which were arranged around a small dining table. He leaned forward, elbows on his legs, both hands clasped around the glass of beer.

"Harry, I want to talk to you . . . but first, if it isn't too much of a bother, I'd like to have you tell me something. All right? I want you to tell me exactly what you think of this Kessler business . . . or rather . . . a more difficult question . . . what you've thought about me . . . about my behavior . . . in reference to this whole matter."

Forsyth was relieved by this request. Grey was obviously prepared to confront the truth.

"I'm quite willing to tell you what you want to know, Grey. There's nothing else to be done."

He paused.

"You've lost your mental balance on this case . . . you've simply lost it. There are some unspoken rules which should govern how all of us act in this insane profession. One of these rules has to do with the extent to which a man can surrender himself to an idea, a suspicion. I'm told that battlefield commanders make bad decisions when they become too close to their men. In our own work, bad judgment is the product of obsessions. Nothing can be absolutely certain in this business, or, at the very least, few things have the status of eternal truths. That's obvious enough since everybody in this kind of work is in it only in order to deceive everybody else. So a rule about keeping one's head and not letting unconfirmed suspicions destroy one's sanity has got to be adhered to rigorously . . . not, mind you, that I think that's easy to do. But you've forgotten that principle, Grey. Your theory about Kessler is good . . .very good . . . but not good enough. Your ideas about Trenchard are outrageous. You've got to give them up."

Forsyth stopped. He wanted to say more about the doubts Grey had expressed concerning Trenchard, but he calculated that any detailed discussion on that subject might only set his colleague off once again. Grey, all the while Forsyth had been speaking, sat still. Only his right foot had moved, slowly, up and down, but striking the floor too softly to produce any sound.

"Yes, I see," he finally said. "I knew that you felt that all along. Good enough. It's just as well that you said that."

Grey leaned back and placed his glass on the table. The introductory talk was over.

"However, Harry, once more . . . just once more . . . I'm going to bring up this complex matter . . . the Kessler business . . . difficult as it might be for you to sit through it. But I will give you my word in exchange for your patience. After tonight, if you wish it, I shall never mention this again. This will be the end of it."

Forsyth contemplated this offer for just a second.

"Fair enough, Grey. I can't deny you that."

He spoke like a businessman agreeing to the terms of a contract.

"But I shall hold you to your word," he added.

"Unless, of course, I find something conclusive." Grey smiled.

"I will be the judge of that," said Forsyth.

"Good. Now, Harry, let me begin with a fact which you do not know. Kessler is dead."

Grey waited in order to observe his friend's response. Forsyth was clearly surprised by the statement.

"How do you know that?" he asked. "How did you learn it? This entire case is supposed to be out of your hands."

"But it isn't. I've been following it."

"Did Atkinson authorize this?"

"No. I did it myself . . . on my own."

"Grey. What are you doing?"

"I was convinced I was right. You know that. So I had to go on with it. I contacted Crowden in communications and he agreed I could have access to the channels. Everything from Frankfurt goes directly through him to me."

"That's illegal. Regulations forbid it. They'll have both your heads for something like this."

"True, but now it's done and that's all there is to it. They can have my head after I tell them Kessler is finished . . . a suicide . . . a suicide observed by agents working under my direction. That's what counts, Harry, not any of this damned rubbish about regulations. The simple fact that

Kessler took his own life demolishes completely the idea that he was working for the other side. Trenchard said Kessler was their man. He can't use that argument anymore."

"And do you take Kessler's death as a final confirmation of your suspicions about Trenchard?"

"No," said Grey.

"It is a relief to hear that," responded Forsyth. He had not anticipated Grey's being so reasonable.

"But Douglas Trenchard is not your friend. What arguments he can and cannot use is only a minor part of your current problem. You've put yourself in a corner, Grey. Trenchard still thinks he has got the truth. Tactically, all he need do is make a point of your having broken regulations. Even Atkinson can't choose to ignore that unfortunate detail."

"Yes, but the fact of Kessler's death by suicide is simply too overwhelming."

"Is it?" asked Forsyth. "A man can take his own life for many reasons. Kessler may have had a host of other difficulties."

"This is just one issue, Harry, and not the one I want to discuss. There's something else I've learned."

And Grey stopped at this point and looked at his friend. The pause was awkward. Forsyth wondered if he was supposed to say something. Again, Grey looked as if he were engaged in an inner struggle aimed at overcoming his own reluctance to continue the discussion. Forsyth was about to speak when Grey got up, walked over to the end table next to the bed, and picked up an envelope that had been lying there. While retracing his steps, he opened this envelope, removed some materials, and placed them on the dining table. Forsyth watched him closely. He felt a growing tension. He knew, absolutely, that Grey was about to escalate the level of his speculations on the Kessler affair.

"First, Harry, I want you to look at these documents. Examine them carefully. Read them closely."

Grey handed him four papers. They were the texts of the memoranda Wolfgang Buchheim had sent from Frankfurt.

Forsyth examined each of them. He read them slowly, but only because Grey had made a point of his doing so. He saw no justification for the request. He was growing impatient. The documents, which he remembered clearly, seemed uninteresting and self-explanatory. Months before he had dismissed them as containing little important information. He was prepared now to dismiss them on the same grounds. Just the same, he felt obligated to perform the gesture of patiently reading each one of them.

Forsyth placed the documents on the sofa.

"No, Grey. What's the point? We've discussed these papers before and agreed that there's nothing in them which merits further attention. Interdepartmental chatter — that's all."

Grey walked over to the sofa, picked up the papers, and returned to his seat.

"Listen to this, Harry," he said, and he proceeded to read one of the memos.

"From SS Gruppenführer Reinhard Kleist to Dr. Otto Kessler, Blocksberg. Dear Herr Kessler. Welcome. I hope that you will find the new research facilities satisfactory. I apologize for the delay in completing the construction. Not everyone responds as you do to my idealism. Those involved in the construction work were told that it was a city government project. Any requests for changes in the facilities can, if you prefer, be addressed to me. I will suggest to the appropriate authorities that your desires be quickly realized. Good luck with your work."

Grey put the paper down on the table and picked up a second one.

"Now listen to this one," he said. "From Standartenführer Franz to Oberführer Kohler. Kohler — Gruppenführer Kleist would like a survey on the work force which can be placed at his disposal for Horselberg. Complete this survey by January 15. This is an urgent matter. Heil Hitler."

"The styles are different," said Forsyth. "We noticed that before. Kleist seems to be rather an agreeable chap."

"Yes. That is what we noticed before. The styles are radically different. But consider the significance of that. Who is the man who composed three of these memoranda? He is a Gruppenführer in the SS. In terms of the Allied armies, that rank is roughly equivalent to major general. But there is more to this than just the matter of rank. This man Kleist is a top-ranking officer in the élite cadre of the National Socialist movement. We must consider the nature of the organization he belongs to. The SS is not simply another example of a standard army. There is not an organization anywhere quite so clanlike, quite so enveloped in mystique as the SS. Not just anyone can qualify for membership. Its men are specially chosen for service. They receive rigorous training in police and terror tactics. Their education is designed to instill in each of them a ruthless attitude toward all those who stand in the way of the movement. You deny none of this?"

"No . . . none of it."

"Good. So let us look at these communications again. What are we to make of them? The really curious fact about them is not simply that the tone, the style, is unusually friendly, or accommodating. The real point, Harry, is that not once, in any of these memoranda, does this man Kleist ever give an order. Read them again. You'll see. He never orders anybody to do anything. He suggests, requests, recommends . . . but never orders. He goes out of his way in making certain that his desires do not interfere with anyone else's responsibilities. An extraordinary display of consideration on his part, you must admit. An astonishing degree of self-effacement, especially for an SS Gruppenführer. How probable is it that such a man would never give orders? He can have what he wants. Surely there are no more than five hundred men in all of Germany who outrank him. The organization he belongs to is built on the very principle of unquestioning allegiance to leader and state. Reinhard Kleist's desires should be part of the definition of national interest. Why, then, is this man so circumspect about his own authority? He simply refuses to exercise it. The force of these memoranda compels the receiver to assume complete responsibility for his actions. It makes no sense. It's inefficient. Compare Kleist's memoranda to the one from Franz to Kohler. The difference is startling."

"The difference is there," said Forsyth. "I never denied that. But what significance can this have? Are you saying that this man is not a real member of the SS? Has some other Party organization infiltrated the SS?"

"No. Not quite that, Harry."

And Grey kept silent again. He was thinking out his next point. He sipped from his glass of beer.

"Now, look at the memos again," he said. "Look at the code words that appear in them. Intelligence organizations have only one interest in code words. They want to know what they stand for, what they refer to. That exhausts the importance of code words."

"Precisely . . . and what else can there be to the matter?"

"Our knowledge of these particular code terms is inadequate . . . or rather, it was inadequate. There is something more to them. Take the two names Blocksberg and Horselberg. What do they refer to?"

"The Blocksberg is the code designation for the research center located in Frankfurt. The other term is the designation for the factory located in the eastern occupied zone."

"Yes. Exactly so. Our search for the meaning of those

words left off at that point. Do you know the origin of these words?"

"No."

"I spent some time in the British Museum the other day looking into them. Both words have their origin in medieval Germany. Both of them refer to locations at which, during the Middle Ages, witches supposedly congregated for the purpose of worshiping their master — Satan."

"An interesting coincidence," said Forsyth.

"And the other term, Harry, the term that designates the secret project itself — Infernal Proteus. There is a fascinating origin for that too. That term was a medieval designation for the Devil himself."

But Forsyth could not respond to these remarks. In what spirit was he to interpret his colleague's observations? There was an unmistakable solemnity in Grey's tone and manner. Had this serious posture been uncomplicated by any other qualifying attitude, Forsyth would have dismissed the whole thing as a practical joke, but Grey's ill-concealed reluctance to be participating in the conversation in the first place compelled the conclusion that his intentions were serious. For a moment, Forsyth wondered if Grey was communicating a move in the chess game. But that was impossible. They were discussing a professional matter.

"All right, Grey. What do you construe out of these code names, or these symbolic code names, if you prefer?"

"Do you believe in the reality of the Devil?"

"Do you want to know if I believe in evil . . . in the existence of evil?"

"No, Harry. I asked if you believe in the reality of the Devil."

"I do not."

"I do," said Grey.

Forsyth regretted that he had agreed to this one last discussion of the Kessler case. But he could do nothing now.

"That is what I think," said Grey. "The Devil . . . Satan himself . . . is there. He is responsible for this . . . the entire business . . . the project . . . the death of Kessler . . . everything. I know it."

His voice faded into a whisper. He had spoken these words without excitement, almost without affect.

Forsyth bolted out of the sofa. He could no longer contain himself.

"Listen to me, Grey. You have lost your mind over this thing. You have lost it. That's obvious to me if nothing else is. There is no Satan, no Devil in Germany directing secret projects. Listen to yourself, Grey . . . listen to what you're saying. The code words are symbolic, that's all. They are nothing but symbolic. They were deliberately chosen by someone who knew their significance, their origin. If it was Kleist who decided to use them, then he did the same research that you did. The man might be a great ironist. You yourself just pointed out that the SS prides itself on its mystique. What, then, could be more fitting than their using code words with occult, demonological significance? The Nazis are great dramatists, they enjoy playacting, they invariably choose to lend political events a mythological significance. There is Siegfried, Barbarossa, the whole bloody Wagner business. We had to listen to mythological propaganda for years before the war started. It's characteristic of them to dramatize their own activities with code terms like this. From their viewpoint, nothing could be more routine."

Forsyth had been pacing back and forth as he spoke. Grey, still seated, did not really listen closely to his friend's desperately impatient words. When Forsyth finished speaking, Grey turned back to the materials lying on the table. For the first time, real fear began to seize Forsyth.

He realized that nothing he was saying was making an impression on his friend.

Grey lifted something else off the table. It was a photograph.

"This photograph was sent from Frankfurt. It was taken only minutes before Kessler's death. Directly after conferring with this man, Kessler killed himself. This must be a photograph of Kleist. Look at it carefully. In case you need help, here is a magnifying glass. I brought it with me from the office."

Grey handed the photograph and the glass to Forsyth. Forsyth took them and stood in the middle of the room, holding the objects as if they were contaminated. The calmness with which Grey, following his long tirade, had asked him to examine the picture disarmed him completely. He felt the helplessness, the awkwardness one experiences in the presence of the mentally ill. Unable to break the momentum of the situation, he sat down on the sofa and looked at the photograph.

"It's difficult for me to make out the man's face," he said after a few seconds. "The picture was taken from too great a distance. The officer's cap hides part of the face — the upper part."

"Don't try to discern the face, Harry. Don't look at the man. Inspect the area around him."

But Forsyth did not even bother to raise the glass to the photograph a second time. He just glanced at the picture for a moment.

"There's nothing there . . . there's nothing around the man, Grey."

"It isn't a question of what's there, Harry. It's a question of what isn't there. Look closely. The figure in the foreground. Kleist. He doesn't cast a shadow."

Forsyth looked blankly at his colleague. His face registered incomprehension. Then he examined the photograph again using the glass. As he looked, he spoke.

"That's not possible, Grey."

"But it is. There's no shadow. It's the one thing that made me reconsider the other evidence. There is an interesting legend about the Devil. It is said that he casts no shadow."

"No, Grey . . . Grey . . . this is insane. It has nothing to do with legends about the Devil. This is a peculiarity of some kind . . . an illusion . . . a chance result of light rays canceling each other out, the product of the man's position in relation to the street lamps, or it's a result of some malfunction in the camera itself . . . an imperfection in the lens . . . or whatever. That's all that's going on here . . . nothing else."

"No, Forsyth. It won't do. Look at it again. The man passing in the background casts a shadow. It's clear. So do the trees near the curb in front of the house. But not the officer, not Kleist. There is no shadow, and there should be. It's an odd thing, Harry. I didn't notice it at first. I wouldn't have noticed it at all unless I had been at my wit's end trying to find something absolutely concrete in all this evidence. I was playing around with the glass, with the photographs, almost as a game. That's when I noticed it. We don't look at people's shadows, not unless they are highlighted in some dramatic, obvious way. We just don't really look at them. They are there a great deal of the time, and yet we do not choose to focus on them. You see? He is there. Satan himself. In the photograph. And the code designations. Blocksberg. Horselberg. Infernal Proteus. They are marks left on the world by the father of Evil, by Satan himself. They are parts of an enormous game of deception, but it is a game he cannot lose. He is enjoying the game. Satan is a great ironist. He can leave the clues that point to his presence everywhere. The code words. The infernal crimes. He litters the earth with them, but he will never be caught. It is a game of deception in which the deceiver does not even bother to cover his own tracks. He succeeds because we are always looking for the wrong things. We never expect him to be there. In the midst of evil, of monstrousness everywhere, no one will believe in him. That alone is his greatest achievement. It is perfect. It is genius."

Forsyth dropped the glass and the picture and got up from the sofa.

"This is mad, Grey . . . it is totally mad."

"He depends on your saying that."

"Mad . . . it is mad."

"But the evidence for it is as strong as it is for anything else you choose to believe. You know it is. You're denying what is before your eyes. You saw the photograph."

"I saw nothing."

"The man casts no shadow."

"Yes, Grey. There is no shadow. But you can't draw this insane conclusion on the grounds of this one damned photograph."

There was rising anger, near hysteria, in Forsyth's voice.

"You've seen the photograph, Forsyth."

"An imperfection in the lens — that's all."

"The code words?"

"Symbolic and nothing else."

"He is there, Forsyth. He is there. The tempter. He never orders men to do anything. He is the deceiver."

"Listen you fool, you bloody fool. What do you think you can do with this crackpot interpretation of a photograph? Where can you go with it? To whom can you take it? Can you bring it to Trenchard, to Atkinson, to Churchill? They'll have you locked away. I have an inclination to do it myself."

Grey said nothing. He had known that the conversation would come to this. Forsyth was not to be blamed. On the night he had discovered the odd thing in the photograph, Grey had decided that the nature of the discovery necessitated that it be both revealed and rejected. Only the confrontation with Forsyth allowed him to feel that the drama had been played out to its end. Now the thing was finished. There was nothing more to be said.

Forsyth was profoundly disturbed by the confrontation. Two things bothered him. First, and most obvious, he was concerned about his friend's mental and emotional condition. But second, and more subtly, Grey's statements disturbed him too. He did not actually believe in the reality of the Devil, but, just the same, his colleague's arguments possessed an uncanny power. It was at least symbolically perfect that Satan, the greatest deceiver of them all, would choose to operate as an intelligence officer. It was perfect too that the father of Evil, sole knowledgeable spectator at a play of his own making, would savor the irony in leaving the clues to his identity scattered everywhere. And Forsyth could not fully accept what he had himself said about the symbolic value of the code words. The enemy's use of words and mythological symbols was not clearly separable from his evil acts. Were the words less real than the deeds? In arguing that the project code designations had been used only symbolically, he had tried to force Grey to dismiss their significance, their reality. But this was surely an error. If the Devil was real, then he would use the code words with a complexity, a wealth of irony, a symbolic richness not possessed by the words spoken by irrefutably real Nazis.

"What are you going to do, Grey?"

"Nothing, Harry . . . absolutely nothing. I'll tell no one. This shall be our secret."

"Good. I am relieved to hear that."

"And not one word more about the Kessler affair. As I promised."

"No. No more."

"But I am going to take this information about Kessler's

suicide to Trenchard, and to Atkinson. Surely you do not quarrel with the importance of that."

"No. I never did completely reject that."

"I'll see you in the morning then — all right?"

To his colleagues, Douglas Trenchard seemed completely obsessed by the vision of the enemy bombed into submission. That was the only subject he ever spoke about. Bombing mission statistics, the performance characteristics of aircraft, the tonnage of explosives delivered to particular targets, the problems of navigation yet unsolved — these were the issues on which Trenchard enjoyed discoursing. Aerial bombardment was the solution. All the rest, he claimed, was a waste of time, energy and resources. Even the complex espionage activities in which he was engaged, at least in his official capacity — these too could be classified as a waste as long as one judged them in isolation from the greater, more important effort. A piece of information here, a piece of information there, what real difference could such things make? It was only sheer force, best exerted from the air, which would bring everything to a successful conclusion. But the bombing campaign still needed its proponents. That was why Trenchard spoke of it so relentlessly. Bomber Command had yet to score a major victory. Other services were anxious to secure its manpower, its equipment. Trenchard's RAF friends appreciated his commitment to their cause. He would not give up until every available aircraft was engaged in the task of delivering explosives to the enemy.

Night after night, the bombers flew. The relationship between this fact and the secret projects which had marked the beginning of Trenchard's obsession grew ever more obscure and tenuous.

Soon the Americans would be over too and they would add their strength to the growing RAF endeavor. It would be the bombers which would devastate the enemy's refineries, destroy his industrial capacity, reduce the civilian population to despair.

Trenchard was invited to attend several Bomber Command strategy sessions. Officially, he had no authority when it came to making decisions, but, as always, his suggestions were warmly welcomed. The planners discussed the Germans' barbaric treatment of civilian populations in the eastern occupied countries. Trenchard argued that this could be ignored. The best solution was an indirect one. Bombs would facilitate a quick end to the war, and the end would bring with it a termination of this barbarism in the east.

Trenchard sat in his office, thinking out the methods for achieving destruction. He studied aerial reconnaissance photographs, circled the areas devastated by night raids, noted carefully the blocks consumed by flames, the zones of rubble left where the victims once lived.

Two days after his night conference with Forsyth, Trevor Grey sat outside Trenchard's office. The secretary told him he would have to wait only a few minutes.

What was he going to say to his former partner? Had he come seeking to justify himself? Grey knew that Trenchard would initially resist his presence. Perhaps he could ease the progress of the meeting by confessing that Trenchard had been within the bounds of reason in refusing to listen to his early arguments about the Kessler affair. The evidence had been scanty. He could admit to that.

Grey was nervous. He could not overcome the anxiety that had been with him every moment since the discovery concerning the photograph. Forsyth thought he was mad. Was he right? That harsh judgment was a repetition of what Trenchard had said some time before. Had he become so preoccupied with Kessler and Buchheim that he had lost the capacity to distinguish the real from the unreal? He had been alone in his office on the night of the discovery. Had fatigue, isolation, the terrible dream, and the force of previous convictions combined to produce an overwrought, hallucinatory "insight"? The hypothesis of an imperfection in the lens had to appear the more reasonable one. It was a resolutely, unashamedly twentieth-century explanation.

He heard the secretary call his name. He walked to the door, opened it, entered Trenchard's office, and shut the door behind him. Trenchard did not seem in the least surprised to see him.

"Good morning to you, Grey."

Grey went to the maroon chair. He had his briefcase with him. In one motion he placed it on the floor, opened it, and removed the Kessler folder. He placed this folder on his lap.

"I suppose the motive for my visit is transparent."

"You rarely surprise me, Grey."

"Then I might as well get on with it. It's the Kessler affair."

Trenchard said nothing. He looked at Grey, his eyes exceptionally bright and piercing.

"I should say we've had rather a strong disagreement about that case. I assume, Trenchard, that you've not been pleased with our professional relationship."

Trenchard would not respond. Grey was trying to provoke an angry outburst. This, he thought, would lend dramatic force to his presentation of the latest information from Frankfurt. Failing in this purpose, Grey shifted tactics.

"I am sorry for all that. I did get carried away by the Kessler business. It was hardly unreasonable of you to reject the notion that Kessler was working for our side."

"It is comforting, Grey, to see a man return to reason."

"But there is more, Trenchard."

"I didn't expect you to leave after an apology."

"Additional evidence has come into my possession since our last chat."

"And how did you obtain that evidence, Grey?"

He asked this question as if he knew the answer.

"I got it on my own."

"We can put you in a military prison for that."

"There's no point in threatening me, Trenchard. The thing is done. Do as you like."

"This obsession with the Kessler affair has not served you well, Grey. I expected better of you."

"Kessler is dead."

"That is a tragedy."

"It was a suicide, witnessed by our own people, so there is no doubt about it. The nature of the suicide is irrelevant, but the sheer fact of it is not. I count on you, Trenchard, to explain Kessler's death as a result of marital problems."

"I do not enjoy being predicted, Grey."

"My view is now as reasonable as yours is . . . or was. A man does not take his own life as part of an intelligence scheme. Kessler committed suicide immediately following a visit from the SS. He was with us all along, Trenchard. I suggest to you then that additional agents be assigned to the Frankfurt project. It represents a threat to us. We must find out what is happening with this project. Kessler told us that a test is scheduled for April. We must either prevent this test, or watch closely for the results."

"You are skeptical, Grey, regarding the use of air power."

"Entirely senseless in these circumstances."

"A pinpoint attack by fighter-bombers would be productive. A great challenge, I think."

There could be no point in staying longer. Grey could read Trenchard's last statement only as an insultingly blatant dismissal of his entire position. He was prepared to go straight to Atkinson.

279

"Tell me, Grey," continued Trenchard, "what other information do you have there? Your folder is quite full."

"Nothing that will interest you."

"My curiosity overwhelms me, Grey. What other data has your private spy ring provided for you?"

Grey hesitated. But why? Even if Trenchard was a German agent, the material in the folder would tell him very little. Grey's old suspicions were not the reason for his hesitation. He feared that Trenchard would notice what he had discovered in the photograph of Kleist. This fear, entirely irrational, was grounded in the belief, held in his heart, that he knew the truth, and that others would now be certain to grasp that truth. If Trenchard discovered and remarked on the peculiarity in the photograph, Grey sensed that he would be unable to keep silent. He would say everything. Even the certainty that Trenchard would greet his explanation with utter derision would not keep him quiet.

"Let me see, Grey."

Grey did not move.

"If your evidence is so compelling, why do you refuse to have me see it?"

What difference could it make? Kessler and Buchheim were dead. Grey gave him the folder and returned to the leather chair.

Trenchard studied each document and then returned them to the folder. No reaction was visible on his face.

"You have examined all of this material, Grey?"

"Yes."

"I am not enlightened by it. Perhaps someone else, someone with imagination and a knowledge of mathematics, will discover the real value in it."

Grey refused to accept this challenge. It was another insult.

"Here you are, Grey," and Trenchard closed the folder and pushed it across the desk.

Grey got up, retrieved the folder, and started to leave the office, but he suddenly remembered his briefcase. He went back for it, placed the folder inside it, and started again for the door. His hand was on the door handle when Trenchard's voice rang out behind him.

"Where can you go with your knowledge, Grey?"

Grey turned. Trenchard had moved his chair back from the desk and swiveled it toward the door. He sat there, imperiously, an emperor holding court.

"Who will believe you, Grey? No one. You have searched methodically through the evidence, looking for the truth. I commend you for that. Unfortunately for you, both your methods and your version of the events are inherently unbelievable in these historical circumstances. Ten years from now you will also see that you have dissipated your energies on an irrelevant question. Of what real import is Herr Kessler's project? Our side shall quickly grasp and copy our opponent's technological advances. Think instead, Grey, of our own achievements in organization, in the employment of technology for the purpose of bringing devastation to the enemy. Thousands of people are receiving training in methods founded on an inevitable indifference toward the deaths of other thousands of people whom we shall never know or see. The cities of Europe shall become an inferno. I act in the name of that possibility. There is no need for me to conceal myself in shame. You are the one who exhausts reason on behalf of a single human being whom you have never met. You should have joined me long ago. But it costs me nothing to leave you to your own crusade. You may possess the truth, Grey, but not enough of it. Good luck to you."

Grey stood transfixed, immobilized by fear, held to the spot by the hypnotic force of Trenchard's gaze. The flames of hell seemed to leap from his eyes. Grey wanted to speak, to meet the challenge of Trenchard's last words, but he could think of nothing. He wanted to resist, to triumph over the force of Trenchard's stare, but his will did not hold. He turned away, opened the door, and was gone.

Not even Harry Forsyth learned about this last encounter with Douglas Trenchard. He had been privileged to share the secret of the photograph, but Grey would tell no one about his confrontation with the individual, the being, who called himself Trenchard. He had been the victim of one last irony.

But Forsyth understood that something had happened to his colleague. Grey sat in his office and did nothing. He drank his tea. He stared out his window. His file cabinets went unopened, his case folders unread. He did not try to conceal his disorientation. The door to his office stood open. Forsyth could walk past and look in at his friend, a man apparently occupied by nothing other than the contemplation of his next chess move.

By the end of March, 1942, Atkinson removed Grey from his position. He gave him a simple desk job over in Desmond Crowden's communications building.

"Trenchard's work?" asked Grey without a trace of bitterness in his voice.

"No," said Atkinson.

This too was not a surprise. Grey's ex-partner had said he would leave him to his "crusade." Atkinson had not even learned of the illegal use of Secret Service communications. At least Crowden would be safe.

So Grey understood that Forsyth was responsible for the change in assignment. Forsyth's motive had been generous. He was worried about his friend's sanity. Nor could he, as a professional, live comfortably with the idea of Grey's holding a position entailing heavy responsibilities. Could part of the running of the Dutch underground be entrusted to a man who thought he had seen a photograph of the Devil? Thus, he had spoken to Atkinson.

Grey sat out the war at his desk. He read mail, typed letters, and answered telephones. He became friendly with the men who worked in communications. In his free time he read novels and played chess with his friends. Grey was not bored. The newspapers provided him with entertainment. He followed the progress of the war in great detail. Grey thought himself a spectator at a play. His superior knowledge was the source of pleasures transcending the joys of patriotism. He knew the "director" of this drama. He thought he could discern the curve of events, a gigantic trajectory which vanished from sight over the moral horizon. But even this vision did not preclude Grey's interest in narrower questions. Who would win the war? He would have liked to have asked his ex-partner that one. But he knew what the answer would be. "Time is on my side, Grey." That's what he would say.

Throughout the war, Forsyth and Grey continued to see each other. "No hard feelings, I hope," said Forsyth. There were none. Grey understood that his friend had acted out of genuine altruism. The two men continued their special chess game. The Kessler case was not mentioned again. But the events corrupted their friendship, at least for Grey. He knew that his relationship with Forsyth was the "instrument" through which he could prove his sanity. This purpose was never far from his consciousness. Grey saw also how simple would be this quest for the verdict: sane. He would just refrain, forever, from mentioning the strange photograph of Reinhard Kleist and the climactic meeting with Douglas Trenchard. This simple expedient would clear his name. That was the only thing he sought. The Secret Service did not interest him anymore.

«11»

The war in Europe ended. Tony Atkinson was prepared to reassign Grey to an active position. Both Forsyth and Atkinson were willing to forget Grey's unfortunate obsession. He was cured now. The entire incident, in their view, had only been the result of the pressures inherent in one complex and admittedly fascinating case. An occupational hazard — nothing more. Indeed, this hazard was liable to claim as its victims the best, the most imaginative, the most competent men.

It was July, 1945, when Atkinson offered Grey the new post.

"No. Thank you," said Grey.

"You're a good man, Grey."

"Thank you, sir. But the war is over, you know."

"You needn't worry about that. There will be enough work for all of us."

"I must refuse."

"I see. Hard feelings, I suppose."

"No. It's that the excitement has rather gone out of it for me."

"Really? It's always business as usual with the Service, Grey."

"I'm sure. I've got my own private battles. We all do, sir."

"Bloody Russians aren't good enough for you?"

"I'm certain you can handle them by yourself, sir."

Grey was at the door when he remembered the one question he had come to ask.

"Sir."

Atkinson looked up from the paper work already claiming his attention.

"Yes, Grey."

"What happened to Trenchard?"

"Ah, Trenchard. You hadn't heard? Forsyth said nothing to you?"

"No."

"I see. In March of forty-four Trenchard flew along on a raid, a big show, over Nuremburg. Perhaps you read about it. A God-awful bloody mess it was. His machine was hit by flak. That was the end of him."

Forsyth had known this, but fearing Grey's reaction to the name Trenchard, he had said nothing about it.

In October of 1945 Grey took a job with a London newspaper. He became a reporter. For years Desmond Crowden, who had been watching him read novels, had said that he should apply his literary interests and skills to social-political realities.

"Are you satisfied now?" he asked Crowden on his last day with the Secret Service.

"Not exactly."

"I thought not. Reporting will suit me perfectly. I prefer to keep my distance from things."

"Good luck to you, old boy."

Nearly a year passed. Then, one day during the fall of 1946, Grey told Forsyth he was going to the Continent. His newspaper wanted a report on the German occupation in the east. They booked him on a flight to Frankfurt. From there he would take the train to Poland.

But Grey stopped over in Frankfurt. He had research of his own that he wished to do.

It took him four days to locate Karin Kessler. He began his search at the university. Two of Kessler's former colleagues told him Kessler's wife was still alive. He did not know her first name. They told him. He asked them where she was living. One of the men told Grey that she had gone to live with a couple, old friends of the Kesslers, immediately after the suicide. Grey was lucky. The man remembered the name of this couple. He went to see them. Karin Kessler had lived with them until 1944. Then she had moved to an apartment. Miraculously, she had survived an air attack which had claimed the lives of most of the people in her building. Now she was staying in new housing located on the outskirts of the city.

Grey found the new housing project. It was surrounded by rubble. Workers and trucks were carting away bricks and shattered beams. Huge machines were scooping up mounds of broken concrete. In some of the devastated lots, still untouched since the day the bombers had come, children were playing. They charged through the ruins. Each battered wall was an opportunity for concealment. Each pile of rubble was a mountain in a fantasy.

Grey introduced himself to Karin Kessler. He told her that as a former member of the Secret Service, he had known her husband, at least in a way. She looked old and haggard. She did not show much surprise at this astonishing visit. Grey thought that either she had been through too much to find his presence worthy of a response, or that, in some way, she expected the ramifications of her husband's fate to pursue her to the end of time. He started to speak to her in German, but his command of the language, which had been adequate for controlling agents at a distance, was not up to the demands of an extended conversation.

"You are the victors," she remarked with ill-concealed cynicism, "so we shall speak your language."

She offered him coffee. He accepted. She told him to sit at the kitchen table next to the window. She wanted him to enjoy the view.

"So," she said to him, "what do you want to know?"

He responded by explaining everything that had happened in London concerning her husband, everything with the exception of his final discovery.

When he finished she said, "You were right, Herr Grey . . . quite right." She fixed him with a cold, absolutely merciless stare. "For you it must be so satisfying to learn that you were right. But, you see, for my husband it would have been better if he had not met your man . . . your representative . . ."

"Buchheim."

"Right. Buchheim. He is dead too. They are both dead. So you see that there can be no pleasure for me in our talk."

He finished the coffee. She did not offer him more. He listened for a moment to the distant sounds of the construction machinery.

"So — is that all you wish to know?"

"Your husband," he said, "knew a man named Reinhard Kleist."

"Ah yes. That is right again. The SS."

"A Gruppenführer in the SS. Did you meet him?"

"We do not speak of the SS anymore, Herr Grey. Do you not know this?"

"What happened to Herr Kleist?"

"How should I know that?"

"You heard nothing about him?"

"No," she replied.

"You never saw him after your husband's death?"

"Once. Just once. He came to the funeral. He was charming. He told me how sorry he was, Herr Grey. He said he would help me in any way he could."

"I see."

"He too might be dead now. He may have been killed at the end when many people died, Herr Grey. Is he the one you are interested in? You wish to find Herr Kleist? He is a war criminal. Sorry, Herr Grey. I cannot help you."

"No, Mrs. Kessler. I am not trying to locate Herr Kleist. It would be quite senseless."

"It would be, Herr Grey. He is vanished. I am certain. If he is not dead, then his friends will take care of him. Like the other SS. Gone. Changed into civilian clothes."

"What happened at the end?"

"I have told you," she said.

"No . . . your husband . . . when he killed himself."

She did not respond. She turned away and looked out the window.

"Why do you want to know?"

"I seek this information only for myself."

She was surveying the ruins.

"For yourself?" she asked.

"That is right," he said. "Not for my newspaper. And I am not here for the Secret Service."

"British Intelligence has lost interest in my husband."

She laughed.

"You must see how amusing that is to me."

She laughed again.

"Perhaps it would be better if I left. Thank you for your time."

He began to get up.

"No . . . no," she said. "You must forgive me."

"There is nothing —"

"You want to know about my husband's last day. Is that right?"

"Yes."

"Good. All right. I will tell you. Sit down."

He sat down again.

"Gruppenführer Kleist visited him just before the end."

"How did you know that?" she asked him.

"There were agents watching the house. They saw him arrive."

"Then they saw the —"

"Yes. They saw everything."

"But your agents did not know why my husband came home earlier that day."

"No."

"I called him at his office. I wanted to speak to him right away. I did not want to wait. It was very good for you, Herr Grey . . . all that information Otto was sending you . . . but I could not live with it. I did not care anymore about risk, about danger. It could have been no worse living apart from him."

"When he came home you told him that?"

"Yes. I wanted a divorce."

"And then Reinhard Kleist arrived?"

"Correct, Herr Grey. That is right."

He was silent. She looked away from him again. Outside there was a muffled roar. He too stared out the window. Dust was rising from where a shattered wall had once stood.

"Do you know what they spoke about? What they said to each other?"

"No. Otto said nothing about it."

"Nothing at all?"

"He looked in shock. He told me nothing about the subject of their talk. I did not expect him to. I was always the last to know about anything."

"Not a word." Grey was speaking to himself.

"When he came out of his study, Herr Grey, he leaned against the bannister . . . there was a staircase . . . he was leaning there. Kleist left. He said nothing. Otto looked at me and said . . . he was speaking to himself really . . . he said that it was the devil . . . or it was devilish . . . he had signed a pact with the devil . . . there was no way out. He said only that. It is hard to remember. It is too long ago. I do not wish to remember."

And it was true after all, she went on to say.

"He might just as well have signed a devil's pact. He was doomed from the start. He and many others. All of them innocent, Herr Grey. But trapped. But there is no point in discussing that. You have learned what you want to know."

In Poland it took the Soviet occupation authorities one week to approve Grey's special request. They could not understand his interest in an abandoned factory. The machine tools had been removed. Only a partially ruined shell remained. There was nothing worth seeing. The authorities thought at first that Grey might be working for the Secret Service, but there was nothing the English could learn by inspecting the remains of a shattered factory.

So they took him to Auschwitz first with a group of reporters, and then drove him down the road in an American-made jeep to the site he wanted to visit. The driver pointed at some woods. Grey walked through them and found what he was looking for. The Germans had not succeeded in destroying the shell of the factory and the Russians had done nothing with the remains. The roof of the structure was gone completely. There were jagged holes torn in several walls. Off to one side of the shell there was a series of ditches which no one had bothered to fill in.

Grey walked through the ruins. Standing in the center of the factory floor, he heard a noise, the sound of rustling in the overgrown grass outside the shell. He stepped out and saw half a dozen wild dogs running through the field. He had surprised them. Their leader turned and looked at him, gave a brief contemptuous bark, and then ran off in a new direction, the rest of the pack following closely behind.

Then he saw something which confirmed that he had come to the right place. Three or four hundred yards from the remains of the factory, he could see a large steel object. It was set against the wooded background. He approached it. This odd structure consisted of two steel pieces which, thrust into the ground about fifteen feet apart, rose vertically into the air. A third piece spanned the distance between the tops of the two vertical bars. Supporting struts had been placed between the summit of this steel goalpost and points on the ground forty feet to the rear. Suspended from this structure by four enormous hooks was a sheet of metal which hung down to within a foot of the ground. This sheet had been pierced through at several places. Both the sheet and the supporting structure were covered with rust. Here was one of those remains of the war, something which, unnoticed and untouched, might stand for centuries.

He had come to see these mute objects, last remains of what he took to be the Devil's own project. Nothing but a half-destroyed factory and a curtain of steel suspended over a field overgrown with grass and weeds. He had been unable to resist making this special journey. He had come half expecting to encounter a messenger or a sign, a sign meant for him alone. There was only silence.

A damp, chilling wind swept across the field. The grass bowed before it. The metal sheet, hanging from its support structure, responded. Grey was walking away, returning to the driver waiting on the other side of the woods. His shoes cut through the weeds. Behind him he could hear the creaking and groaning of metal rubbing against metal.